ANECDOTAGE

ANECDOTAGE

A SUMMATION

TRANSLATED FROM THE GERMAN
BY SUSAN BERNOFSKY WITH THE AUTHOR

FARRAR STRAUS GIROUX
NEW YORK

Translation copyright © 1996 by Farrar, Straus and Giroux
Originally published in German as *Greisengemurmel* copyright © 1994 by
C. Bertelsmann Verlag GmbH, Munich
Printed in the United States of America
First edition, 1996

LIBRARY OF CONGRESS CATALOGING-IN-PUBLICATION DATA
Rezzori, Gregor von.
[Greisengemurmel. English]
Anecdotage : a summation / Gregor von Rezzori ; translated from
the German by Susan Bernofsky with the author.
p.   cm.
1. Rezzori, Gregor von—Biography. 2. Authors, Austrian—20th
century—Biography. I. Bernofsky, Susan. II. Title.
PT2635.E98G7413 1996   833'.912—dc20   [B]   95-45963 CIP

AUTHOR'S NOTE

The author confesses that while rereading the finished manuscript he scratched out all the commas in a fit of pique—except those contained in quotations from other writers and a small number whose presence was perhaps indispensable. These pedantic myrmidons of syntactical order, these irritating traffic cops, served only to temper a text whose curmudgeonliness could be more clearly expressed by the sole means of colon, semicolon, dash, and parentheses. Admittedly the reader is now in danger of losing his bearings in a labyrinth of clauses, and at times will be forced to retrace his steps and begin the work of reading anew. Forced, in other words, to participate actively in the careful crafting of the text. The reward will be a greater intimacy with it.

ANECDOTAGE

And Ifrid the Fisherman began: "Know, O Demon, that in days of yore and ages long since past, a king called Yunan reigned over the city of Fars in the land of Ruman."

—FROM THE FIRST OF THE *THOUSAND AND ONE NIGHTS*

Since my return from the hospital I've become aware how much my eyes have deteriorated. Writing and reading eighteen twenty hours a day and half the night (sleeping pills hardly do a thing anymore) have taken their toll. I don't want to get used to wearing spectacles all the time (my colleague Goethe didn't like them either). For short-range viewing they've been indispensable for years (as they were for him as well). Things look hazy as though they lay behind a pane of fogged-up glass. But my long-range vision always used to be quite good. Good enough at any rate to let me drive a little faster than most people. Now I'm beginning to wonder. And I'm not the only one. I've had quite a few comments lately on how heavy the traffic can be (as though I were already having to tap my way through it with a cane).

I've begun to play a game that keeps my mood appropriately bleak. A sort of auscultation of my existence in this world. When my eyes come to rest on some particular object—the huge insect skull of a biker veering abruptly around the corner a green left-turn arrow by the flashing red of a traffic light the white of the eye of a daredevil pedestrian in the metallic roar of the city's bedlam—I look at it distinctly but not as part of what surrounds it. It detaches itself from its context then becomes more perfectly isolated the more tightly I narrow down my lids to fix its contours. It presents itself in meaningless importance like a recruit who steps out of line bellows his name and then leaps back into ranks. He is announcing his own essential anonymity. It's only the categories that count.

At home I practice this game as a sort of optical calisthenics. Other sorts have been recommended to me: for example pumping away on a stationary bicycle to promote good circulation. Fortunately the bicycle is in the big house along with all the other fitness equipment. We live in the tower. Supposedly just for the time being. Though it's beginning to feel permanent. For my optical gymnastics it's just the thing. Each window offers a splendid view. The days are glorious: skies blue after gray weeks in which a wintry spring dabbed the countryside with stingy bits of green. Not what one would expect of Italy. But even changes of climate can be gotten used to. It's as if the weather were under EC jurisdiction. Naples gets the same as Scotland; one place is just like the other. Not long ago the nights were still frosty but now things are shooting up all over. A gleaming sun hidden intermittently by the diminutive clouds gliding past—all at once it turns bitter cold—coaxes up a glimmer of new grass whenever it reappears. Nature giving a polite biological smile as if to reassure us that it will be some time yet before we have the ozone hole gaping open directly above our heads. Suddenly flowers are everywhere—wisteria on the walls above the golden-yellow fields of rapeseed a froth of cherry trees in the vegetable garden—a horticultural hi-de-ho! Only the summery hum of insects is missing. The bees are dead. A plague wiped them out say the padres of Vallombrosa who lost dozens of colonies. (Colleague Milton's "Vallombrosa, where the Etrurian shades / High over-arched embower." *Paradise Lost.* No wonder: the fellow was blind.) Even so: the walnut tree doused with acid rain now has buds popping out of its unharmed limbs.

4

I direct my optical gymnastics to the south where you can see the farthest—nothing but forest. Or rather what goes in these parts by the name of *bosco*: a tangly profusion of stunted oak beech ash chestnut acacia. Nothing like a proper timber forest. No unicorns stepping out of the morning fog into the Caspar David Friedrich light. (Childhood's enchanted forest: " 'Twas brillig, and the slithy toves / Did gyre and gimble in the wabe . . .") To be sure, the view from above does give the impression of a woodsy mass thickly matted with an underbrush of laurel elderberry holly. Here and there interrupted by the yellow explosions of broom and ornamentally overgrown with the Art Nouveau tendrils of wild ivy anemones and blackberries. I take in the landscape in leaps and bounds adjusting my pupils from near to far and back and forth and to and fro darting from detail to detail as if twisting the lenses of a telescope into focus. The region is mountainous hilly—furrowed lengthwise with deep ravines where the earth has subsided into crevasses in which slender rivulets cut into the rock. The red clay walls are as steep as the cliffs of a coastline. They are what have saved the countryside for miles around from the construction craze that has taken over Italy's fresh-out-of-the-oven industrial society.

We live in the tower because the perpetual process of renovation and refurbishing has finally succeeded in transforming the big house into a junk heap of a construction site for the manufacture of its ideal form. I admit the house does invite tinkering. Like many others of its type—the so-called *case coloniche* being the homes of tenant farmers dating back to the period of Tuscany's settlement in the fourteenth sixteenth and eighteenth centuries —it was originally devised for two families who lived cozily with all their livestock beneath a single roof. It was half caved in when we took it over twenty-five years ago: bedded in knee-high meadow grass beneath a snow of acacia blossoms. Swallows that had encrusted the roof with their nests swarmed about

5

the house (as the bees had once swarmed about their hollow trunk). By the time we got it back in shape the nests had been destroyed and the swallows were gone leaving us with a maze of stables rooms hallways closets whose functions and furnishings are still under discussion. No sooner has perfection been achieved in one corner than something in the next is in need of repair and the mere thought of some necessary operation is enough to get B.'s aesthetic juices flowing. I keep toting my things from one niche to the other: the paradox of a domestic nomad. The swallows never returned.

The tower stands at a distance of one hundred paces from the house: the stub of a medieval signal tower one of whose missing stories we have restored. Furnished as a guest suite it has turned out to be much cozier and better suited to our needs than the big house. Bruce Chatwin wrote several chapters of his novel *On the Black Hill* here; he loved the tower. So do I. The only nuisance is traipsing back and forth to fetch the items I've forgotten to bring with me from pieces of clothing to reference books. But this too is secretly part of my strategy. I'm doing my best to avoid getting settled in one spot for good. Not only because the doctor has ordered exercise and the trips from tower to house and house to tower replace the walks he emphatically prescribed (I admit more symbolically than anything else) but also because I don't want to give up my freedom. An old man's hardheadedness, I know. In all likelihood motivated in part by superstitious sleight of hand. Overly rational systems of order make me feel rebellious. I shy away from all forms of planning; I don't trust them. All my life I've subscribed to the principle of *carpe diem*. Which doesn't mean my life was all luxurious leisure. (Is there anyone out there who remembers what this means? Leisure . . . how distant now is the age when days offered themselves up to us as vessels made of light that we might fill as we chose! . . . Does any such thing exist for young people today? I don't know. I don't know today's young-

6

sters: I know only youthful oldsters and the sort who were old the day they were born.) In any case I've practiced *carpe diem* for three-quarters of a century. Not always in idleness. Not always at leisure (in the best sense of the word: having free time at one's disposal). But always on the alert ready to adapt to changing circumstances. This is a necessity. The second half of this century—compared with the first—was suspiciously quiet at least at the sites of major conflagrations. (Gathering strength for another shot at the Final Solution?) Now things are beginning to stir again. It's time to be on the lookout for surprises. The hours might change their shape and makeup without warning. The situation taxes one's existential adroitness. "Life is a white-water boat trip" my father used to say. Time whisks us through treacherous rapids shallows whirlpools. I like to think I've been a skillful canoeist. I'm not old enough to give it up yet.

Superstitious sleight of hand (I'm repeating myself) for conjuring up reality. Household magic. In Italian the word is *scaramanzia*: you speak of bad things to conjure up good ones. I'd like to preserve my youth by acting like a cantankerous old man. (Actually it's more the opposite: I behave in a rigorously youthful manner so as to cash in on sentimental credit for my age.) I accept the touching solicitude of the women in the house (Anna and Fedora and recently also Aisha and Leila from Marrakech) with the equanimity of a pasha at the same time making it clear I can be moody if provoked. Certainly I'll defend myself against crass violations of my property rights over my own physis. They've given up trying to ply me with miracle cures as well as belated prophylactic care. (It's alarming how obsessed German family periodicals are with this. The "strength and beauty" wave of my youth has subsided into a decaying emaciated corpus of homespun pointers on avoiding skin-cancer-promoting sunburn heart attacks sweaty hands and stress-induced ulcers. My colleague La Rochefoucauld says there is no more burdensome illness than constantly being concerned about one's health.) The hybrid blossom of natural medicine (correlative to the destruction of Nature). All wasted on me. I don't need herbalist quacks and thalassotherapists to point out that my body is showing signs of wear. Standard scientific medicine is quite adequate to the task. It has convinced me that my life hangs by a thread. Supposedly this thread can be lengthened by carting me from one operating room to the next. The operations produce so-called side effects. These must be eliminated with the help of additional operations (which in turn produce side effects). Tasks for a mechanic. For herb teas birdseed diets acupuncture and yoga eye hair and foot-sole diagnoses it's too late for me. I have also refused to change the position of my bed which is possibly located above a subterranean rivulet. Nor will I let them give me injections in my various scars to get the blocked circulation of vital magnetic currents flowing again. (What would be the point? A youthful blunder that landed me in a dueling fraternity left me elegantly carved up; though not nearly as generously as my recent encounters with surgeons. But as the Viennese like to say: it adds up.)

Nevertheless I am prepared to make concessions. Treatment by autosuggestion. (In my day this was called the *méthode Coué*.) I tell myself I'm still hardy enough to withstand the next surgical procedure. Whenever I walk from tower to house—for instance to fetch a new stack of books to strain my eyes with—I thrust my shoulders back and my chest forward and take several deep breaths: the starting position for all calisthenic activity. That's plenty of activity right there. After all it's the psyche that produces the therapeutic effect. I do grouse a bit (recalling similar tortures in early childhood) when my clothing is laid out for me according to the weather reports on television (once it was the coachman's rheumatism). (B. displays an energetic decisiveness that would make her the envy of a

Swiss social worker.) I drag my heels but in the end I'm grateful. I despise undershirts wool scarves warm headwear—but I admit they're warm. (Senile contradictions: I also hate nightshirts but have gotten used to them in hospital beds.) I don't make a fuss when they tell me how all these things are in my best interest and that I really must show some consideration for my advanced years and fragile health; and I do understand that taking one's pills regularly is a matter of conscience. I've also accepted the strict rationing of my alcohol consumption though I reserve the right to go just a bit overboard on occasion. But all the commotion about my deteriorating physis gets on my nerves terribly. I am more than just an ever more infirm body. Mythological phenomena can be observed in me. For instance the quickening of the spirit with Dionysian flames. So that extra drop is sometimes essential. B. takes it personally: she's being wronged.

I find all this doubly irritating since I am overly self-involved to begin with. Perhaps egocentrism is a sign of old age. Perhaps navel-gazing is the essence of a writer's existence. (The self as focal point for both short- and long-range vision.) At any rate my life these cool spring days is marked by an unambiguous symbol of dotage. Emblem of an old man's decrepitude and his right to special treatment: the bedpan. It is my own personal contribution to my senescence. I brought it back with me from the hospital (in Italian they call it *pappagallo*). It too is linked to many a childhood memory though it isn't the same as the good old *pot de chambre* ("*Potschampa*" we said in German) of weighty porcelain that became the object of the bitterest nursery-room power struggles between my sister and me and that modern-day interior decorators purchase from antique shops to use as vases in their living-room designs (household gear of yesteryear). When I was a child the chamber pot was a standard feature even stowed beneath the bedside tables at provincial hotels where it summoned up visions of traveling salesmen's erotic exploits. (Voluptuous beauty in Victorian *dessous* squats bare-bottomed above it as the delighted voyeur observes.) Now this association-rich item has been replaced by a feather-light piece of plastic. (The pseudo-English governesses once sporadically involved in my education would have called it "flimsy"; but not only the material has been modernized but the design as well: the *pappagallo* is olive-shaped with a short tubular neck attached to one end; the Germans call it a "bed duck": *Bettente*—and indeed it does resemble an abstract duck by Brancusi more than the parrot the Italians see in it.) In any case: it says something that I use it with a bad conscience; my embarrassment further prodded by the shy ceremony with which Anna Fedora Aisha or Leila as the case may be slides the *pappagallo* beneath my bed at night then takes it away warmly filled in the morning after depositing my breakfast tray on my stomach. A fine testimony to the reverence and empathy mothers bring to the shortcomings of their charges—a specialty of Mediterranean women who have managed to remain naïve. An archaic level of civilization. Folklore with antique-shop value. Sometimes it makes me want to box their ears.

In a word: I am adapting to my age of nearly eighty. Still there are my eyes. They sting when I open them. As I did not in my youth I now read far too much. (An utter mishmash: Norman Mailer and the Bible Panofsky and Handke and again and again *Elective Affinities* and *The Man without Qualities*.) I'm not sure if this is merely escapism or a full-blown addiction. (If I wanted to be thorough I'd read up on what colleagues Pascal Kierkegaard and Heidegger had to say about boredom.) In any case a certain loss of reality does result (with a gain of reality in another dimension). My reading glasses narrow down the concrete world to precisely the same extent that they offer me access to the abstract world of black on white. Now that I need glasses even for long-range viewing I worry about losing myself altogether as a sleepwalker in the never-never land of abstract realities. A belletristic existence. All my life I've found disciples of the printed page suspicious (the sort who read Proust at thirteen and devote the rest of their lives like colleague Borges to collecting literary rarities). Mandelstam's cultural pensioners. But what else is left for me to do? I've done enough traveling. Had enough chaotic love affairs. Truly worthwhile pastimes are hard to come by.

Naturally I'm not the only one inundated with unacceptable quantities of paper. The Brazilian rain forest isn't being razed for my sake alone. Printed matter is a hot consumer item. Without it our world wouldn't be what it is. (Bravo!) Let's not even mention literature and its hybrid proliferations. The amounts of paper routinely and daily consumed are staggering. During my sojourns in New York I'm always shocked at the hundreds of jumbo-sized pages in the Sunday edition of my newspaper. A heavy armful of paper black with printer's ink. An utter mockery of the laments about the dying forests in Maine regularly reported on in this most 'provincial of metropolitan papers. (And when it comes to the news the breakup of the U.S.S.R. is allotted twenty lines at the top of the page followed by a foot and a half of department-store ads. All the text is confined to a narrow strip atop each page. A sadist in Virginia slays seventeen black youths. Rarely anything at all about Europe. Seventeen death sentences in China. Scads of victims slaughtered in Peru in Chile in Nicaragua. The zoological species human being is hard at work on all fronts to complete the mission the Creator devised for it. Twelve full pages of film ads. Corruption scandals in the Senate. The news that red beets reduce cholesterol.) And this journalistic excrement isn't the only thing conjuring up a highly questionable reality. Every morning the mailbox overflows with a flood of mass mailings brochures circulars pamphlets announcements that sweeps away all doubts as to the reality of this "reality." (My colleague Nabokov says this word should be used only between quotation marks.) I too am susceptible to the hypnotic power of the printed word. These runes work a strong magic. I direct my revolt against their rapidly accumulating carrier the paper. At times the thought of this insane wastefulness can put me in a rage. I cram the fireplace with every kind of paper in reach (never books: they don't burn well). Struggling in vain with the smoldering bits that won't catch fire properly. My autos-da-fé do not cleanse me. I remain a slave to the printed page. Even here in this Tuscan wilderness largely untouched by culture we subscribe to a plethora of periodicals three daily newspapers as well as four weekly and six monthly magazines. Often the day is over before I have absorbed its printer's-ink precipitate. On top of this I myself participate in the production of scrap paper. I too sully page after page on a professional basis. I too attempt to conjure up "reality" by means of runes. A self-consciously fictional reality to be sure (as if that made things any better). In any case I am one of those magicians who turn out fetishes with the help of the rotary press. It's my duty to take my magician's work seriously. I owe it to B. She loves me. (The writer.) The point of my striving to achieve a sensible lifestyle conducive to good health is to enable me to write as much and as well (and as successfully) as possible. I willingly submit. My writing is my life. Constructing a fictional reality comes naturally to me. A dreamer by temperament. A prestidigitator by birth (or vice versa). So I construct my own abstract world. Paper is patient. Over the years I've written my way to the professional title "writer." I'm very conscientious about living up to it. I write regularly (when I'm not reading).

To be sure there are moments or rather hours days weeks when I am incapable of writing. (When I was seeking the hand of my first wife Priska Klara in marriage—preparing for the miscarriage of a bourgeois existence—and was forced to confess to my father-in-law presumptive that I was a writer he gave a worried look down the length of his nose and said "And what do you do when you can't think of anything?") Today this is no cause for apprehension. Half a century of monitoring my own creative psychoses like an orderly at an insane asylum (that's how long I've been writing: half a century!) has taught me patience. B. is anything but patient which makes her tolerance all the more admirable. I placate her with parables (which she sees through). One suspiciously visual analogy was suggested by my pupil calisthenics. The hours and days marked by lack of motivation writer's block and empty-headedness (I say) are perhaps as beneficial to my creative powers as the ravines that protect the landscape here from the threat of cement and mortar. (An appeal to romanticism: B. is a Green Party advocate.) In reality the opposite is true. I fill up these sterile stretches of time with reading matter. Not sparing my eyes I pack sixteen eighteen hours of the day with the fictitious worlds of other prolific navel-gazers. With no thought to what I ought to fear: literary infection. Fictions giving rise to fictions. Literature born of literature (preferably cribbed from the newspaper). Incestuous intellectual. (My colleague Gombrowicz once said he'd rather be seen as a false count than as an intellectual.) I know I'm a con man in the reality racket. I'm one of the shamans of the runic arts. But I wouldn't want to pull the usual sort of wool over anyone's eyes without at least getting in a wink or two.

This makes me think of Ugo Mulas. His obsession with cleansing photography of the photographic. Of the con game of fictitiousness that its nimbus of objectivity lets it play out even more deceptively than the other arts. (The unreality of reality.) He made prints not only of a motif but also of the image of the film on which it had been captured. He'd have liked best to have photographed the camera as well and behind it himself: as an informer denouncing the eye that kept the lens (the so-called objective) from being objective. I can remember just such a self-portrait. (I don't own it: I don't collect souvenirs.) His Etruscan head the almost Slavic boyish face with the full-lipped mouth the short turned-up nose the high cheekbones and far-spaced gently slanting eyes ("his wide brow wreathed with curls of hyacinth" is perhaps how it goes). A young forest-dweller a faun. In the museum in Volterra such a head is on display. It crowns a narrow blade of green-patinated bronze. A well-developed sexual organ in front and in back the gracefully sinuous trace of a spinal column along with a naturalistic pair of naked feet at the base show it unequivocally to be the figure of a youth. Abstract and elongated like a Giacometti sculpture. It is called *Ombra della sera*—evening shadow—and there was something appropriately dusky about Ugo's sharp-eyed mildness: a slight sadness that could be brightened by his vivacity but never banished altogether. How amiable he was became apparent in New York. He had come there to photograph the protagonists of the American artistic epiphany: Rothko and Barnie Newman Stella Jim Dine Oldenburg and Rauschenberg Lichtenstein and Jasper Johns (Pollock was already dead)—in short the New York art scene of the 1960s. He spoke not a word of English and crept around their studios in the guise of a smiling camera-clicking deaf-mute and they all adored him and gave him their work although even in those days the zeros on their prices were beginning to proliferate like carp spawn.

He once told me the story of his father: a *carabiniere* who'd found his way from Sardinia to Lombardy and whose dream it had been to own a bit of land on which his family might prosper. The first part of the dream came true but he got into trouble with the other part. Sending his children to college proved to be costly and long before their educations were complete his property came under the hammer. Ugo described this with a smile: in his eyes that slight sadness that never left them. This was still in the days before his illness. Once he visited us here. The house was far from its recent state of imperfect perfection (before the start of the devastating process of perfecting it definitively). It still stood in the shade of two immense elm trees that eventually fell victim to Dutch elm disease in the late 1970s. The tower was a mere stump. Ugo walked around with his sharp-sighted dreamy eyes and almost forgot to take pictures. At the time there were still a few abandoned *case coloniche* left in the region (the tenants having traded country for city during the seven fat years of industrial prosperity). He toyed with the idea of buying one for his daughter. The only obstacle being that this would put her too far away from her schools. Soon after he fell ill.

My early companions here: Ugo and Bruce. Both died young. Both fulfilled their artistic promise at an early age. O.W.A.s: the Ones Who Achieved. Young sacrificial victims at the altar of the Great Fetish Art. But even so. (What am I trying to say?)

The king was much amazed and said, "Verily this is a matter that cannot be kept secret, and as for the fish, they must be bewitched."
—FROM THE SECOND OF THE *THOUSAND AND ONE NIGHTS*

*A*mong my friends there isn't a one who doesn't envy me for living here. I conduct every visitor to the highest room in the tower. The view there is stupendous. Undeveloped countryside all around; a scant handful of houses scattered in the direction of the Arno Valley the closest one a half hour's march distant. To the south are only two buildings a dozen or more miles away as the crow flies: the farcical Moorish palace of Sammezzano tucked brick-red into the evergreen obscurity of its park like a comb in the hair of an Andalusian woman; one leap farther is the Torre del Castellano simple as a child's drawing of a knight's castle tiny smoke-blue silhouette in the airy pigeon blue that the Pratomagno paints on the sky's seam. Both the Moorish palace and the chivalric castle are historical fakes. The Sammezzano palace is the product of the Oriental craze around 1850 which the then landowner (who claimed to be descended from the royal house of Aragón) all too eagerly followed. The ruins of the Torre del Castellano were purchased after 1945 by a local collector and done up along strictly medieval lines. But this does nothing to spoil the splendor of the panorama. On the contrary. It lends an Italian note to the Etruscan countryside.

I spread all this out before my guest with an inviting sweep of my hand. Please do help yourself to all the Tuscany you could ask for. The motherland of architectural high culture. Botanically noteworthy as well with its sublimely showy graveyard vegetation: laurel pine and cypress above the violet halberds of the wonder flower *giaggiolo*—the iris in the Florentine coat of arms. (In our garden the porcupines scoop the bulbs from the earth quicker than we can replace them.) A landscape full of art-historical allusions. Here and there a rickety farmhouse of the *macchiaiuoli* here and there on a hilltop a Michelangelesque villa (wine bottle vignette) here and there a Böcklin-like Isle of the Dead knitted up in dog rose. Even the region's hilliness is illusory. In fact the land rises in solid rolling waves from the depths of the Arno Valley and only looks mountainous thanks to its many precipitous chasms. Though with the drama of a mannerist landscape. This was once all farmland wrested at great effort from the barren earth (the wonderful frugality of Tuscan husbandry is well known to have arisen out of poverty). That the region has been left to go to seed is a product of the industrial boom. Country-dwellers racing to the cities in the 1950s and '60s. I point out the lighter hues in the *bosco*'s protective camouflage: the silvery shimmering foliage of the overgrown olive trees not yet smothered beneath the thick tangle of ivy and blackberry vines. Once these were olive groves and vineyards now abandoned with no one to do the tilling. *Tant mieux pour nous*—

and then I ask my guest whether he isn't as troubled as I am by all this luxuriant but ecologically questionable splendor produced by the land's former cultivation. Doesn't he too get the feeling the whole thing has been staged so as to create the illusion of a form of existence unconnected to any truth? The truth of the past even less than ours today. I for my part distrust this grandeur. Even leaving out of account what it's hiding: the enormous service stations on the highway that is too far away to be seen in the daytime but at night creeps out from between the indigo-blue foothills a glittering worm wriggling off toward the southeast. The old cities rapidly filling up with cars: Figline San Giovanni Montevarchi Arezzo. Crumbling mortar above fashion boutiques and electronics shops; juvenile proletarians in leather jackets perched atop cacophonous motorcycles; coat-of-arms-encrusted Gothic town halls spun into the disorderly web of telephone wires; and on all sides the metastases of shoddy new buildings factories garages; the mange of construction sites trash heaps. That awful workshop where an ever more perfect world is being produced—

to bewail this is futile is embarrassingly behind the times I say. Already the laments for a world that has disregarded its own blueprint so willfully that the plan's original sense has been reversed make for plenty of material in my three daily four weekly six monthly periodicals. (Each column rubbing shoulders with glossy-paper-bright exhortations to make purchases that will speed the downward spiral into catastrophe—Lord forgive them for they know not what they do!) We'll press our accusations all the same. Against whom? As if we were really prepared to give up our indoor plumbing to restore God's undefiled Nature—we impatient passengers of thundering airplanes we ignominious children of the single earth-encompassing stone megalopolis that evening after evening is transformed for us into the fairy-tale kingdom of myriad light bulbs—

can't help giggling I say. Tuscany! Long-horned white oxen hitched to two-wheeled carts wobbling heavily beneath their load of grapes—isn't that it? Vintners rejoicing at harvesttime —ah the chianti! Let's put the folklore aside. A nature conservation area without trash cans for the plastic bags soda-pop cans and used-up cartridge cases (you can see them lying around). God's and the construction planners' undefiled Nature. A hedonist's reserve colonized exclusively by owners of vacation homes pensioners retired British army men artists fleeing the world. Refuges of this sort are among the lies we live; I wonder how long it will take our brothers and sisters in finally liberated Eastern Europe to see through them. They'll be showing up here anytime now. They had their own lie to live and in the end found the courage to repudiate it. Heroically (with improved consumer product availability and new vacation spots in mind) they shook off the yoke of the inexorably perfectionist will to fashion an ideal world and now seek the truth among us. Will they be quick studies when it comes to the more sublime forms of deception—and self-deception?

My sisters and brothers in the East move me to tears. I have taken a good look at their plight. I mean the plight of their purported liberation. In Romania for example just a few days after the overthrow (and murder) of Ceaușescu. In the bloody dawn of freedom that promised a day dark with clouds. As the heroes of the so-called revolution were beginning to figure out that it hadn't been their revolution. That it hadn't been a revolution at all. Pure fraud. A coup de theatre to cover up the

appalling truth. For ten days I observed the bewildering leg-
erdemain whose ostensible goal was to restore some semblance
of order to this intentionally induced chaos. The only order it
produced was of course the same inexorable order that had been
there before: after all someone had to get things in order again
and the only ones up to the task were those who had established
the first order to begin with. So it made sense that everything
should remain just the way it was before. In the ruins of a
decimated city in a country stripped of all its treasures in a
thoroughly corrupted and now ideologically sterilized society.
At the expense of a people that from the start had been trained
to wear its yoke submissively and in which God forbid some
rebellion might ferment. (Though harmlessly. The providers
of order have a firm grip on the reins.) Immediately afterward
I found myself in Cologne where I spent four days following
Prince Carnival and his retinue around. There I observed how
hard Germans have to work to organize a bit of whimsical chaos
for their own enjoyment. For the respite of their overtaxed
nerves in this world of fastidiously regulated prosperity in which
no risk is too great when it comes to making windfall profits
buying up potential sources of prosperity from their less prosperous sisters and brothers in the finally liberated German East.
A fortnight to observe and make comparisons isn't much. But
it was enough to make me swiftly plunge in the wake of my colleague Nietzsche to the deepest possible depths. (The depth was
not my doing: the depressing circumstances were responsible.)
After this I went to India where my encounter with The Mother
of Pondicherry prompted even more perplexed contemplations
and then it was back to the hospital. The year 1990 was packed
with event. And for me with experience as well (not all events
affect us). At first my experiences seemed even to me to have
nothing to do with one another. Does it make sense I ask that
I should have mixed feelings observing the outbreak of spring
here and in Eastern Europe and everywhere else in this world

barreling swiftly downhill to its own demise? Certainly I look on this with sympathy even empathy. But also with the alienated curiosity of one who has undertaken to juxtapose a fictional reality to this implausible one. Popular fiction. And no matter how well it turns out how well crafted . . .

and though I relish the discomfort with which my guest is squirming his way out from beneath my questions I am burning with impatience to be rid of him. My own babble bores me to tears. Utterly ordinary babble of the sort you find in the newspaper. I can't wait to be alone again and put on my reading glasses and reenter the enchanting irreality of the world of words and letters: still the coziest corner in this limbo of disconnectedness.

And as he drew nearer, he found a palace built of dark stone plated with iron, and one half of the gate stood wide open, while the other was closed.
—FROM THE THIRD OF THE THOUSAND AND ONE NIGHTS

The dubious spring outside my windows is a gift bestowed by March. (A song from my childhood my father used to warble "The poplars in the avenue sway in the Ma-arch breeze / My winter dream dissolves like snow that from the rooftops flees.") Indeed not even a month ago the weather was still decidedly wintry. Or what passes for winter here. Sleet coming down in the fog now and then a nasty wind churning up the olive trees. None of which bothered me a bit; I didn't set foot outside. I preferred to stay glued to the television screen. I've been glued to it since January 1991. What was taking place on it then (as though it really were happening right here before my eyes and not several thousand miles eastward in the fabled land of Arabia) was the Gulf War. A winter dream of the mass media that dissolved not with the snow but in the fog-gray of the glimmering screen. The fascination exerted by the events conjured up on its cathode-ray tube was remarkable. I said to myself this is finally real reality (though not my reality here). I plunged in. My books lay forgotten. The realm of the seven pillars of wisdom had been transported to my room. The logical continuation of the adventures of *Lawrence of Arabia* was unfolding before my eyes. I was watching world history in progress: the Iraqi dictator Saddam Hussein had occupied Kuwait and (as we're all sick to death of hearing) was driven out after heavy bombing by the Desert Shield of Mr. Bush and the Desert Storm of four-star General Schwarzkopf. For television reporters as well as my three daily four weekly six monthly periodicals a perfect example of what is now known as a scoop even in German journalese. But what a sad flat fart of a scoop! I gazed my way from one disappointment to the next. The pictures were stupefyingly empty though commentators worked hard to boost the sensation value. Patter is the customary aural backdrop for the moving image. And these were images that had no business on the screen. At first hour after hour of nothing but airplanes taking off and landing as in movies when you're supposed to believe the hero or heroine has moved to a new location. When they land something or other usually happens. But not here. The planes were bombers but where had they dropped their bombs? CNN eventually showed us their target: Baghdad city of Caliph Haroun al-Rashid at night ultra-pitch-black darkness ringed at the distant edges with St. Elmo's fire. All well and good but yours truly had witnessed these phenomena firsthand between 1940 and 1945 (a few thousand miles

21

to the north and west—in Berlin): an infinitely more dramatic experience (and louder). Real live reality. Here it was abstract. Occasionally one was offered a bird's-eye view of an infrared image of a bomb target vaguely bobbing in the crosshairs of the (apparently unchallenged) attackers. Grainy gray-black like an underexposed negative. An indefinite something suddenly extinguished by a snowball splatting right on top of it. That— said the commentator—was the bomb. (And anything that had been alive down there had "a snowball's chance in hell" just like me in Berlin in 1943.) Here and now the process was nebulous like a sort of blueprint of the horrific. (In my room in the tower things were nice and cozy with a dandy little fire crackling away on the hearth and I held my evening glass of whiskey in my hand.) Only once did an amusing interlude break the monotony of this abstract warfare when one saw a tiny figure no bigger than an ant managing to scurry over the last bit of a bridge before it too vaporized beneath a splatting snowball. Finally the human touch. Of course this scene was re-broadcast over and over. As was an oil-smeared cormorant: witness to the satanic contempt this foreign brute this brutal tyrant showed for the environment! Followed by the oil-laden waters of the Persian Gulf: Sinbad's sea shimmering with jewel-like fish Scheherazade's world of emeralds and rubies and vales of turquoise smothered in petroleum. To break the power of this fiend and see him wiped off the face of God's earth was considered a matter of honor for all civilized nations. All right then that is what I wanted to see. That's what had been promised. Damn it I wanted to see the thing with my own eyes! Like the barrage of bombs in Berlin. The deadly human touch. But what one saw on television was a rip-off. The disproportion was exasperating between the suspense built up before the raids and the dribs and drabs of action eventually parceled out. The human species wasn't working hard enough to accomplish its mission here.

The media tacticians seemed to sense this. Ordinarily the

world's mood dances on the scoops of the moment like a Ping-Pong ball on a jet of water and if the water doesn't keep bubbling up vigorously enough the ball tumbles down. Mr. Bush's political future in his own country was at stake. The media bigwigs patched the holes in their visuals with meaningless patter. Every half hour the poker-faced commentators chimed in with theoretical–drivel analyses of the situation. Specialists did their abstract work. Live reporters equally far from the scene of action filed inconsequential reports (supposedly they weren't allowed to get any closer) while full-time intellectuals dished out verbal porridge at round–table discussions of the ethical moral political economic ethnopsychological and international–law–related aspects of the event. These all seemed very familiar. But where was the event? I watched it vanish in the sun-swathed banners of desert sand behind the departing tanks. Would they soon come upon Saddam Hussein's murderous lines of defense? If so, I never saw or heard about it. Nothing that deserved the name "action." (Ryszard Kapuściński described the process in *The Soccer War*: ". . . Gregor Straub of NBC said he had to have a close-up of a soldier's face dripping sweat. Rodolfo Carillo of CBS said he had to catch a despondent commander sitting under a bush and weeping because he had lost his whole unit. A French cameraman wanted a panorama shot with a Salvadoran unit charging a Honduran unit from one side, or vice versa. Somebody else wanted to capture the image of a soldier carrying his dead comrade. The radio reporters sided with the cameraman. One wanted to record the cries of a casualty summoning help, growing weaker and weaker, until he breathed his last breath . . .") Here before my eyes (and ears) was nothing of the sort. Not the slightest hint of action. This war was either at a standstill or else so devoid of whatever gripping reports are made of that I caught myself wishing Saddam Hussein would hurry up and deploy his poison-gas grenades and infernal rockets.

Something fishy was going on. Hadn't the mass media

themselves—television above all—constructed this desert marvel of a scoop and tossed us onto the water jet of their world-historical up-to-dateness? (In any case the diplomatic corps of Iraq Saudi Arabia Israel the United States—Mr. Bush needed his toy war—and God knows who else exploited the situation for their own purposes; people all over the world had interests in the conflict.) The water jet had been turned on but alas not full force and we couldn't dance on it. Before my eyes the sensation (presumably also the purpose) vanished beneath hands that were unskilled or tied somehow.

I myself am an old pro at this trade. In prehistoric times—from 1946 to 1956—I dabbled in radio. In Hamburg-on-the-Elbe. The historical events of that era—the ceding of the Bukovina to Russia the Second World War and so on—washed me up on those shores as a radio journalist. Not amid a rough-and-tumble competition among stations as one finds today in the commercialized news reporting of world events but rather in the cushy caveman days of the German mass media: when it was still just us out there in the bombed-out field. But even this taught good lessons in the tricks of the trade: if you smell a scoop somewhere you've got to put it together yourself the way a heavyweight champion constructs his opponent in the ring. Then a give-it-all-you've-got uppercut to the jaw (the jaw of the media consumer to be precise). All right. But now everything was reversed. I stood there in the corner of my own free-will ring waiting for blows that never came. Something was odd about the whole arrangement. This soon became readily apparent as the mother of all battles went into labor for the precipitate delivery of a pyrrhic victory which came so abruptly and as it were underhandedly that even for the commentators and round-table gossips sloshing breathlessly about in the wake of the latest events the present reality kept slipping into an irreal past. What took place was purely abstract. No one seemed at all certain what had actually happened. It was not accessible to the senses: a war in which one was told that on one side there had been scarcely a few dozen casualties (mostly victims of traffic accidents and friendly fire) and only a few hundred thousand rumored dead among the enemy forces. But damn it! I'd have liked to have seen at least a few dead piled up somewhere. As witnesses to the just cause (if that's what it was supposed to be). Hadn't the enterprise been sanctioned by the united nations of the civilized world as ethically and morally impeccable and supported in every way (for example by letting the oppressed people who were to be liberated starve)? Emotionally it was hard to make it all add up. The visual element was missing. Something that could be grasped (physically or mentally). The so-called realness of it all. The mission accomplished for our species. As long as we couldn't sense the reality of the lives once lived by the enemy dead this *drôle de guerre* was an abstract war. Without the evidence of heaped-up cadavers it existed only in statistical terms. True they tried to make up for it later with footage showing the destruction of trucks of the retreating troops and former occupiers of Kuwait. Grotesquely devastated convoys that seemed most of all to express how modern man has identified himself with his vehicles. But this too was not necessarily how to bring the distant events closer. I kept lagging behind with uneasy questions. Why was reality being kept under wraps? Was it embarrassment at a preposterous overkill? What had become of Saddam Hussein's infernal war machines? Were they being saved for the next scoop? Waiting in the wings until the Oriental devil was in a position to deploy truly deadly force? *Ex oriente lux*—even the light of an atomic flash? Had the media put their scoop together so as to bash me in the nose once and for all? Now that they can bring world history live into the home (no matter how abstractly) no doubt they're trying to produce it with as much breathtaking reality as possible. Definitively breathtaking. Knowing that I and people like me will be there to consume it in good faith. Greedy for reality. In euphoric commiseration like a mild drug high. Following these events in a no-man's-land between realities. Simultaneously exhilarated and paralyzed. In a sphere beyond reality that lifts me out of myself. What a strange addition to life here in my Tuscan tower! But an addition it is.

At this point Shahrazad saw the approach of morning and discreetly fell silent; but when the tenth night had come, her sister Dunyazad said, "Tell us the end of your story," and she replied, "With the greatest pleasure . . ."

Isn't it astonishing that I'm still reading books? Even writing them? Incurably spellbound by these runes? Both priest and sacrifice in the cult of the printed page? Stalwartly defending my own private realm of demons against the unleashed fiends of virtual reality? (Bruce Chatwin in *The Songlines* revealed Pulcinella's secret: the poet sings the world into existence.) Courageous navel-gazer. Steadfast worshipper in the temple of the Great Fetish Art. Heroically struggling against the shadow play of the present so much less real than any reality conjured on paper. (Colleague Thomas Mann's "murmuring imperfect"— how old hat!) For my part I harbor no illusions. I know I'm defending a lost cause. Not as heroically as the O.W.A.s who fulfilled their artistic promise before their early deaths. More shrewdly. Sybaritically. A hedonist in the hedonists' corner. An epoch-embezzler with eyes wide open. A nineteenth-century man of letters on the threshold of the twenty-first. A late singer-into-existence of the world. Tempted by the cult of runes to commit acts of deception. But not self-deception.

On occasion when I gaze out my tower window at the rolling Valdarno hills that reach to the gray-blue distant Pratomagno I fill my lungs with air and feel alive. Despite the more or less natural disintegration of my physis I remain (more or less) in possession of my mental powers. An indefatigable Cartesian. *Cogito, ergo sum.* Warbling my way past the question what's the point? Can my thought still hit the mark and what does it miss? To what extent is this world still obedient to my singing? One thing has become ever more clear to me: I with my rune game (like my colleagues with theirs) am nothing but a joke. We are playing to the void. Ancestral father Onan. The mass media sing today's world into existence CNN first and foremost. When the tube (quintessential apparatus for the production of reality) is turned on in the evening—this happens with tormenting regularity—a sort of communion occurs. B. and I and our occasional guests sit in silent unison our gazes meeting at the vanishing point of world-historical perspective. We know that in their rooms Anna Fedora Aisha Leila and Ibrahim are engaged in prayer much as we are and the abstract events flickering across the cathode-ray tube before all our eyes draw us toward the end point of a common fate where we find one another. We are united in the shadow play of "reality." Soon all humankind will be united night after night in the experience of the Gulf War *Perry Mason Dallas Dynasty* German reunification. And yet no one is allowed to say: I am not alone.

(The consequences are common knowledge: a mass-psychotic need for communion. Collective kowtowing before the Great Fetish Art. Metastases of compulsive self-expression Everyman and Everywoman wanting to write. Painters supplement their troglodyte philosophemes with elucidating inscriptions: bastard poetry. Potters rise to the rank of psychoceramicists. Musicians become semiologists. The will to survive makes inroads in abstract fields.) My own affliction is becoming worse and worse. It kicks in with particular force whenever it's time for some repair job on my deteriorating body. I'm never more diligent than before one of those procedures to eliminate this or that side effect. (My colleague Dr. Johnson: "When a man knows he is to be hanged in a fortnight, it concentrates his mind wonderfully.") Of course given my utterly irrepressible optimism I assume I'll wake from the anesthetic. But—as rosy-cheeked mentors across the globe so like to bleat: *Be prepared!* Prepared I am. And when—unexpectedly after all—the familiar old world is there again posthumously as it were my reunion with it leaves me euphoric and drained. Reborn into the tedium of everyday factuality. I have a sense of somehow having been cheated. Time goes along doggedly from each used-up yesterday to each listlessly hoped-for tomorrow. The boredom gradually building up during reconvalescence is paralyzing. Empty morning hours in bed writing tablet propped on my knees and before me all the livelong day utterly devoid of responsibility (and ideas). Now and then an intuitive insight pops up like a totem pole surrounded by a flock of thoughts that soon take wing again like swallows fleeing a troubled house. I'm supposed to be resting up. They feed me bland invalid fare designed precisely not to stimulate the brain: bleached-out chicken for lunch porridge for supper. They don't take me seriously here. I've been to the other side. But no one's willing to accept this. Death has no place in our world of prosperity. So they nurse me back to health on an invalid's diet. Peristalsis as unobtrusive as perestroika. (I know this is bad wordplay but it's a disgracefully deep-seated flaw in my character that I can't pass up a chance to indulge in it. Especially not when in a state of acedia.) My restlessness increases as my health returns. My mind mistakes its own impatience for a dancer's gay abandon. (Grete

Wiesenthal's School of Dance they called it in Vienna before my sister's early death. Today the name Wiesenthal is more likely to call up associations of the hunt for Eichmann and Dr. Mengele.) The mission of mankind coming back to haunt us. The fear of procreation with the end of the world so nigh. Let's live for the next final operation.

"Now, the cause of that knocking, O King," said Shahrazad, "was this: the Caliph Haroun al-Rashid had gone forth from his palace to see and hear the latest happenings."
—FROM THE ELEVENTH OF THE *THOUSAND AND ONE NIGHTS*

*B*efore the last one too I'd expected that the fair chance of my soon ceasing to exist except on paper would hasten my efforts to immortalize myself in this medium. A promise not lived up to. That final (for the time being) correction of the so-called side effects of an infirmity caused by a side effect from years and years ago was minor. At least according to my doctor who was seconded by the surgeon. So the operation was taken lightly by all concerned and no one showed less respect for it than me. I checked into the hospital feeling frisky. The nurses there have known me for years. They didn't even bother to bring the *pappagallo* to my bedside. I could stand up and trundle to the bathroom under my own steam. Nothing about any of this prompted the sort of suspenseful apprehension I had enjoyed before past operations (foretaste of the great adventure

I'll be embarking on any day now). I was distracted. I had stocked up on books and magazines and now started out with so-called light reading: reality. For example (so as to get as close as possible to the concrete world now that I was close to the end) the weekly journal *Der Spiegel*. From my linguistic homeland Germany an issue devoted to the sensational theme of the side effects of German reunification. Heaping scorn on my sisters and brothers in the East. Other German periodicals were more entertaining. *Die Bunte* reporting on the eccentric behavior of the Princess von Thurn und Taxis and the erotic menu most recently enjoyed by the daughters of the princely house of Monaco. (Plus health tips: treatment of kidney stones and of pustules on the mucous membranes. All sorts of weight reduction programs.) Let's flip to the world of letters arts culture politics: in *The New York Review of Books* Timothy Garton Ash writing not (say) on the reality of books but on the "reality" of the most recent events in Poland and Czechoslovakia—which stirred up my recent memories of Romania. Back to Europe: *Paris Match* reminding me of Pondicherry and Carnival in Cologne. My Italian homeland: *Panorama* and *Espresso* highlighting the procession of clowns in the circus of Italian politics. *Gente* offering photographic reports on Lady Di and the sixth marriage of Sandra Milo. *Novella 2000* announcing Liz Taylor's upcoming eighth. Scandal-sheet material with a touch of class: *Vanity Fair*. I longed to get my hands on a real television set. This mere husk of the televised world could not induce in me the heightened receptivity to be enjoyed by a man condemned to death.

The doctors made up for this in the preliminary examination. I found myself lying flat on my back (Kafka's bug) my legs raised and bent like those of a woman in labor while a long tube was inserted into my rectum and my guts were pumped full of air. This is how the French extracted confessions from Algerian freedom fighters. I had nothing to confess beyond my own skepticism about various matters including scientific medicine. Though people say you can always trust a surgeon's knife. Especially given the latest technological advancements. At the end of the tube a lens is mounted like the nauplius eye at the tip of the arm of a starfish and beside it a tiny lamp to illuminate and examine the wall of the intestine. The unrelenting advance of this miner's light into the body's innermost cavities not only is extremely painful but comes with its own set of psychological side effects. I hated the interns who had seemed so friendly on their morning rounds and who now appeared to be taking malicious pleasure in my torments like small boys skinning a frog. I was no longer the easygoing old gentleman (*lo scrittore*) in a private patient's room with whom they had exchanged pleasantries while glancing over the temperature chart at the foot of my bed. (I never had a fever since except for the side effect of my various intestinal complications I am in perfect health though if I weren't so healthy I would have to think myself a gravely ill man.) Here in surgery I was a subject like all the rest. Meat for the scalpel. The results of this examination would determine the relative distance between this or that piece of my anatomy and the garbage can. Even my nakedness alone was enough to show I had no right to expect to be treated with any semblance of human dignity. (The point of view of Christian colonial gentlemen: the naked "savage"! Once in New York as I sat with various other subjects in the waiting room of the Department of Radiology—black mothers Nicaraguan salesgirls Irish truckers Bolivian peddlers African street sweepers old Jewish immigrants all lumped together in green smocks closed in front and tied together in back; legs bare brown legs white legs black legs fat legs thin legs hairy legs smooth legs varicose-veined legs athletic legs flabby legs—one smock with bare legs below suddenly had a fit: the man inside had been forced to undress and wait but when they told him he could get dressed again since he was in the wrong department he shouted "And why did I have to strip naked? You do everything to humiliate us!")

The interns—two of them one tall and haggard one short and fat like Mutt and Jeff—had their eyes pressed to the viewing apparatus at the far end of my rectal tube and twisted its knobs like submarine officers at the periscope. This activity went along with inarticulate but loquacious remarks like "Tsa tsa tsa!" and "Hm hm!" and once the short fat one threw in a *"Mamma mia!"* After they had peered all they wanted and liberated me from the tube (the air hissed out of me like steam from an old express-train locomotive) they set about making a drawing of my en-trails. I lay there on the orthopedic bed respectfully covered with a sheet and watched as they shaded in the questionable zones. We waited for the head physician to arrive.

The head physician is a surgeon with an excellent reputation and a philosophy of life devoid of romanticism. While he pored over the blueprints of my innards he licked his lips in antici-pation. Then he came over to me and began to elucidate the shaded bits. A single procedure to clear up everything was no longer possible, he said. The damage was too extensive. Not only had the morbid growth to be taken into account but also the fragility of the tissue itself. These were side effects of cobalt radiation that had doubtless been well intended but probably given in too high a dose. Nowadays such treatment is no longer used at least not here in Europe said he. The Americans have their own ideas about it. (His American associate had said "The decision is risky. But with a man of your status we don't want to make a mistake." Blessed are the poor.) Be that as it may: he said it's lucky for us the body automatically works to over-come its own illness for even in my case a certain *status vivendi* had thus been reached that could be stabilized with only a few minor adjustments. I could count on having at least a few more years ahead of me. No problem.

This announcement left me somewhat dissatisfied. Disap-

32

pointed. Ever since my first major operation whose side effect (caused it was said by an anesthesiologist's error) had been a heart attack that occasioned a memorable stay in the intensive-care unit I had promised myself the same drama each time. Before my second-to-last surgery I kept the orderlies who'd come to cart me off to the operating room waiting for almost half an hour because I was finishing a book. This time there was nothing to finish. The *mene, mene, tekel, upharsin* of my final hour ought to have spurred me on to new creativity. There is nothing to touch this sacred impatience. I saw the same impatience in Bruce's eyes just a few weeks before his death. Sapphire-blue visionary's eyes glittering fanatically in a boyish Anglo-Saxon head that had already become a skull. (It was poignant how his youthful curls had thinned. Damp with fever like the down on the skull of a new-hatched chick.) He was too weak to write but obsessed with the thought that he was about to succeed in pinpointing the cause of his illness. Somewhere in Africa, he said feverishly. He was in touch with all the most swiftly sprinting researchers in a race against time. It goes without saying that he wanted to win so as to be able to write.

(It was the same with Ugo Mulas: the cancer spread through his body as part after part of it was trimmed away and he hung like a spider in a web of tubes and hoses and was grateful to the doctors for giving him the time to write his theoretical study of photography. He too had the eyes of a fanatic. Visionary's eyes. Prophet's eyes. They were not a radiant blue like Bruce's but shone with a dark glow glowed with a fervor that sanctified his pain. His hair went white. His hazelnut-brown Mediterranean robustness became wrinkled and silver-nitrate gray like a photographic negative. His lips were stretched taut with the effort of wresting just a few more days of life from his cancer-ridden body.)

Bruce Chatwin and Ugo Mulas: quintessential O.W.A.s. Neither of them lived much past forty. They'd had to hurry.

I arrived here this very night, and was standing there uncertain where to go, when suddenly I saw this second mendicant; so I salam'd to him, saying: "I am a stranger!" and he replied: "I, too, am a stranger." While we were conversing, our third companion appeared and saluted us, saying: "I am a stranger," and we replied: "We, too, are strangers."

—FROM THE THIRTEENTH OF THE *THOUSAND AND ONE NIGHTS*

The uppermost window of the tower where Bruce wrote some of *On the Black Hill* (constantly speaking of his next book project) gives on the southeast. My onetime friend Ernst Schnabel (naval hero former convoy leader with the German Order of the Gold Cross also an obsessive writer and dead too though at the age of seventy-two) would have computed in a flash the difference in degrees of latitude between my position here and my legendary homeland. Which no longer exists even in name: the Bukovina. Once a crownland of the Dual Monarchy later part of Romania today in Ukraine. (In agriculture one says "The fields migrate to the best farmer" but in politics it seems to be just the opposite.) I can still hear the hodgepodge of languages spoken in this fabulous land: Romanian Ukrainian German Yiddish Polish Russian Magyar Turkish Armenian Gypsy. A Babel where the indigenous amalgam of deeply felt mutual sympathies and cynical worldliness enabled everyone to understand everyone else (which doesn't mean he opened his heart to the others in true fraternity). Bruce questioned me on the subject in his own way by coaxing out anecdotes. Bruce the collector. Once I discovered what became of these treasures he hoarded. In the days before the advent of Anna Fedora Aisha and Leila a certain Giuliana saw to our well-being. One morning she went to the tower to straighten up and returned distraught. "How many people are staying in the tower?" Just Signor Chatwin. Why? She had overheard an entire assortment of voices: men women children. It was Bruce writing. Reading aloud the many-voiced chaos at a country fair in Wales. When I read the passage in *On the Black Hill* one of these voices was from the Bukovina.

A great deal of ink has left my pen since the days when I still worried over the value or lack thereof of the anecdotal episodic mode. I remember having heated discussions with friend Schnabel in our sanctuary in the former studios of the North West German Radio Network in Hamburg (where I was eventually thrown out—by him). The year was 1946 '47 '48 and Schnabel looked up to his namesake Ernest Hemingway with the most fervent reverence. We spoke about this a great deal and preserved our differences of opinion to the last. Bruce and I never exchanged a word about our craft (with one exception on the day we first met) but contented ourselves with batting anecdotes back and forth. I would like to have had him with me on my last trip to Romania. Ever since my return home (a paradoxical homecoming from my homeland) I've been having the sort of monologic conversation with him that the living have with the dead with whom they have unfinished business. (Which applies to any deceased writer-colleague worth comparing oneself to but since the real comparison is always with oneself the results are never satisfactory.)

In reaction to Romania I had similar difficulty getting myself under control. My relationship to the land of my origins proved to be quite troubled. Which is to say my myth no longer fit. My trip took me not to the Bukovina proper (or the part of it still in Romania) but to Bucharest. The focal point of historic events. After all I wasn't traveling around in search of my own past self but on the trail of the ostensible revolution. Yet of course I kept tripping over my own feet. I couldn't shake off my own past there (nor anywhere else for that matter). It was ridiculous the way I kept leapfrogging my own shadow. Instead of Bruce my (younger) friend Tilman Spengler was with me. One of those brilliant young men who have reality here and there and everywhere perfectly under control (one can only admire this). Like a ghost I walked beside him through the streets of Bucharest and was accompanied by my own ghost who wouldn't stop haranguing me. On and on it went about the difference between simultaneity and present time. And there I was after half a century's absence (with only two lightning-swift belated exceptions) in the land of my own mythical pre-history where even the blue yellow red of its national flag had become my mythological banner. I walked over the same cobblestones on which I'd worn my soles down years before as a youthful *flâneur* with a carnation in my lapel past the sites of old dreams and dreams-come-true joys and miseries conquests and losses triumphs and defeats . . . and all these things now existed simultaneously within me in a dimension of time that was neither present nor past. Nothing was past but everything was now and here within me yet was not the present. I gazed up at the blue yellow red Romanian flag from which the Communist insignia had been cut and thought that the hole in the middle was me.

January 1990 was not the first time I'd returned to Romania since my departure in 1937. I'd been back once in 1980 for a week and another time in 1986 for a few hectic days. Both were in the days of the cold Cold War when Ceaușescu was at the zenith of his dazzling career. He was praised on all sides as a great statesman (for his supposed independence from Moscow) and Madame Elena for her scientific achievements. (The Queen of England received him as a head of state equal in rank to herself while renowned universities conferred honorary doctorates on the half-illiterate scientist.) Even in those days there wasn't much to eat in my homeland and even less to warm oneself with and the winters were bitter as they could be only there. Lovers used to quip "Love me but don't undress me!" Nevertheless I couldn't muster any pity. These brothers and sisters of mine in the European Southeast lived their lie with such hard-nosed defiance that I couldn't tell whether they were trying to fool me or themselves. They knew the police rule of thumb that everyone is under suspicion and the more unobtrusive a person is the more suspicions there are. So they wore the official lie in their faces as openly as an archduchess might have worn her Catholicism at a Corpus Christi procession. I knew I was seeing only the surface. I also knew I would never see anything but one sort of half-truth or another and it would be purely a matter of chance if I got a glimpse behind the veil. Only once did I encounter the truth and then it was *en passant* on the street. A couple straight out of a Dostoevskian vision: an old woman reduced to tatters hunched far over and supported by a young man of savage romantic beauty aquiline nose burning eyes a waxen pallor—he too starved to the bone; pitifully shielded from the biting cold by the threadbare folds of an ancient ankle-length coat and a thin rope of a wool scarf around his neck. Atop the chestnut-brown curls that hung down regally to his shoulders he had placed a jaunty cap of rancid fur that might have been scavenged from the garbage. The couple proceeded in slow motion through the undulating streams of pedestrians who disdainfully ignored them. (The streets of Bucharest are always packed even today.) The old woman paused exhausted after every other tottering step. The young man solicitously patiently matched his stride to hers and the enormity of the contempt expressed in his aquiline profile his ramrod posture his eyes fixed straight ahead avoiding even the most fleeting contact with those around him the pride with which he guided the ravaged hag on his arm as though he were escorting a beautiful woman onto the dance floor made my heart miss a beat. This was the living image of contempt for an entire species. Pure misanthropy. Self-hatred in all its dignity.

A few days later I drove with my friend Venier (head of the Italian news agency) to Curtea-de-Argeş where the Wallachian princes are buried. We drove through the lowland plains of the Bărăgan where as a twenty-year-old doing military service I had participated in various cavalry exercises (sometimes in-volving farmers' daughters). Earthy youthful memories to last a lifetime. But now there was no sense of homecoming. I kept telling myself I was home again if only for a visit. Yet a tem-porary homecoming is not a real one. It was as if I'd never left but also as if I'd never been there before. Nothing I saw struck me as foreign. Yet I had no sense of being at home either. I was numb inside. And so I experienced the trip literarily: as a journey under the guidance of the *Surrealist Manifesto* according to which the real and the unreal intermesh to produce the surreal. I was in Romania all right. We drove westward. The country-side was flat. On our left to the south the Danube flowed; on our right to the north lay the Carpathian Mountains. We could see neither. Both were many miles distant and the horizon lay beneath a wintry haze. The road was lined with grotesquely twisted willows gnarled trunks bristling with bunches of thin stubby twigs like witches' brooms. It was very cold. The mother-of-pearl-gray sky took on a peach tint around the edges. From snow-covered fields flocks of crows rose up. That was Romania as it had always been. (As I had sung it into existence.) But whenever we passed through a village things became pre-posterously exaggeratedly Romanian. In place of the traditional white-and-blue-and-yellow-painted mud huts of bygone days that had huddled beneath gently sloping hipped roofs like rab-bits in warm hutches we found a series of pointily gabled stubbily turreted petit-bourgeois villas in the hybrid Balkan-Byzantine style characteristic of the Romanian nationalist movement that flared up around the turn of the last century (architectural jargon calls it the Brancovean style). They had been built in the late 1940s and early '50s with the dawning of the optimistic Stalinistic brand of Romanian Communism. That these gingerbread houses fit for boyars were to be occupied by kolkhozniks was curious enough. (Even the Conducător Ceauşescu found this inappropriate. Two decades later he had most of the villages razed and sky-high housing developments built in their place.) Still the inhabitants gave evidence of their agrarian origins for the walls of the loggias at the foot of the stairs (two stocky arches divided by a column as thick around as a drum coiling massively upward like a turban drawn out into a cylinder) had been adorned with murals of primitively stylized spruce forests framing deer. Floral bouquets. Crowing cocks. Mountain sunsets. Here and there a clumsy memorial to the good old ornamental embroidery of the good old days on blouses cushions coverlets sheepskins (no longer part of Romania's image). All the more curious that this folklore-tinged proletarian idyll should show such close kinship with Ceauşescu's post-Stalinist edifices in Bucharest. Linked by the same spiritual phenomenology—just as Park Avenue and Disneyland are.

We turned off to the right and toward the mountains to the north. At the edge of a hamlet bristling with icicles a Securitate patrol stopped us. I had a sinking feeling in the pit of my stomach. Venier got the necessary documents together and managed to make the destination and purpose of our trip seem plausible. But my passport (I hadn't yet contritely exchanged my stateless person's status for Austrian citizenship) gave my place of birth as the Bukovina which made me a former Romanian. My papers from the foreign citizens' office looked insubstantial in the black leather glove of this member of the state security force. ("Flimsy" the pseudo-English governesses of my childhood would have called it and the patrolman "beefy.") He looked unnervingly Muscovite in his fur cap and massively belted uniform coat. "You were born in Romania?" he asked me. At the time the Bukovina was still part of Austria I explained. I took great pains to sound affable and added that I had been a Romanian citizen between the two major wars. "War" in Romanian is *râzboi*. I'm not sure why the word sounded so intimate when I said it as though it were something linking me to this man (something apocalyptic: violence blood cruelty devastation death). He appeared to sense this too. He returned my passport and said "C'me're I want to show you something!"

A few paces away a small group had gathered: a shriveled little man of perhaps seventy and a handful of boys from very young to adolescent. My state security cop took the old man by the shoulder and showed him to me. "Have a look. This here was our priest. But now we've shaved him!" The boys hooted and the man reproached him. "You should be ashamed of yourself! I baptized you. I taught you to read and write!" The officer gave a hearty Stalinist laugh (the "terrible joviality" of the head forester in my colleague Ernst Jünger's *On the Marble Cliffs*). "And in exchange I've shaved you!" To me: "He had the most beautiful beard of the lot of them. The patriarch couldn't help being envious. And I shaved it off." The boys hooted. They belonged to the generation that would march to meet the Securitate's bullets in December 1989. But not because they wanted to have their priests' beards back.

In January 1990 I saw their freshly dug graves at the edge of a public park. Shabby rough wooden crosses and the bedraggled poorhouse flowers in a sludge of snow and trampled earth. Stumpy candles constantly blowing out in the draft from passing cars. Clumsy farewells scribbled by mothers and siblings. Live human suffering. Pictures of those who fell in vain: all heartrendingly young. Passport photos. Amateur snapshots. To preserve them from the vagaries of the weather their relatives

40

had placed them beneath turned-over drinking glasses. Tilman Spengler thoroughbred journalist that he is discovered the grave of a lad of whom apparently no picture existed and instead the bereaved family had placed under a glass a newspaper clipping with a photo of his greatest hero: Sylvester Stallone as Rambo.

Anecdotes of the sort Bruce Chatwin loved. Though I'm sure he would have resisted the desire to put them to literary use. Maybe (stepping back to hide behind himself) in the cultivated impersonality of a newspaper article (a tried and tested trick). He drew a sharp dividing line between journalist and novelist. The journalist can allow himself all sorts of things that would be inappropriate for the novelist (like firing off the Roman candles of sensationalism). And he preserved a strict division between Chatwin the novelist and Chatwin the journalist (not to mention Chatwin the irresistibly charming conversationalist). One of his obvious virtues was discipline. Which was also the cause of his well-concealed exhaustion.

Indeed, mistress, neither was I born with one eye only; and the story which I am going to tell you is so marvellous that, if it were written with a needle on the inner corner of any eye, it would serve as a lesson to the circumspect.

—FROM THE FOURTEENTH OF THE *THOUSAND AND ONE NIGHTS*

The thankless task of perpetuating culture! Reading the correspondence between Hugo von Hofmannsthal and Carl Jakob Burckhardt I realize what has been lost in my lifetime. The world's riffraffization impresses itself upon me to the point of physical distress. An awkward fate has befallen me: sharing in the decline with open eyes. A contemporary of morbid vintage. I see the lost splendor that most of those born after me are— lucky for them—blind to. Not merely the wealth and depth of knowledge not merely the sharp-sightedness foresight world-view of disciplined epoch-embezzlers intent on smuggling the nineteenth century into the early twentieth nor their worldliness (not to be confused with the cosmopolitan provincialism of today). It's *le bon ton* not only in how friends behave to one another but in everything they refer to in their conversation. Reading becomes a way to linger in excellent company. (In this respect I admit I'm a hopeless snob.) From the most profound to the most trivial—whether ideas about religion history ethnopsychology literature theater politics or characterization of individuals description of circumstances or sketches of a city and travel reports (in pretty well all of which Burckhardt cuts a better figure than Hofmannsthal in political matters almost uncannily prophetic) or an invitation to breakfast sickbed updates news of the sale of a picture or exchange of vacation plans—each expressed with a grace that may be attributed to mutual esteem good form discretion and urbane reserve—in short with an objectivity that bears so civilized a pedigree it can make the likes of yours truly gnash his teeth in shame. Embarrassing enough to be an epigone but living in the gutter with a view of uninhabited palaces makes the cup still more bitter. The only consoling thought is how much self-deception it takes to inhabit a palace. What makes my colleagues Burckhardt and Hofmannsthal so admirable is their firm belief in the world they and their predecessors sang into existence. Death song of dinosaurs. (Perhaps that was equally beautiful.)

I won't be so incautious as to measure myself against my colleagues Burckhardt and Hofmannsthal. (Comparison with such exalted dead can be literarily fatal.) Gnashing my teeth I'll content myself with the thought that I belong to an unfortunate generation caught in the middle (even old men have childhoods behind them). Hofmannsthal was two years older than my father (their birth dates 1874 and 1876) and I was fifteen years old when he died (1929: I was then—unwillingly and unpropitiously—at a boarding school near Vienna in Mauer which is not far from his estate in Rodaun). For most of my life (until 1974 when I was sixty) I was a contemporary of Burckhardt's. Admittedly the break between fathers and sons had long since been made (Freud's Oedipus is a document of its time). There were not only rebellious sons but idiotic obedient ones (epoch-embezzling small fry). Some wanted to sing the world into existence in a striking new way. Small fry who devoted their cracking voices to the service of mankind by inverting mankind's models and values. And others (born curators) saw anyone who wanted to pocket culture's golden treasures as a scoundrel. The role that fell to them reminds me of American slapstick comedies (I'm a product of my time): as the iron horse rushes snorting into the future the bad guys uncouple the cars in which the cultural treasures of the past are being transported and the good guys—heroic Buster Keatons—try with their hands and feet to keep the rapidly receding coffers attached to the locomotive. The scuffle ends but not without losses the least of which seems that of social decorum. Worse still—with all the conflict between self-deceivers and with the villains pulling the wool over their eyes—everyone forgets to ask what's fueling the locomotive and where it's headed. That's how things are in this world. The ways of God are not so mysterious as is generally assumed; it's just that we lose sight of them.

Bruce and I met sometime around 1974 in London at a Western. Clint Eastwood was shooting from the hip. Bruce was touchingly young—the "Golden Boy" he remained all his life. I actively seek the company of young people. (My colleague Hofmannsthal quotes Marshal Lyautey: *"Je m'entends rarement avec un général, toujours avec un lieutenant."* That's easy enough to see given that the lieutenant clicks his heels.) The soon-to-be O.W.A. Bruce and I (already somewhat worn down) promptly agreed that manners are the most striking indices of an age. Hand-me-down fustiness in formal dress old texts restored to youth in the new generation's handwriting. Fathers eliminated. *Plus de pères. Rien que de fils!* Social etiquette changed in precisely the same way as the salon gave way to a Western saloon: you enter by kicking open the swinging doors' truncated wings and with an icy glance from beneath the brim of the Stetson shoved halfway down your forehead make it clear that you are quicker on the draw than anyone else. No aestheticized curlicues please. Anyone who insists on emotion can imagine the passionately glowing heart behind the steel façade. For the world is still moved by love hate power humility. What counts is the unscrupulous reprocessing of the old clichés. Otherwise no one will swallow them anymore. This was the only conversation in which Bruce and I laughing contemptuously touched on our métier. Throughout our friendship the impassive avenging-angel face of Clint Eastwood hovered between us and behind it I glimpsed the young generation's suffering and the painful compulsion to sing this ugly world into beautiful yet also truthful existence. Knowingly and unsentimentally. So to speak between clenched teeth. No bellyaching permitted. As though to question the sense and purpose of this singing would be bad form. Bruce needed his discipline. He knew the face value of elegant social conduct.

(Ugo Mulas the Sentimental: mulling over the plan for his book on photography—it grew in him along with the cancer he would die of—he became fascinated with my old pictures goods embezzled from the past. Prints dating back to my childhood: my sister and I in various poses and costumes. They had been taken by my father. Using primordial cameras that without doubt had represented the latest technology around the turn of the century. Ugo made me describe them in detail: the costly behemoths of mahogany fine black leather brazen fittings ground glass and thick lenses; mounted precariously on awkward tripods of lightweight wood the legs telescoping stalks of interlocking segments each smaller than the last like the legs of an easel. These tripods reminded me the wartime child of the crutches of an invalid—this too a genre picture from this epoch: machine guns were propped on similar stands though these were made of iron. My father hated everything military. For him these tripods were fragile struts in the landslide of our civilization. He didn't see the connection. If occasionally he changed from the hunter he was in every fiber of his essence into an amateur photographer it was in the getup of the landscape painter: *Bonjour, Monsieur Courbet*. Like baggage on an expedition the gear was carried by porters. The tripods were encased in linen pouches that could be buttoned open and shut; the cameras reposed in the green felt linings of sturdy calfskin cases with stout straps brass hinges brass locks. They made their appearance compressed into flat heavy mahogany boxes. Only when they had been screwed down firmly to the tripod did my father unfold them: their innards caterpillared out into the daylight as rails hinges little brass screws little bronze wheels extended toward us their elephant's trunk a black leather bellows in a reverse perspective of zigzag stairs so as to mesmerize us with a round dark mirroring Cyclops eye ringed in blackened metal. We trembled in expectation. The lens's aperture was pointed at us ready to fire. Our father—a powerful magician preparing an astonishing feat—draped a black cloth over the instrument so that it covered the plate of opaque glass as well as his head down to the shoulders. We knew—he had allowed us to peer through the lens—that he now saw us reduced in size and upside down in adjustable distance and focus. We didn't stir. The camera covered by the black cloth with Father hidden underneath looked like a surrealist bird on three thin fragile and two sturdy legs. It suddenly took a step aside then another backwards in order to find the right position. Father's hands emerged from beneath the cloth to turn the wheels and screws: the caterpillar-like accordion folds stretched out and contracted;

the enormous insect eye of the lens glided silently on precise steel rails back and forth and back again finally coming to rest. Father stepped out dramatically from beneath the black cloth and covered the lens with a round leather cap. From one of the instrument cases he retrieved a metal cartridge and slid this behind the ground glass. When he had pulled out a thin metal tab we knew the camera was loaded. The picture's moment had come. Our clothes were tugged into place; hair brushed back from foreheads; hats adjusted. We were given a last stern warning not to move a muscle. Father positioned himself beside the camera. With a ceremonious slow gesture he reached for the leather cap concealing the lens snatched it away quick as can be counting under his breath as though summoning a spirit "twenty-one twenty-two twenty-three" and drew it in a circular motion away from and back toward its starting point then slapped it just as quickly back on its lens. We knew that in the flourish of this gesture—while under the spell of his counting we dared not breathe much less blink—a magical act was being performed that later in the darkroom in the blood-spilling red of an alchemical kitchen would become visible: with the gentle swirling of the acid bath in its porcelain tray in which on the milky glass plate a hazy magma was forming that in ever deeper tones of gray to black gave birth to shapes whose outlines were ever more clearly emerging we—my sister and I—were plucked out of time as witnesses to the questionable truth of a sunken world. The lie of photography sang this world beautifully into existence.

My sister has been dead for more than half a century. But the grief in Ugo's eyes was not for her. It increased when I told him that even my father—captivated by the stunning new technical developments—had soon banished the prehistoric monster cameras so as to photograph with the luridly sharp little gadgets with which one can so to speak shoot from the hip. Of the many hundred snapshots that resulted I have saved none.)

46

When day broke I set out again, walking on until I reached a lovely, well-fortified city. It was the season when Winter had just departed and the roses made one gay-hearted and all the blooms were gleaming and the brooks were sweetly streaming.

—FROM THE FIFTEENTH OF THE *THOUSAND AND ONE NIGHTS*

*W*hen I returned from Romania in January 1990—my skull full of bleak images and my spirit weighed down by the gravestone of the past—no trick of self-discipline could help me give literary form to my experiences without my needing to question the sense and purpose of amateur eyewitness accounts. As a reporter I was always a disaster. I kept running out of anecdotes. And then there was nothing left to tell that hadn't already been told. The ostensible revolution was over. The tyrant Ceauşescu and his ghastly wife had been butchered. Even their contribution toward completing the mission of mankind was but a flyspeck in human history. There was nothing more dramatic to report. All sorts of rumors yes but so unreliable you couldn't use them for a scoop. And anyway how many dead were there "really"? The first reports on television (taking into consideration God knows what technicalities of revolution) exaggerated the facts so deceptively that audience interest soon flagged along with the story's credibility. What? It wasn't sixty thousand dead but only several hundred in Timişoara and a few dozen in Bucharest? Someone flip to a good soap opera. I could have written my fingers off describing the horrors preceding the Revolution—torture chambers hair-raising prison conditions death cells murderous work camps cesspit hospitals orphanages dripping with AIDS—in short what one would expect from the enemy camp. But then hordes of my reporter colleagues sharpened their pencils and even with the most horrifying statistics failed to achieve the effect the photojournalists had evoked with a handful of images: that sickening swell of pity barely strong enough to produce the enervated sigh: "One really ought to do something." Forget all that. In the end what it all came down to was the grand insight that socialism had been a bust: an attempt to perfect mankind that had cost several hundred million lives since 1917. How pathetically old hat! Where was the scoop?

What had I wanted in Bucharest? To take part. In what? To do what? I'd made the spur-of-the-moment trip not wanting to miss the hour when the shackles fell: when the blue yellow red flag would not just be a mythical banner signifying my disreputable origins in an operetta Balkan land—free at last of the hated insignia of the hammer-and-sickle dictatorship—but proudly unfurl above a homeland emerging from the darkness behind the Iron Curtain to lend its voice to the concert of free democratic nations as a trade partner on the open market reliable comrade-in-arms and popular tourist attraction. Direct access to reality. That wasn't such a good idea. Romania is a surrealist country. It's no coincidence that such prominent Church Fathers of Surrealism as Tristan Tzara and Eugène Ionesco were born there (as well as Ionesco's Moldavian guru Urmuz who in twelve pages composed one of the most important prose works of profound nonsensicality).

It is a magnificent country: rich with ore-veined mountains rustling forests vineyards heavy with fruit grain-golden fields. Farther on begin the steppes from which over the millennia streamed shaggy-haired nomads their ancestors and descendants Gepidae and Cumans Petchenegs and Avars Huns and Hungarians and finally Russians and—from the opposite direction —Germans. For centuries Turks kept the country in servitude and the Orthodox Church kept it in ignorance. Dandified sons of boyars who'd gone to study in Paris brought back the Enlightenment and syphilis while German and French engineers plundered the land's riches and gave it weapons. The only defense this people of serfs bent beneath the lash had against these indignities was a spunk that like Antaeus they drew from the earth beneath their feet from the soil beneath their laboring hands. Until the epidemic nationalism of the nineteenth century broke out in the awakening land of Romania and armed it with the myth of its origin in the union of Roman world masters and proud Daci. Throw in a healthy dose of megalomania. From which the changeling Nicolae Ceauşescu then profited. (For which his people despite their hatred loved him.)

With this sketchy quick gallop through history I am only trying to elucidate something essential for those to whom Romania is as distant as the fairy-tale land of Cipango (or the Maghrebinia I sang into existence): a people living in full awareness from one moment to the next that it might lose everything see everything destroyed that was built up with such great effort never experience lasting order whose views are constantly invalidated plans obstructed efforts undermined who always have new masters to serve—such a people, I say, does not believe in a one-dimensional realm of fact. It believes in absolutely nothing at all. Except the profundity of the nonsensical. (That is another way to sound out the sense of the world.) A people of great artistic talent. Artists of the existential.

As I say I made my trip to Romania not alone but in the company of my friend Tilman Spengler. He too had to endure my ditherings about the mythic land of my birth. Romania I said to him does not belong entirely to Europe but even today forms a part of the legendary empires of the Ottomans and of the

Tsars (including the Communist Tsars). It is closer to Byzantium than to the Rome it so often invokes. The population is violent in an Asiatic way but like Slavs submissive to Fate. Hand in hand with this go unscrupulous opportunism sly-fox intelligence generosity and a happy-go-lucky spirit. Also most prosaic sobriety and—yes—surrealist wit. A feel for the absurd. But all this is well known.

None of it can have been new to my young friend. He had visited Romania often. The last time had been during the heated days of the coup d'etat only a few weeks before. He had many ties there with young people who like himself had been born into a new world. Ready to fool themselves into thinking as so many had done recently that a newer better one might be produced. I knew neither them nor their projects. My only knowledge of the world these days is from hearsay. More than half a century had passed since I'd lived in Romania. The stories I had to tell of it were an old man's ruminations. Yesterday's realities with their realness worn thin. At this young man's side I was like a useless supernumerary waiting in the wings for a play that hadn't been staged in donkey's years while the drama now on the boards was quite different. I trotted along observing with what energy and competence this young man carried out his tasks both journalistic and philanthropic (he was coordinating an aid project). Even my Romanian was too rusty to be of use to him. It grated at the joints. Only when I could sit down with someone in a corner and chat about old times did it become fluent.

Mine wasn't the only stomach that turned to see the fantasies so many were caught up in. We paid a visit to the painter and sculptress Silvia Radu and her husband Vasile Gorduz (himself a sculptor and painter). They live in a studio cottage in an artists' colony which the regime established in the 1950s (before the outbreak of the Conducător's merciless campaign for urban reorganization) in a fit of patron-of-the-arts ambition. The television-station buildings are just across the street (one cultural institution deserves another). It was no secret that the weal and woe of the so-called revolution depended on television and the battles for control of the station were accordingly fierce. The artists' colony had been in the cross fire between the Securitate and the military forces hoping to replace it and the muses' retreat bore the scars of this conflict. We picked our way over heaps of broken glass through doors sagging on their hinges into studios whose walls had been transubstantiated by bullet holes of various calibers into works of preconceptual art à la Fontana. Admittedly much of this chaos of works-in-progress tools work clothes damaged furniture fractured plates could be put down to a bohemian (not to mention Romanian) lifestyle. But the general devastation went beyond even this. Clearly it would take a double measure of courage to endure a Bucharest winter in these ruins. The damage to the artwork was in many cases insignificant. In one of the neighboring studios the first salvos had severed the cords on which the pictures hung. They had fallen on top of unfinished works now damaged of course but salvageable once they'd been exhumed from beneath the rubble. The studio of a fellow sculptor named Ovidio Maitec whose medium was wood had gone up in flames along with a lifetime's work. But art as we know is like a phoenix. The prevalent mood was optimism marked by desperate humor. These survivors had nothing more to lose.

Tilman had brought along coffee a yard of salami and several chocolate bars: a stopgap attempt to enhance our diet (what diet?) over several days. But the generosity of the Romanians (artists no less) precluded such selfishness. All the coffee was immediately brewed up in a bucket and doled out the chocolate broken into chunks for distribution the salami sliced down to nothing. Neighbors and friends dropped in. At every moment someone entered or stood up to leave and everyone was offered refreshment. Our host had pressed a sort of wine from the grapes on the trellis (now shot to pieces and covered with frost). Everyone gathered around the little stove that produced heat from window frames and similar architectural scraps. And naturally the conversation turned to the man who had the most recent bout of misery in misery-steeped Romanian history on his conscience: Nicolae Ceauşescu the Conducător (in German: Führer).

This was in point of fact (and in the piles of shards the cold the doors sagging on their hinges the shortages the generosity peculiar to times of crisis the grim humor of the hopelessly courageous survivors) just like the Age of Rubble in Germany immediately following the end of the (for the time being) last full-scale effort to accomplish the mission of mankind: destruction. Then too in the bitter-cold winter of 1945–46 the survivors had huddled around cylindrical iron stoves fed with household goods starved drank home-brewed turnip schnapps and tried to explain the incomprehensible events that had occurred by means of the psychological profile of a larger-than-life demon. Adolf the Führer. The German Conducător. Had he been insane? Was it possible for Evil to enter into a human being of flesh and blood like you and me with such unfathomable intensity? Could the demonic the satanic be concentrated in such monstrous proportions in a single person who was in every other way no more than average? Or had mysterious circumstances intervened to make this individual the focal point of all the Luciferian rays in us all? Converging as if in a lens. A Chosen One of our own choosing? A true Führer on the road to the Final Solution? I couldn't suppress a giggle. The young people around me had no idea how old the world is. How deep-seated our will not to see the truth.

Naturally I was careful to keep these old man's words of wisdom to myself. Among other things it occurred to me that although parallel situations are never precisely identical they tend to come about for the same reasons and ultimately bring the same results. Bucharest in 1990 and Hamburg in 1946 bore an uncanny resemblance to each other yet the situation in Bucharest was marked by something specifically Romanian which was the participants' sense of reality. Their calm in the midst of abstruseness. Their equanimity when confronted with the bestiality of existence. As we sat there drinking lethal home-pressed wine and bringing up age-old questions only to drown them out again in an endless wash of idle talk suddenly a child appeared among us: a boy of eight nine ten years. No one knew whom he belonged to or where he'd come from. He seemed to be perfectly at home as though his presence were a matter of course. Intently he examined pictures and sculptures listened to our conversations (someone was just saying that people were stripping their telephones of the bugs they'd always assumed were there in the Conducător's time but had had the good sense not to remove) casually accepted a slice of salami and piece of chocolate chewed swallowed and gazed. When asked his name and whether he lived in the neighborhood he replied with composure that his name was Vasili and he lived not far off though only temporarily. His father had lost his life in the days of the upheaval and his mother had business somewhere in the city center. Yes he had sisters and brothers too but he didn't know where they were just then. He looked around a while longer and then was gone as inconspicuously as he'd arrived. When I remarked how odd this seemed to me our hostess said "Yes. And yet what he says may well be true." True in any case was his brief epiphany. Thick-skinned heir to a decimated civilization. Child martyr of the surreal forces at work in this world of ours.

The artists' colony and television headquarters lie in a district that in my day—the early 1930s—was only sparsely populated. At the outermost edge of the diplomatic quarter located between the two elegant *allées* radiating out from the Piaţa Victoriei: the

Şosea Khisseleff and the Şosea Jianu. There used to be nothing but open countryside beyond them. Bleak apartment complexes now crowd the landscape where small huts once lay tucked away beneath the branches of elm and ash trees in whose crowns wild doves cooed. One hut out of three was a barbecue shack. The air was thick with the charred garlicky smell of *cărnaţi* and *mititei*. Gypsies played their fiddles. Beneath the straw-covered awnings quail in willow-twig cages beat time. Everyone drank watered wine and sang along with the Gypsies' fiddles. (*Îmi dai o litră şi un sifon . . .*) These were outskirts still free of the mange that spreads around big cities: prosperity's dumps the destruction that results from the progress devouring man. The Şosea Khisseleff laid out on a grand scale by the Russian occupying governor around 1840 (two riding tracks parallel to the broad roadway two footpaths beneath imposing lindens and plane trees behind which massive villas were set back in dark gardens) sliced through the undeveloped land from the Piaţa Victoriei (where today tanks of the Conducător's successor guard the Stalinist government fortresses) to a Triumphal Arch miles distant (which once collapsed when the army marched too forcefully beneath it). Out here you could still find old caravansaries left over from the days of the Turks their stables still housing full-blooded horses. I too had a horse (which had never won a race) and I actively participated in its training. Early in the morning I would ride out with the others to the racetrack that has since vanished beneath the gigantic complex called the Palace of the Press. In my memory this ample forest-rimmed grass oval is not only a site of heart-swelling equestrian adventures but also the quintessence of the mythical blue yellow red epoch of my existence. Now more than half a century later I and Tilman Spengler prowled up and down the marble staircases and kilometer-long corridors of this colossus whose only service had been to disseminate mendacious legends about the historical human and intellectual greatness of a former cobbler and Party climber named Nicolae Ceauşescu.

Tilman had come to dispose of two hundred typewriters that a privately organized aid project had brought here from Munich. They had been earmarked for the postrevolutionary Ministry of Education and the Arts. Just getting them into Romania had been difficult. The stalwart young ladies who had undertaken the transport (steering an old truck for five hundred miles) had overcome the obstacles placed in their path by the still mercilessly bureaucratic customs and police checks only by lipsticking a red cross on a white handkerchief and pretending to be doctors and nurses. And in fact their transport did include—along with the typewriters—urgently needed medical supplies: milling cutters for skull operations rib cutters (my surgeon would have licked his lips) possibly even an intestine-scope with a nauplius eye (I'm not sure but why pettifog about such matters). Anyway the supplies had to be shipped back to Munich: the Romanians had no use for them. "Too complicated for the medical technology at our disposal" was the official reply. (I've since wondered whether I shouldn't have my various side effects treated there.) The Ministry of Education and the Arts was kind enough to accept the typewriters. After appropriately bureaucratic negotiations with the building superintendent's office permission was secured to unload the cargo in one of the rear courtyards of the titanic complex beside a snow-covered coal heap. Their future was to be decided by someone higher up.

The recommendation for this came from our old friend Dan Haulica. If it had been up to him things would have been settled without a hitch. But the newly installed higher-up was not to be circumvented. Him I knew as well from the Venice Biennale and remembered him as an anxiously high-strung intellectual posing rather stiffly as a dissident. Now we found ourselves standing before a buttoned-up ministry official whose chief-clerk glands were clearly doing overtime. (No proper suit yet but of course a necktie of Lenin red and intellectual's ringlets still adorning his head in conflict with his newly fastened shirt collar.) A Man of Reality fresh out of the oven. No longer the piously ingenuous sleepwalker in the Niflheim of the intellect but possessed of clear insight into the power-play value of Culture. I stared at him so absently that he tossed his head and gave me a questioning look. I averted my eyes and glanced out the window. These grounds that had been green fifty-three years before among the hodgepodge of buildings and courtyards had thanks to the generous distribution of horse dung in its racetrack days borne a profusion of mushrooms. An old jockey who'd lost his wits in a bad fall and had his license taken away used to gather them for me in the evenings. We'd have them grilled on the spit in one of the pubs drink *o litră şi un sifon* listen to the fiddling Gypsies and the quails beating time beneath the awning. (Haven't I already described this in some other context?) What I can hardly have described was the marvelously naïve faith in the future typical of those years. Not only mine. Everyone was expecting a new world. Improved. Perfected by whatever means and at whomever's expense. Plans rose like constellations and kept the ideological firmament vibrant with conflict. In those years I was a college-educated illiterate. All that could move me to enthusiasm was horses their breeding and their breeding for speed. Nevertheless I too was burning with eagerness for the new world. To me too it had been promised those summer evenings nearly sixty years ago now when the sky turned inky blue and a yellow moon came up above the ponds and lakes of Băneasa "myriads of frogs hammered so delicately and incessantly on their silvery strings of bells it was like a tissue of sound veiling the landscape." (I quote myself: old men repeat themselves.) I might make so bold as to speak of the tattered veil of my illusions—all the world's illusions save one. And to this one illusion mankind clings: the ludicrous belief that human beings can resist their destiny and construct a better world than this one which they are destined to destroy. (Admittedly an old man's insight.) Once more I began to observe the fresh-out-of-the-oven despot. I thought: if the frogs are still alive the hammering of two hundred typewriters in the new ministry will soon silence them. Perhaps this was accomplished years ago by the two thousand typewriters of Ceauşescu's propaganda machine and the lakes and ponds around Băneasa have been filled in with concrete. I was unable to confirm this since it was bitter-cold winter in January 1990 when I was permitted to return. The frost had a firm grip on the land of my youth. As is described in a Christmas carol I remember from my childhood. *Earth stood hard as iron, / Water like a stone.* It by and large came down to the same thing except that concrete would not melt. There was no spring to look forward to. The frogs' silence was for good.

And I passed three days with him; at the end of which time he said to me: "Do you not know a trade by which you might earn your living?" "I have studied law and the holy texts," I replied, "and am trained as a scribe, a mathematician and calligrapher." "These are not arts that are valued hereabouts," he replied.

—FROM THE SIXTEENTH OF THE *THOUSAND AND ONE NIGHTS*

When I gazed out the window of the newly established Romanian Ministry of Education and the Arts I was looking into the past but I lingered only briefly on the distant past. *("Qu'as-tu fait, ô toi que voilà, pleurant sans cesse? Qu'as-tu fait de ta jeunesse?" . . .)* My gaze was more clearly fixed on an object situated in the middle distance within my internal stockpile of images: Hamburg in 1946–47 (admittedly almost a lifetime away—though not my lifetime—and already the focus of a sentimentality I was struggling to keep in check.) It had been then that a model for the transformation of intellectual into chief clerk had impressed itself on me for all time. A mini–model as it were. Germanically straitlaced inside and out. Displaying so pure a distillate of provincialism that I carry it within me as an amulet against the no longer surprising phenomenon of human metamorphoses.

Hamburg nearly two years after the end of the war but still the Ptolemaically flattened world of bombed–out German cities. A familiar world—familiar (though now forgotten despite the many times it's been described) wasteland of detritus with skeletons of buildings poking up here and there airy expanses of sky in the window holes of bare walls. (Memorials? Not at all! Cassandra remains eternally unhoused.) Paths trampled out amid the piles of rubble speak of the astonishing hardiness of the human race. (It never gives up. The moment the destruction is over it sets about rebuilding for the next round: naturally enough along the lines of the world that was just destroyed.) Above the exposed asphalt ribbons of former roadways streetlights dangle from bent concrete poles with makeshift cables. Signposts pointing the way back to the roads of the old order. At night their faint cones of light pick out neatly stacked still lifes of mortar scraps furniture crockery shards cement children's toys crumbled brick and bent iron bars from a darkness crisscrossed by scurrying rats. A surrealist landscape. (Man is less imaginative than he supposes. Also less free in his actions. These things are given to him.)

As my doctors assure me the body has a natural tendency to heal itself only the noblest cities disappear entirely from the face of the earth. O.W.A.s themselves. What remains of Babylon? Elsewhere life goes on. Amid the rubble tidied up and put away the old madness germinates in preparation for its rebirth. The world of the so-called Age of Rubble has often been depicted in word and image and we've seen no dearth of reminders that even cities that have temporarily collapsed into their own cellars are "silent outcries." The nature of these outcries is subject to debate. In any case the outcry of Hamburg remained unvoiced and had no repercussions although the chorus of admonishers warners preachers starry-eyed idealists and apocalyptics had already begun to sing believing they could bring this outcry to ears that refused to hear (including their own). For a while I was one of them.

This singing club found its niche in Hamburg's radio station (under British control). A handful of leftover intellectuals (as well as several persons aspiring to this status). As motley a crew as one might find on any self-respecting pirate ship. Even today almost half a century later I can still make them leap out of ranks like recruits at roll call:

Bruno E. Werner: formerly a fashion magazine editor: tall handsome elegant Saxon man of the world winds of culture fluttering his snow-white hair. Head of the division on "The Cultural Word."

Dr. Kurt Emmerich: once a doctor then a convert to popular fiction known throughout the German-speaking world by his nom de plume Peter Bamm. Sharply profiled gentlemen's-tailor's-dummy figure like a steeplechase rider recipient of the medal *Pour le mérite* in World War I and thus affecting a certain gallant jauntiness when speaking or writing. Editor of commentaries on miscellaneous news items.

Peter von Zahn: also a Saxon well-built redhead with an at-ease way about him civilized and Anglo-Saxonified by affinity and marriage a class valedictorian of natural intelligence and ambition but with nerves too delicate for later developments in the German broadcasting industry. Head of the division on "The Political Word."

Glib Dr. Heidtmüller: chief-clerk type of the executive class expert in business matters with administrative talents that sent him flying up to a top bureaucratic-hieratic position though he soon departed—I can't remember if it was a political or physical death.

The emotional well-being of our listeners was taken care of by the family-paper-aesthete Walter von Hollander who gave the inhabitants of rat cellars and Nissen huts helpful instructions to be followed in case of marital conflict difficult children menopausal crises shyness and similar disturbances in the harmony of life. Of Baltic extraction mild-mannered and slick like someone in a champagne ad amicably old-maidish ideal companion for a fireside chat.

Equally poised on spiritual tiptoe and with literary pretensions was Gerhard Bahlsen: better groomed than he was schooled and as easily digested as the cookies manufactured by his family. Intellectual with a subscription-library education and dwarfed by the director of the ambitiously high-brow division for evening programs:

Jürgen Schüddekopf: every bit the intellectual of that mythic sort whose aesthetic ethical and moral conscience is subjected to painful ordeals (private tutor Bigum in Jacobsen's *Niels Lyhne*). Tall heavyset with a massive Luther head and a Paul Klee sensibility one of those whose respect for quality forbids them to participate in the production of consumable culture but who are forced by their sense of personal responsibility to intervene whenever culture is in danger of suffocating in the silt of mediocrity and who thus wind up in the culture industry after all. As a logical consequence he drank himself to death.

The "Echo of the Day" was overseen by Elef Sossidi: a delicately Germanicized Greek—a Faiyum painting—military and political scientist who concealed a sharp ironic intellect and biting wit behind his Levantine mask.

Last but not least our two antagonists: Axel Eggebrecht whose literary Mistinguette affectations allowed him to bob atop the radio waves as the figurehead of our institution (for the dissemination of information and knowledge maxims and entertainment political backbone and you name it): long-limbed ungainly and skittish with a profile straight out of Punch and Judy and a voice like a cheese knife; and

Herbert Blank: an early Nazi follower of Gregor Strasser who had paid for the deviant non-Hitlerian alignment of his nationalist sentiment with eleven years of prison and a death sentence commuted at the last possible moment and who now labored under the illusion that the renewal of Germany might be brought about through radio: an asthmatic of middling height and burly in the sailor's garb of a laid-off first mate (which he never was).

Ernst Schnabel was not yet a member of this staff: a nautical hero of Napoleonic diminutiveness and author of poetic prose whose ethical fortitude was always lying warily in wait ("guardian spirit aboard the good ship *Categorical Imperative*" as Sossidi called him) with the romantic aura of the youthful round-the-world sailorman. For a while he and I were friends. Until he too became a staff member.

When I think of this time I think of a saga. Even the climate was Icelandic: legendary Ice Age of the so-called Reichsmark years in bombed-out Germany. (It is noteworthy that the propped-up currency of the monetary reform of 1948 brought with it the chronology and thus also the climate of a new epoch.) The buccaneering crew that signed on aboard the radio-wave-cruising ship then known as the North West German Radio Network were no doubt just as intrepid and carefree as the pirate Störtebecker's cohorts must have been (and more boisterous more uninhibited in their plundering). In the middle of the city's lunar landscape the station headquarters stood glittering on Rothenbaumchaussee lit up like a Christmas tree with music streaming from the cracks in its bombed-out walls. Classical music under the baton of Hans Schmidt-Isserstedt and derivative (in both senses) "easy listening" tinkling away under the auspices of Harry Hermann Spitz. The Age of Television had not yet arrived. Radio alone lifted the inhabitants of the rubble above the horizon of their ruined world. A beaten starving people of homeless former Party members and sullen willingly unwilling fellow travelers were to be transformed by means of acoustical entertainment (symphonies dance music radio plays cabarets lectures news stories) and massive doses of deeply cautionary cultural chatter into democrats in the British Labour Party style. Mass-media reality. (Just look at the results.) And we the chatterers and cautioners were not the only ones who believed in our calling for even outside the radio station's metastatically proliferating complex we enjoyed a prestige that today almost enables one to speak in melancholy retrospect of a local "intellectuals' interregnum." The monetary reform that changed time and weather along with the currency ended this. Thereafter so-called economic factors dominated every form of life especially politics. And took over the so-called cultural sphere with the delicacy of a whale eating plankton. Developments were progressing full speed again.

At this point Shahrazad saw the approach of morning and discreetly fell silent; but when the seventeenth night had come she went on.

$\mathcal{B}$ut as long as it lasted this brief (and only) intellectuals' interregnum in German history was marvelous. The British occupying forces kept tabs on it with a light hand. Fraternization was frowned on of course but soon established de facto by the eager-beaver secretarial staff. (Sororization.) For a while the door to the rest rooms on the executives' floor bore a little plaque with the inscription "British personnel only." But as soon as dear old Sossidi added "Rule, Britannia, rule the waves!" the degrading sign disappeared. The radio staff was like an elite corps and I was proud to count myself among their number. I was bursting with belated youthfulness and hysterically youthful enthusiasm. I loved the North West German Radio Network. Even its symphony of voices was enough to put me in raptures. An haute école of hearing. Axel Eggebrecht's schoolmasterish screechings (straight from the larynx) contrapuntally alternating with Herbert Blank's barked-out gems of free-youth-movement wisdom. (His teeth had been knocked out in penitentiaries and camps: whenever he got excited which was often he barked his sentences from naked gums like an aging hellhound yelping in a grotto.) In comparison Peter von Zahn's down-to-earth commentaries drawn out to mannered length thanks to frequent brief pauses seemed urbanely and circumspectly uplifting. The *feuilleton* was assembled by Peter Bamm and spiced with crystalline witticisms offered with a slight Saxon burr each offered as it were on kissed fingertips. And nothing could stretch the scale of expressive possibility further than Jürgen Schüddekopf's discriminating late-show announcements—irritably extruded from beneath the burden of existence—and the exquisitely surreal puns and bursts of inspiration served up by the comedian Heinz Erhardt. ("So here's anudder pome.") The actual content of this polyphonic chatter on the airwaves was absolutely irrelevant. The staff fulfilled their roles as witnesses of faith. They drew attention to the religious character of the media. Idolization of concepts. They'd have let themselves be crucified for the higher truth of the chatter they broadcasted: the Great Fetishes at the dusk of Creation: Culture. Art. Human Rights. Human Dignity. Freedom. Equality. Democracy. They believed in them as human be-

63

ings artists intellectuals and paid employees with retirement benefits.

The Wunderkind among all these regular staff members was indisputably the free-lancer Ernst Schnabel. His manly talk poetically hoarsened by a Saxon accent ("Dam-dam on the Gongo") made him the epitome of the courageous survivor to our hollow-cheeked listeners: a stalwart lad a very model of the "Good Comrade" mini-hero of great sea voyages straightforward upright poetic sensitive and (as circumstances would have it) choleric. Even the British controller could not fault him: an antiseptically spotless political past with none of the usual whitewashing about having felt the need damn it to perform his duty to his fellow citizens and fatherland. (I repeat: the German Order of the Gold Cross.) He fed succulent morsels to the perpetually ravenous microphone: eyewitness reports from distant continents high-seas adventures educational supplements in the style of American youth journals poetic sketches about the situation at hand. Everything that crossed his lips was ready for broadcast: brief easily comprehensible well written with a musical touch. Pieces that not only sounded good but had literary and above all ethical class. The breezes of his apprenticeship on a training ship wafted through them with fresh salt-tangy air. His wartime experiences as leader of a seaborne convoy lent an extra measure of respectability (a man who has looked Death in the eye). When he called on the radio audience to describe how they spent one particular day during the transitional years of 1946–47 (bitterest heart of the Ice Age) tens of thousands of letters poured in. He incorporated the most powerful of these in a sort of collage documentary radio play of heartrending immediacy. Live human suffering. One of the most moving radio broadcasts of all time. In this abstract world of ruins surrounding us we experienced reality through the medium of radio waves.

In contrast to all his qualities successes and achievements stood Schnabel's existential angst. He had a family to support:

a charming wife and two little daughters twittering gaily away like parakeets and he was plagued by fears of being unable to satisfy the growing demands of all this condensed femininity. This erotic fear which was gradually developing into a full-blown neurosis was joined by a metaphysical one about the possible failure of his own self-fulfillment (what Americans call looking for one's identity). Like every young writer out of the closet or not friend Schnabel was haunted by the inner compulsion to write a—*the*—great novel. The novel of the century. The conscience of our race. (He admired Joyce but had to struggle to read him.) Needless to say his plan like those of countless other epigones was laid out on too large a scale ever to be put into effect: a fate shared by all hands aboard a dozen ships that sank somewhere in the Pacific in a hurricane. (*"Ni plus, ni moins"* as Schwab would say.) Ernst Schnabel however carried this dream around with him as a mother does a child though at the same time he was tormented at having to choose between ambition and conscience between laurels and hungry mouths to feed. One would have to be betrayed for the other's sake (as would he in either case). Naturally his fear of letting down his womenfolk was stronger than that of not seeing the name Ernst Schnabel on the list of the epoch's great authors. ("Whoever marries and has children is putting the scourge in fortune's hand" says colleague Montaigne. No not Montaigne it must have been someone else La Rochefoucauld or Montesquieu or some other member of that clan. Montaigne didn't have so light a touch. He said "A man who starts a family seems to me like someone who shits in a basket and then claps it on his own head." The first warning is most definitely from colleague Bacon.)

Friendship too is an act of identification—though also of comparison. When I left the permanent staff of the radio's hallowed halls Schnabel preached at me for being irresponsible. (I too had a family not to mention—of course—the urgent need to write *the* great novel though my ambitions weren't quite so high as his: "Doggy shouldn't try to pee any higher than he can lift his leg" is a useful maxim from not colleague La Rochefoucauld but my hunting father.) My friend Schnabel warned me not to be foolhardy. He kept at me so persistently for so long that his own duress was clear. I went to the highest-ranked of our British controllers and made a case to him that Schnabel's literary work including what he wrote for radio would flow more freely and produce even finer results if he were no longer plagued by the financial fears of a free-lancer with a sporadic income but could sit and write with the peace of mind of a regularly salaried employee. My petition was successful. (What bizarre youthful folly!) Ernst Schnabel was hired to head the division for features and radio plays.

During the years the two of us spent as half-stowaway free-lancers aboard the radio ship of fools we shared a berth: a tiny room in an out-of-the-way corner off a back corridor for which an administration just beginning to find its bureaucratic sea legs had not yet found a use. For nearly a full year we had lived as brothers on that half-floor of the old radio building on Rothenbaumchaussee hammered on the same typewriter used the same telephone the same electric teapot the same bench for a quick nap after having worked through the night (or a quickie with an eager typist). We had spent countless hours exchanging thoughts incidents experiences foolishnesses gossip philosophemes reflections on the times and future plans and in the poorhouse generosity of those most peculiar years shared a last cigarette or the single stick of chewing gum snatched up on the black market. On the day Ernst Schnabel was named division chief I was about to sit down as usual at our shared desk when suddenly he bellowed "That's my desk now! In fact this is my office! Get out! I have work to do." A fresh-out-of-the-oven despot. (Mini-Hitler I used to call it: a product of atomization. The spirit of the Führer redispersed among the people.)

The transformation was so perfect I didn't even take it personally. What I held against him was his betrayal of the cause. For this I owe him an apology. What particular cause did I have in mind? The esprit de corps of anarchistically liberal intellectuals? The wool we the socially "committed" were pulling over our own eyes? Our lame attempts to open the eyes of others through the art (and power) of the word? After all we were colleagues. Had propped up the great values shoulder to shoulder. Jointly devoted to the Great Fetishes Culture Creative Genius Human Dignity Freedom Equality Democracy (and the Fraternity of Cain and Abel). But I realize he was able to serve this lie better in his new position. At the time I couldn't yet see this. Blindly committed. I didn't yet hold in my hand the key to the well-kept secret of the true destiny of man.

Schnabel's work from that point on had more to do with bureaucratically administrative than literary matters (a result of more general developments but it was my mistake to have pushed my friend into their current). In any case the current took him far: he became the director of the good old North West German Radio Network. (Whose development wound up shrinking it in the paradox of its own monstrous expansion. Now it is known simply as the North German Radio Network having given up its "W" to Cologne and employs not the dozen madmen of the Reichsmark years but several thousand regular staff members with retirement benefits. This too can be seen as progress. In my newly discovered sense of the word that's just what it is.) Still: the kaleidoscope of voices soon vanished. Herbert Blank passed away. Peter von Zahn emigrated. Schüddekopf drank himself to death. Axel Eggebrecht was only occasionally heard screeching in the empty halls: a sort of acoustical skeleton jiggling in a death dance. A sterilized perfected radio German was developed. Immaculate diction took the place of local color. Television in any case was quickly working its way to the forefront drowning out the magic flute of the spoken word. No one would claim that dear old Schnabel with his exemplary administrative competence could be blamed for this. It was part of the general course of development in which he was a pawn. But to his honor let it be said he did not let himself be blinded by power for long. He soon handed in his resignation and returned to writing. On clipped poetic wings to be sure.

"The black tomcat that is with him in the temple," said the good spirit, "has a white spot the size of a dirham at the tip of his tail; he must pluck seven white hairs from it and burn them over the sick man."

—FROM THE EIGHTEENTH OF THE *THOUSAND AND ONE NIGHTS*

I think back now to this legendary age because in Bucharest (and then in India and at Carnival in Cologne) I kept having my nose rubbed in worrisome questions of power and powermongers and the protean forms they take. Not new or even surprising phenomena. At least not for someone who was robbed of his homeland by the crooked pact between Hitler and Stalin. He just experiences them at closer range more intimately than beneath the onslaught of millennial personalities like comrades Joseph Adolf Benito and consorts. On a smaller the smallest scale. Laced up even more tightly (as one sees in every sphere these days). The nausea this provokes makes me sprout the most curious blossoms. Once I came right out and asked B. whether she could discern in me (the proverbial henpecked husband) any traces of the power instinct. (Women have an extremely personal even chummy relationship to power. One confessed to me once that she liked it so much when a man had an orgasm inside her because it made her feel powerful.) B. countered my question with the remark "You're too playful." And in fact I did have to suffer an embarrassing confrontation with my own lightweight status during a brief visit to Vienna in the year of our Lord 1990.

My friend Franzi Goëss brought me along to a conference on the Pan-Europe movement at which Otto von Hapsburg spoke. The topic was the reopening of the countries of Central or rather Eastern Europe. The Danube region in other words. My native land. Where my childhood was played out and most of my books as well. Probably with an eye to symbolism the conference was held in the main building of the Danube Steamship Company. A severe edifice set in strikingly barren grounds. We grouped in a sort of tearoom with a large bar and a semicircle of veranda windows overlooking the gray river and various factory complexes on the opposite bank. Not a cheery picture. We sat with our backs to the panorama gazing up at the bar behind which the speakers sat enthroned on a podium. The first to speak was Archduke Karl the son of His Imperial Highness who enlightened us as to the program and objectives of the Pan-Europe Society (which have been well known since their formulation by the society's founder Count Coudenhove-Kalergi but today in the view of the imperial grandson were closer to being achieved than ever before). He was followed by a Czechoslovakian minister in Slovak (or Czech?) charmingly interpreted by a Countess Waldstein. He too shared the opinion she fluently translated that great things were in the offing above all with respect to improvements in the strained relations between Czechs and Slovaks. A similar tone was struck by an exceptionally elegant Hungarian minister one Count Bethlen. His family was from Transylvania where Romanians roast Hungarians on the spit. Nevertheless, he said, it was Hungary's goal to achieve peaceful coexistence between the two national groups. It was to be hoped that the Romanians would show an equal measure of goodwill. No delegate from Yugoslavia was present but it went without saying that similar brotherly inclinations held this ticklish assemblage of Serbs Croats Slovenes Bosnians Montenegrins and Macedonians together. Then the floor was turned over to Otto von Hapsburg who up till then had been listening with a practiced ear making a solid impression thanks to the integrity one associates with a prominent individual who never tires of repeating that he lays no claim to his legacy as heir apparent to one imperial and several royal crowns (including those of Hungary Bohemia Galicia and Lodomeria as well as the crown of the duchy of the Bukovina). He too spoke of the auspicious prospects opening up in the countries of the Danube. The militantly piebald character of the region's mix of nations was rapidly giving way to unified planning for the future. His observations substantiated what had been said on the subject by earlier speakers with the additional note that the countries of the European East which had at long last been reunited with the West showed clear signs of a return to religion—that is to the Christian Church—and thus also to the true fundamental values of Occidental civilization. He spoke clearly using well-chosen words and immaculately constructed sentences and after a suitable length of time brought his topic to an orderly conclusion. The president of the Pan-Europe Society Archduke Karl thanked His Imperial Highness Dr. Hapsburg his father. Then the floor was opened to discussion.

And something highly embarrassing occurred: no one said a thing. The last echo of the invitation to debate died away. No one stirred. The audience of elderly monarchists coincidentally available journalists and a female cheering squad (students of journalism and political science no doubt) remained silent. This excruciating silence implicitly challenged the noble utopianism of the claims made earlier and debunked the integrity of the speaker (no one believes in innocent fools anymore). The silence settled on our most sensitive nerve endings. The heir apparent to the largest number of vacant crowns in the region of the Danube stood there motionless and waiting. You could hear the watch ticking in his vest pocket. His dignity was unassailable his patience no less so. I however was suffering. Not for him. He waited with practiced grace sleek and slim in his plain dark suit trying not to give anyone an encouraging glance but directing his gaze above our heads at the Danube gray behind the veranda windows. His head was so emphatically lacking particularity of feature mien expression as to seem to announce the intention to be indistinguishable from that of any other man of culture of well-preserved advanced age with an Austro-aristo mustache and well-shorn thinning hair. It was a head of the smooth well-shapenness and high-born elegance of an aristocratic Jugendstil bust. Countless heads whose owners could be looked up by name in the Almanach de Gotha had aspired more or less successfully to a shape this noble. Here it was perfect. The proprietor of this excellent head did not allow it to smile but nonetheless gave off a general impression of benevolence toward all persons and things. Even this embarrassing silence. Still I was suffering. Suffering from the futile suspense that was gradually filling this silence to bursting. All of us expectantly awaited the words that might release us—anything except the awkward half-ironic "Well then if there's nothing left to say . . ." though even this would have broken the bands that the silence was cinching tighter and tighter around our gullets. We dared not even clear our throats.

Tormenting childhood memories began to stir within me: the malicious silence maintained by adults while I waited for a word of release that came sooner or later and broke the spell leaving one to awaken as if from a stupor. Its arrival was always preceded by the steadily increasing agony of *it's expected of me.* As though something were at stake in a game I wasn't allowed to play but whose outcome would conce i me so that I was obliged to take a stand. As though a word from me could avert disaster and change it to good fortune but I didn't know the word and was racked with guilt. Now it was the same thing all over. I imagined everyone's eyes on me. Absurd assumption. Psychoanalytically revealing. It would have given a shrink grounds for embarrassing views on my sexual behavior: narcissism onanistic tendencies and similar transgressions. Considering my age this was ridiculous. I was taking myself too seriously. As though I owed it to my rank as human being and artist to add my two bits to the hogwash. This set my teeth on edge. Nevertheless I was seized by a nearly overwhelming compulsion to say something anything at all. For example I might have said something about Romania. About the revolution that hadn't been a revolution but a disguised coup d'etat whose strings nearly slipped from the manipulators' hands; about how it seemed to me—now that the will to freedom had been stirred up among the Romanian people—that the only possibility for reestablishing order and guiding the government toward a democratic future was to reestablish the monarchy. Could one hope and believe such a possibility existed?

It would have been a more than tactless question touching the most sensitive nerve of the individual to which it was addressed. But I could have countered the extravagant (and contentious) utopianism it implied. I could have said: Romania has been a nation for barely a century and a half and never tasted freedom before. So Romanians are still in a state of political infancy and will have to work their way through all the various phases of development before reaching maturity; among these are a reprise of the constitutional monarchy Romania enjoyed during the single Golden Age in its history (which let me note is still functioning perfectly well in the West—in Britain Spain the Netherlands Denmark Norway Sweden; but in Romania it was violently interrupted—half-digested as it were). I could have said such things with unabashed optimism. They are what I believe. Not only because I believe in the irony of the world spirit, but because as an epoch-embezzling Occidental I stubbornly believe that reason has no choice but to accept the mystical. I wouldn't have cared if people thought me a lotus-eating Romantic daydreaming hard-core reactionary and/or an old fool. I'd have provided what everyone was so expectantly awaiting even longing for in the general hush: material for discussion. Paleontology. Contemplative scrutiny of dinosaur bones. Prehistoric Great Fetishes still imbued with an echo of their former magic. Even if it had only inspired more blather it would at least have broken the silence. Somehow I blamed myself for letting the blather about the future of the Danube region get stuck halfway through (I mean before it reached the point of utter absurdity).

Lord be praised: a Belgian journalist beat me to it. Using that lovely form of address reserved for royalty *"Monseigneur"* he posed a question in French and Otto von Hapsburg Duke of Lotharingia replied to him in equally fluent pure French. The upshot of his well-chosen words and immaculately constructed sentences (not to mention the question) escaped me for I was already deep in my own musings. I'd missed my chance. What chance?

How many moons ago was this? I don't recall. Time keeps zipping by and here I am still musing. Though I knew perfectly well why I hesitated vis-à-vis His Imperial Highness in Vienna until I'd missed my chance (it's possible I hadn't hesitated all that long before the Belgian beat me to it—the silence may have been much shorter than it seemed to me in the suffering inflicted by my own hysteria—but these are so to speak the embroidered borders of my musings) for my intention to raise my hand had already succumbed to paralysis before it was fully formed. What paralyzed me was the thought of having to stand and confront

Otto von Hapsburg. Two notorious personalities (for very different reasons) face-to-face. On one side a phenomenon unique in world history a monument to the elegant renunciation of power the epitome and personification of human probity. Doubly first-class prewar goods; the man who took the loss of half a millennium's imperial legacy as a call to practice and teach politics as simply as any low-ranking lecturer nobly renouncing all personal claims. The very model of an aristocrat patriarch cosmopolitan clearheadedly content with his place in everyday reality yet also actively participating in the *Great Dream*: improving mankind's lot. Worlds removed from the vulgarity of run-of-the-mill idealists who set out to save the world. No straitlaced perfectionist he. A generous man. A high aristocrat of reality. True: not an artist. Not one who sings worlds into existence. Unruffled and decisive in his dealings with given concrete possibilities among which he counted the possibility of mankind's coming to embrace reason and insight.

That was *him*. And on the other side *me*. A hack writer. A cynic who sees in everything only devastation and the will to perish and doesn't hesitate to joke about it. Author of scathing social criticism. Parodist who takes mankind's most noble causes as an easy target for ridicule. Ironist who sees politics as a game played by charlatans and crooks. Mocker of Culture who would rather call himself a baron than an intellectual. In a word myself in the dubious glory of an image I owed to the success of one of my books: *Maghrebinian Tales*. Prototypical product of a fairy-tale land of ill repute earning me a host of epithets: man without a homeland bad-mouther rabble-rouser —what else did they call me? Oh yes: snob dandy unscrupulous ladies' man irresponsible talented. Yes a great charmer an entertainer bubbling over with bons mots a literary lalapalooza a fine judge of whiskey a shoe-polish connoisseur. But a ne'er-do-well dubious disreputable shady . . . The realization crashed down on me: how right B. was to warn me against this image.

74

Wouldn't people who recognized me when I stood up have to expect some malicious jest cryptic frivolity challenge? The author of *Maghrebinian Tales* offers us his opinion on the Danube region. Would it be a couplet? "On the steamship *Pischtakisch* déshabillée above the fish there sailed a ravishing duenna from Nagypalavach to Vienna . . ." Well? That was my "reality" in the German-speaking world. As both artist and human being I'd cut my hamstrings. The satirist's scourge I'd been swinging so adroitly had struck me in the eye. Half a century of an epoch-embezzler's efforts to illumine dunderheads (as well as defend the purity of the German language) hadn't done much for my image. Even if I could admonish myself like Rilke before his fragmentary Apollo that it was about time to change my life: it was too late.

Certainly I should have realized this sooner. If not back in the prehistoric times of my brotherhood with Ernst Schnabel and the other Church Fathers of the postwar German culture industry then at least in the early 1960s when the "miracle of postwar reconstruction" made its mark even on German literature. The illustrated journal *Quick* to which I eagerly and profitably contributed (it was one of the sidelines I was unfortunately forced to pursue. Let it be said for the benefit of those who consider working for the popular press unworthy of a serious writer that it isn't easy to raise three sons when a ballpoint pen is the only tool you have to earn your living)—*Quick* gave me the job of interviewing certain of my writer colleagues who had done their fatherland proud and risen to true literary fame: the triumvirate Heinrich Böll Uwe Johnson Günter Grass. Voices heard around the world significant contributors to cultural history and thus also politically relevant. Böll on the telephone when asked if he would be prepared to make a few statements about himself politely declined. I met with Grass and Johnson in Berlin. In a little pastry shop in Charlottenburg they downed coffee and cake at *Quick*'s expense and declared they would not dream of appearing in the mass media next to advertisements for toothpaste and brassieres. With the unanimity of Rosencrantz and Guildenstern they announced their intention never to contribute to consumer society (which let it be said also consumes books) then consumed a few more slices of cream torte and stalked off proudly. I ought to have followed their example. Consumer society rewarded the purity of this sort of image management. Uwe Johnson died under circumstances befitting his eccentricity: almost an O.W.A. So he continues to survive on paper as a good German writer with a strong sense of values. I ran into Günter Grass years later. In Frankfurt at the hotel Hessischer Hof during the International Book Fair. He was wearing what used to be called a "Stresemann" in prewar years (black jacket with a many-buttoned gray vest with gray-and-black-striped trousers and a silver necktie) and trotted so nimbly down the main staircase that I mistook him for a head porter rushing down to welcome Lord Weidenfeld. Only by his mustache did I recognize him. When I tried to have a word with him he had no time for me: he was on his way to a reception for the then Chancellor Helmut Schmidt. He'd found his world-historical niche. With his sturdy nimble legs planted smack in the middle of real-life reality. He would have stood up to Otto von Hapsburg—oh yes! My ex-friend Schnabel would no doubt have done the same. He'd have squared off with him face-to-face man-to-man despite his short little legs. The image these two shared as vehicles of culture not only allowed this but virtually demanded it. No point trying to keep up with them. In those years I too wore a mustache but this was the only thing I had in common with Grass and Otto von Hapsburg. The missing link. Nothing else connected us. I was separated from the one by his naïve purity from the other by his artistic will to power and from both by the dubious gift of irony. Laughter born of hatred.

76

Presently the demon set me down on a mountain, and taking a little dust,
over which he muttered some magical words, sprinkled me with it, saying:
"Leave your present shape and take the shape of a monkey!"

—FROM THE TWENTY-FIRST OF THE THOUSAND AND ONE NIGHTS

$\mathcal{P}$lease don't misunderstand me. This is a summation, a
report made in my own defense. A highly personal document.
If the reader likes he may take it as a work of literature building
on the tradition of the *Confessions* of my colleague Jean-Jacques
Rousseau. Back to the true nature of man. This requires patience. Man—including this specimen here *me*—is as everyone
knows a complex item. Produced over time. Modulating in its
course. But within man time stands still. He is approachable
only by way of detours into the past with the sweeping con-
jurer's gesture with which my father about to expose the plate
in his antediluvian camera removed the leather cap from the
lens and after chanting the spell of enumerated seconds replaced
it. To describe everything circumscribed in this action I will
have to digress: I have been musing over these matters for many
moons. Ever since Bucharest Pondicherry and Cologne. This
is where the exposure began. It then developed its pictorial
character in the acid bath of television. This time not in front
of the television screen but in front of the camera and *on* the
screen. In Berlin. For it was there I'd been invited to participate
in what is known in the troglodyte jargon as a talk show (even

in German). Ignoring B.'s judicious warnings I went. (I imagined that by conducting myself with an old man's dignity I could correct my German image.) Naturally it was a bust. I'd never heard of the moderator and alas had no idea how prominent she was (more prominent than I would have thought possible). When she came up to introduce herself before the show I absentmindedly took her for a makeup girl and said I didn't require her services. She revenged herself on the air. She had studied my German image well enough to be able to focus her attack on its brittlest spots (womanizer and so forth). To take me properly to task she reached deep into the arsenal of feminist platitudes. Soon the two of us proved to differ as to the distinction between man and woman. (She stuck to the party line claiming there was none and eventually called on the female members of the studio audience to relieve me of my false belief that there was.) When the idiotic spectacle was over I went back to my hotel on foot. It was winter and bitter cold. What with all the preparations and waiting around and the show itself hours had passed. Night had fallen and Berlin was covered in snow. A thick fur lay upon houses trees roads and every exposed object. The streets were dimly lit pure white illuminated darkness. The roads were empty of cars and not a soul was in sight. The snow swallowed my steps. Berlin offered itself up to me in a never-before-experienced virginity: white in the dark expanse of night like a photographic negative. I saw it with Ugo Mulas's eyes (pure eyes).

That was very beautiful. Even three-dimensionally it was a negative of the city a mold I could fill with the moods and sensations of my various encounters with it (a literary lost-wax process). First the Berlin of 1938: still a metropolis but already spiritually sanitized. Capital of a kingdom of barbarians. De-Jewed and brought into line with the healthily average. Rendered abstract in preparation for events triggered by this abstraction. No longer fluorescent in the rotten decadence of the 1920s (the curse-laden age of the Weimar System, as the Nazis called it, now relegated to the past). Conscious of its calling. Anticipating the future in a kind of transparent futuricity: its buildings containing the skeletons of their own ruins. There shortly after the Walpurgisnacht of 12 March 1938 in Vienna (the annexation of Austria to the Third Reich) I spent an anxious summer and began to write. Blindly. A walking dreamer among sleepwalkers. Later beneath the steel storms of falling bombs I experienced firsthand the inner ordeal of the passive participant in world history. The human touch. Live human suffering. And then Berlin of 1945: city of ruins necropolis of a threefold legend—Berlin of Schinkel and Varnhagen Berlin of the saucy 1920s Berlin the luminous (though spiritless) capital of the Third Reich. It didn't take it long to become a legend again as the war invalid in imitation George Grosz style: amputated ragged shit-spattered crusted-over but still irrepressibly Berlin. Pioneer city that cultivated its isolated Western half bloated with hunger edema as a "bridgehead of freedom" (the Eastern half remained more Germanic). Pioneer city for colonists of the abyss. Which in many respects it then became.

So Berlin is still part of my spiritual bone structure. The city shaped me as Bucharest had before it and Hamburg-on-the-Elbe in later years. I carry Berlin within me through every present moment in the contemporaneousness of all past experience. Piebald as the various historical developments. I captured something of that first Berlin—the Berlin of 1938—in my novel *Oedipus at Stalingrad*. Another novel—*Death of My Brother Abel*—contains snapshots from heroic times. I hadn't yet written anything about Berlin of the post-1945 years. In that snowy night in 1990 I could feel how heavily it weighed on me. Rather than going straight back to the hotel I strolled through part of an old district in the west of the city where certain significant moments of my life had been played out (including the start of my first marriage). I was on the trail of my own pupation in 1938: the state of paralysis between the reality-devouring caterpillar stage of the aspiring writer and his unfolding (this last in the post-1945 years in Hamburg). It was after midnight when I returned to my hotel room. I sat down and began to jot down a few key words to record the thoughts and expressible feelings I had experienced during my nocturnal stroll. Since my flight back to Italy left at eight the next morning I got up before dawn packed my belongings still half-asleep and got a cab to the airport. High up in the air I discovered I'd left my notes in the hotel.

A serious loss. Though of course I know how to take it: if not as a metaphor for man's experience of reality in general then at least as a shabby consolation that it's probably all just a delusion. Surely nothing in those notes was irreplaceable. I know how this ghost does its haunting. You think you've lost God knows what and when you find it again it turns out to be utterly banal. For decades I've been waking up with the vivid impression that just before falling asleep (at last! after long hours of lying awake staring into the darkness) I'd had an idea that contained a flash of ultimate insight not only for whatever piece I happened to be working on but for myself as well: the secret of my existence. A word that would unlock the universe—and I couldn't remember it!! It was lost! I spend days racking my brains over what it might have been. Once years ago I decided to keep a notepad within easy reach beside my bed so that I could record my thoughts even when already half-asleep in those moments just before gliding off into the wonderful underworld of my ego. For years now I've been trying to capture that crucial moment when the verbal thought and the sensation linked to it become like the two rails of a train track and meaning detaches itself from word and then disintegrates altogether: transformed into images that possess their own pictographic syntax and grammar—and I tumble down the dark hole . . . Naturally I've never succeeded in catching myself on the threshold and the notepad remains blank. One morning I woke up certain that I'd once again found and then lost a phrase that would have unlocked the universe and the secret of existence. I hadn't had the strength to hold on to the vanishing moment and record it. And again I racked my brain for days and this time it came back to me. The thought I'd had as I was slipping off had been that if I were ever really to have an important idea I should make sure to write it down.

Inglorious delusion. An anecdote that would amuse Bruce Chatwin (and irritate B. an old man's jokes: colleague De Quincey's "anecdotage"). Certainly my Berlin notes had contained passages that were irreplaceable for me. My thoughts had been as clear then as the snowy night I'd wandered through (my heart icy with mourning for the city of Berlin: this is a condition of fertile receptivity to the literary seed). What I was wandering through had once—before my time *hélas!*—been one of the mythical cities of the century quintessential metropolis Babel of the thousand tongues contending to dominate. Life-pulsing life-bubbling life-inflaming capital of the front-runners of our epoch . . . and it had offered itself up as a site for the most sinister of powers. The whore of Babylon betrayed Art. She betrayed the cult of the Great Fetishes of the twilight of the West. Her love affair was no longer with Jewish intellectuals and the flourishing magma of Rhineland howitzer-factory shareholders Junkers black marketeers pimps stage actors and world-worn officers but with the real dregs of humanity: rabid demagogues from back-alley hovels and allotment gardens: like-minded like-tempered low-life comrades-in-arms of the Führer from the foothills of the Alps and his superhuman greed for power power Power. The splendidly many-tongued language of the decadents was brought into line. After which the words of the powerless survivors were drowned out by a single word: POWER.

Then with the collapse of this power Berlin contritely tried to become the spectacular battlefield where this defeat was staged (though still secretly working to produce a stylized version of itself). It presented itself as the bravely patched-up war cripple—oh sure no longer in the style of its starry-eyed son George Grosz (he too had been sanitized) or to the tune of a Bertolt Brecht song (his music too had gone sour in the face of this worldview-come-true). No: Berlin was reborn in the cellophane wrappers of department store goods. Pioneer city colonizing the abstract rebuilt atop a pyramid of skulls that spoke of millions of dead and neatly halved to produce a good division of labor. One half a training ground for petit-bourgeois mindlessness and mulishness the other half a spearhead of the Cold War. And the whole place just as saucy as ever just as brash and culturally ambitious (in vain). Irrepressibly self-intoxicated harlot who borrowed her slogan from one of the world's most ignominious pullers of wool over eyes (and most self-intoxicated powermongers): *Ich bin ein Berliner!* . . .

All these issues (and I myself as well in the robust bloom of youth that had seduced me into my affair with writing in the summer of 1938 then left me to flail amid falling bombs) now appeared to me in star-bright clarity that late snowy night. I quickened my steps to get back to the hotel and write them down and left them on the desk in the dazzling well-polished barococo hotel and presumably they were thrown away. All that is left is the title: *Anecdotage*. But titles can be changed. No problem. In any case it was already a sketch for a summation of sorts with a vanishing point offered by history for the junction of close-up and long-range vision of power and its relation to reality. (How worn-out! Old hat! It's all the fault of the situation that my colleague Gottfried Benn encouraged me to recognize.)

But I signed to them that I could write. The captain then said to them: "Let him write; and if he scribble and scrabble we will kick him out and kill him; but if he write fair and scholarly I will adopt him as my son. For surely I never yet saw a more intelligent and well-mannered monkey than he."

—FROM THE NINETEENTH OF THE *THOUSAND AND ONE NIGHTS*

Our house in Tuscany stands on a rib of land between two ravines in the furrowed landscape of the Arno Valley. I can watch the earth crumbling away on either side. The only thing that seems firmly rooted is the tower atop its cone of earth. I haven't bothered to investigate the tower's history. Presumably it's part of the cordon built by the Florentines as a line of defense against Siena and Pisa. (Is history even imaginable without acts of violence?) In any case all such structures are monuments to power. Aisha Leila and Ibrahim (not to mention Anna Fedora Raffaello and Enrico whom we employ) don't need reminders to see us as the powers-that-be. That's what we are for them though the only basis for our power is our checking account at the Banca Toscana (which is as unreliable as the ground here —clay and sandstone on slate). At most I could see my *pappagallo* as an insignia of lordship and its removal every morning by the Moroccans as a feudal ceremony. But symbolically it is my tower. Emblem of the power of advanced age. Just the right place to take stock of things here on the verge of completing my eightieth year of life: sheltered from the world in nerve-sparing isolation; elevated to a goodly height above all the profane events of life below and with an unobstructed view in all directions: the tower *c'est moi*. At a tranquil remove from the fools' game of clashing forces.

Thanks to the surgeon's assurances I'm expecting a few more years of my current *status vivendi*. What are "a few" years? A chain quickly rattling over a gunwale each link a sigh of relief heaved in bed at night before the hoped-for onset of sleep: morning and evening once more having joined to form a completed day (one of the dwindling number remaining). Having heaved many many such sighs in the longed-for bliss of bedtime I anticipate my own last breath with good cheer: "Long night watch of my life your course is done!" Naturally I miss the glandular freshness that gives young people their air of fulfillment long before they've achieved it. Skin glowing with good circulation ("good turgor" in medical terms). Thick hair *joie de vivre* in white-toothed laughs testicles bursting with hormones (fear of procreation!). I too once enjoyed these things in the aura of future promise. I still know them (I haven't forgotten) and don't mourn their loss. What I've come to miss is my old sense of wonder vis-à-vis the world.

By the way I've lied to you. It isn't true—as I claimed at the beginning—that I still drive faster than most people. On the contrary: I drive more slowly. ("Slowness is art" were supposedly Rodin's dying words; with the mysterious postscript "Thus the birth of the Virgin.") My reasons are less metaphysical: I detest the vulgarity of reckless speeding. It's not that I'm worried about safety. By now every child knows it's just as dangerous to drive slower than average as to go fast (most accidents are produced by the average itself). All the same: when I lie in bed at night unable to sleep my old heroic deeds of the past keep coming back for one last twinge of shame. From my years in the Germany of miraculous reconstruction: racing against a Porsche amid snow flurries after dark in Christmas traffic on the Autobahn between Frankfurt and Cologne—egged on by my three sons aged twelve eleven and nine. ("Who's faster? Mercedes or BMW? And how much faster than that can our Jaguar go?" Well let's show 'em!) This sort of thing belongs to a phase of my existence that now seems incomprehensible to me. I turn away from it as from something unclean. (I find various episodes of my past unsavory but you'd be surprised which things I put in this category and which I exclude.) Driving slowly is one of the privileges (and signs of dignity) of old age. I who no longer have much time left to me take my time. A luxury I can afford since I no longer have to outstrip anyone.

Especially not the O.W.A.s. I think of how Bruce once years ago (shortly before he fell ill) arrived here to do some writing in the tower: he climbed out of a fire-red *Deux-chevaux* to whose roof he'd strapped a surfboard. Golden Boy. He had just come from Greece. In his eyes the Aegean the wind of a long road in his close-cropped blond hair (a tiny crocodile on his polo shirt). His shorts—which came to just below the crotch—revealed his hiker's legs in all their splendor. No one would have thought this belated youth capable of writing anything more than his own name. And yet he was virtually glowing with promise. I went to meet him (as always his smile was the slightest bit crooked) and thought I was never like this. Never so all-of-a-piece. Though naturally less fucked-up than I am now. Less complicated. Today I am the putty holding together my piebald biography. (A man we were thinking of hiring for the house before the days of Aisha Leila and Ibrahim wrote in his application: *"Ho un passato poliedrico"*—"I have a polyhedral past." I like that.) But even as a young man I was older. More cunning. More enigmatic by nature. I felt for Bruce the same indulgence tinged with tender melancholy that I feel for my sons (but not for myself at the same young age). For the golden aura that surrounded him and surrounds all young people of promise: the nimbus of a sublime martyrdom (which for my part I was well able to avoid). The defenselessness of pure souls. Bruce Chatwin the writer in his glass-clear fragility was utterly vulnerable. Which explains his restlessness and his antiseptically pure poetic sense. (Like the rhapsodic one of my friend Ugo Mulas.)

The race driver Jackie Stewart once made B. the present of an anecdote. Once during a race a gust of air blew into his face containing the essence of all the summers of his lifetime. The impression was so vivid that after the race he drove the same stretch again slowly to discover its source. At the point where he had been struck by that quintessence of summer air the guard wall of a curve was padded with straw. The scent of it had struck his senses with the highest possible intensity at two hundred miles per hour. How beautiful! How profound! I like discussing this incident with B. (She admired and loved Bruce. And Ugo was perhaps even closer to her.) I ask her: was it the infinitely intensified impatience of his desire to win that had sharpened Stewart's senses to the point of making it possible for the scent of straw to become the quintessence of a life's worth of summers? Or was it the resolute patience with which he retraced the race course step by step to which he owed the revelation that it had been nothing more than a bundle of straw? An old man's ruminations.

And lo and behold: there stood the king's daughter before us; she had consigned the demon to the flames, and he had been changed into a small pile of ash.

—FROM THE TWENTY-FIRST OF THE *THOUSAND AND ONE NIGHTS*

That B. is descended from an Armenian mother a French grandmother and an English great-grandmother shows in her face in the loveliest epoch-embezzlerish way. A creature from the Age of the Crusades as if she's just stepped down from atop an early Gothic church portal. The strong and the delicate solid and fragile sensual and chaste united in a single image—this is what makes her seem to belong in a niche beneath a pointed arch. The compactly modeled nose and amber eyes are Oriental; the clear broad forehead and faintly cruel mouth come from the Burgundy of the early Middle Ages; the chin chiseled of the finest steel displays an English determination. Italian—from her father—is the neck: her most beautiful feature. The grace with which it bears her well-shaped head takes its example from the best centuries of Italian art history. What else? Yes: her character too is a mix of strength and fragility grace and hardness Eastern wisdom and Occidentally idealistic self-deception. She blushes in anger when I say that young heroes are mythical figures only because they died before their balls shriveled up. When I claim that even art is a matter of hormones and the death of O.W.A.s probably nothing more than an unfortunate coincidence. But sometimes lucky: ostensible fulfillment thanks to a presumably well-timed interruption. *Presumably* and *ostensible*. It's uncertain whether a point of unsurpassable climax was reached or whether we should be mourning the loss of what the artist might have produced in later years. Could Bruce have surpassed himself? What would his life's work have looked like if he hadn't died in his forties after *Utz* but had gone on living and writing until the blissful age of eighty? (Or should I credit him with the wisdom of Rimbaud? After all he loved nooks and hideaways far from the pandemonium of our civilization.) What if I had died at forty after the publication of *Oedipus*? If a haphazard but nonetheless insightful Death had amputated the rest of my paper existence with one snap of his scissors? (After all you can always trust a surgeon's knife.) When *Abel* appeared after fifteen years of work I said to one of my sons "Now my book has been published and the world is just the same as ever."

I weep for my friends who died young and for the possibilities they left unfulfilled. How I'd have loved to see them enjoy full lives and robust creative powers. I'd have liked to challenge them to contests. How deftly they eluded my challenge. The advantage the O.W.A.s have over us survivors is simply that they don't have to keep proving themselves. We have to keep proving ourselves to them but that's a different matter. They did not quite achieve the rank of those dead greats whom it can cost you your life to measure yourself against. (The enticing sublimity of silence.) All the same they placed depth markers indicating various ranks. Measurement addicts can gauge themselves by this scale but for their part they're out of the game. Farewells are always poignant. Our grief over the loss of something irreplaceable that was prevented from coming into existence has something of the melancholy of a folksong. The sounding board of our soul resonates with a primal fear: an inkling of the monstrous wastefulness of Nature. From the fanatic's eyes visionary's eyes prophet's eyes of O.W.A.s Kali peers out at us (the most convincing of India's thousands of deities).

This is why we the hardy survivors mistakenly suppose the O.W.A.s have something over us—their devoutness. They served their deities with all they had (though they—like all of us—really only serve the one Great Goddess) and with outward signs of devotion (Bruce Chatwin's discipline) they allowed an extraordinary toll to be extracted from them by the forces of divine destruction. Their sacrifices are pleasing to Kali's nostrils. We survivors are plagued by subconscious feelings of guilt. We are heretics living beyond our existential means. We want to draw an advance on our immortality this side of the Beyond. As if we wanted to defy Kali. We betray Death to Life. (Nowadays even corpses are plundered to save the living from death.) We disregard our duty to keep singing beautiful worlds into existence to cover up for the fact that we are all of us merely helping to build the pyramid of skulls atop which the Great Goddess has her throne. The O.W.A.s hover before us like angels in a dazzling vision. They speak of the world's splendor. It is as if they had sowed themselves as seeds of hope upon the killing fields and made us a gift of the eternally nourishing harvest of these well-fertilized plots. We the stingy hoard our seed for survival. We are not magnanimous enough to sow ourselves as martyrs in this game of hide-and-seek with the truth. We go on puttering about with the dullard equanimity of cud-chewing cows. If my grim sense of humor hadn't been provoked to speak out against this world of blind groping I'd hold my peace. If my garrulous tongue had not accepted the challenge not to let the mole-blind course of events go on all around me without at least voicing my contempt I would surrender myself to the care of Anna Fedora Aisha and Leila like a child peacefully urinating in its own warm bathwater. Not even the thought of B. who has summoned this exotic troop of women to ensure my well-being would suffice to stir up a few sad dregs of professional ethics. To be sure I certainly keep in mind all I owe her. Basically everything: the ecologically questionable splendor here (including the rainless early summer outside my windows which is just about to turn into a full-blown scorcher) the freedom from tiresome everyday cares my recent ability to work steadily (bringing in a lifetime's harvest whether that means a thing to anyone or not) last but certainly not least (crowning it all as it were) my very survival. Without B. the various side effects of treatments tried out on me to treat side effects of yet earlier therapies would long since have had me lying beneath the three lindens I planted in the hollow beneath the tower: one for each of my sons. (Everyone knows one should father sons plant trees and write books. Is that all? Oh yes and believe in mankind and make others believe in it as well! Worshipper in the temple of the crepuscularly Occidental Great Fetishes Life Love Freedom Equality Spirit Beauty. And again and again Art.) All this would be reason enough to create a literary monument to B. but gratitude and a husband's love are not enough for the production of literature. One also needs that basic emotion fear of death (even if unconscious like the fear of procreation in those blissfully testosterone-soaked youths) or else hatred.

Hereupon the Caliph spoke: "In Allah's name, how beauteous! O Jafar, in all my years I have never yet heard so enchanting a voice."

—FROM THE TWENTY-SEVENTH OF THE *THOUSAND AND ONE NIGHTS*

One insight to which my encounter with myself in front of Otto von Hapsburg led me was valuable: that hatred has been my constant companion. Smoldering hatred. Not brightly pure like that hate inflaming the young man in Bucharest leading his tattered old mother through the verminous crowd as though escorting a beautiful woman onto the dance floor. Good clear hatred belongs to the pathos of youth and a young man bursting with testosterone can afford it. The misanthropist's proud hatred of the riffraff who go on and on about how good how noble how gentle and pleasing in the sight of God how full of brotherly love they wish to be yet who don't stop killing torturing and harassing one another lying stealing and slandering. Hatred of the stupidity that believes in everything good beautiful and true while participating in every kind of wickedness hatred of the base subservience that over and over grits its teeth and bows its head to power hatred of greed envy falseness and everything else that runs counter to the beautiful good and true that everyone believes in . . . Hip hip hurrah! My colleague Chamfort says that anyone who doesn't hate humanity at the age of forty never loved it. My development took a different course. I never loved it but this didn't stop me from hating it with all my heart though my hatred lost its sacred fire in the earliest years of my childhood. Long before I might have produced as guarantors colleagues Sartre and Moravia and all the rest of them my hatred had lost its edge and become nausea and eventually when the nausea became unbearable withdrew to that sanctuary of cowards: irony. It spares me direct contact with things I find truly repugnant and at the same time serves a physiological function since I enjoy laughter. Laughing fulfills my need for pleasure. It is an essential component of my well-being as is (or at least used to be) sex. Or wine. Irony processes the nausea so that I can laugh at it. But occasionally even my irony fails me. This was the case in India.

I was in India in late February and early March 1990. After Bucharest and Cologne. With B. of course. She adores India. We've gone there so often that our trips have taken on the character of pilgrimages. The shrines we visit are predominately of art-historical significance: crumbling Mogul palaces in the North; Hindu temples in the South swarming with beggars. Nor do the exotic charms of Nature receive short shrift. Flowers everywhere. Color at long last. Women like hothouse blossoms. Men like shepherds right out of the Bible. A remarkably vivid world at least for the time being. (We don't even feel obliged to ask how much longer?) Marvelously inexpensive textiles handicrafts galore and bizarre forms everywhere you turn. Temples of a carnivalesque panoply of gods exotic but aesthetically exemplary pure art everywhere transcendence in concrete form. And then the climate! Nourishing air sauna-like heat (just the thing for me: old men like to have it toasty). This time we were in the South. We'd rented a car in Madras and were managing as many as five temples on any given day. Imposing edifices. Symbols of divine power. Gigantic stone pinecones. Encrusted with gods. Overloaded with gods like the dangerous country buses with their umbels and clusters of passengers: monkey gods mouse gods louse gods elephant gods snake gods cloud gods cannibal gods. Surrounded by great quantities of cavorting monstrosities: giants dwarves gnomes angels devils chimeras demons—all manner of sacred deformities. I had a skullful of wayward mythology and scorched soles from walking barefoot over sun-baked stones. My feet cooled off again in the crypt-like dark of labyrinths between whose forests of columns blossoms glowed and oily flames flickered and priests with oil-glazed bald heads and oil-dripping naked torsos anointed massive basalt lingams with milk and oil (vegetable oil of course: environmentally correct). Beggars straight out of legend in the arched entryways to the outer temple walls: tiny systematically maimed cripples with such cleverly folded-up limbs they were so to speak multipurpose and could be put in your pocket like a Swiss Army knife. And some who were perfectly intact except for a leg like something thought up by Ionesco growing rampant across the floor and through several archways. There were also very beautiful begging children. Entire swarms of begging children and begging old hags and begging pregnant women and begging old men of Bethlehemite beauty and begging hippies. And begging elephants. I scattered rupees around and bore wreaths of flowers around my neck and betel leaves between my teeth and cloves between my lips and blossoms behind my ear and dots of red white and mustard-colored powder on my forehead. A tourist. (Though without a camera. I—my father's son—detest the way laymen run around poking their cameras into everything.) In a town called Pondicherry I stumbled into a highly refined and thus particularly vexing system for pulling wool over people's eyes. Interesting as an instructive parable: a miniature model for the exercise of power (and the exercise of art in the service of power).

Pondicherry is an attractive town in a former French enclave of the colonized subcontinent and has such a distinctly French look about it you'd hardly know you were still in India. If you

don't look too closely the dark heads on the shoreline prome-
nades might belong to Moroccans or Congolese—dark-haired
people at any rate out of an exotic world stenographed by Dufy
in the middle of which a policeman in a red kepi directs the
tumultuous traffic and ocean breezes finger airy garments and
the hair of young women glimmers pitch-black from the crowns
of their lovely slim heads to the smalls of their backs and monkeys leap about on the rooftops of officers' casinos built in the
classical style and old men (my contemporaries) poke out from
beneath their shrouds arms thinner than the sticks on which
they prop themselves and old witches grin yellow-toothed
from skulls embedded in a tangle of white locks like spun sugar
at a country fair. In the middle of town stands a gravestone.
It serves a double purpose: memorializing the guru Sri Aurobindo and his companion in life and work the mouthpiece of
his wisdom and herald of his prophetic eye the (thoroughly
secular) executrix of his spiritual power *La Mère*. The Mother.
Together they can be credited with having founded the first
international ashram in 1926 thereby beginning a worldwide
movement that has possibly shown a chosen few the path of
the just life as willed by God and plunged tens of thousands of
others into the questionable bliss of existential mysticism. But
they share this originally unanticipated outcome with more or
less everyone who ever started an avalanche of faith with a
careless foot.

You can't go anywhere in Pondicherry without running into
a memorial a picture an inscription a commandment or pro-
hibition of The Mother. The cult of personality cultivated
around her (or that she herself cultivated) surpasses that of the
late Herr von Karajan in Salzburg. Sri Aurobindo was without
doubt an important man ("the last great visionary" Romain
Rolland called him). Learned in many languages and sciences a
poet journalist dynamically active politician until the liberation
of India. After independence was declared he withdrew to live

a purely spiritual life. Essayist: prominent interpreter of the Vedas and Upanishads literary critic whose scope ranged from Shakespeare to Rabindranath Tagore but above all theosophist in the original not the sectarian sense of the word: a bard of God who takes the precaution of not naming him directly but rather makes use of oblique phrases: *the Overmind. The Divine* is so to speak inferred allowed to remain in the rough form of a spirit of the highest positive potentiality which occasionally imparts itself to certain figures who are particularly well suited (such as Buddha Jesus Christ or himself Sri Aurobindo and through him The Mother) and issuing from their mouths eventually leads mankind down the true road to salvation. But the message he had to proclaim is not immediately accessible. Minds which (like mine) were still too firmly fastened to the material world desperately required The Mother's translations and explications (as well as the occasional retouching I suspect). Unfortunately she had the opposite effect on me. She stood regrettably in the way of my lame efforts to enter into the sphere of Sri Aurobindo's thought.

But I admit that if my account of Sri Aurobindo's qualities and achievements is superficial and inadequate there's another reason for it: I'm an intellectual lightweight (of all the good spirits my favorite is Ariel). Simply too frivolous to immerse myself in Sri Aurobindo's writings (I was supposed to be on vacation!) and too impatient. Besides which I can no longer endure someone offering me the sublime banalities of the profound good beautiful and true along with the impending salvation (or end) of the world as though he held sole distribution rights to them. My mind disengages the moment anyone starts speaking to me in tongues. My brain has built-in bulkheads that automatically close whenever the verbal torrents of eschatological experts threaten to sweep me into the presence of God. Especially when these torrents come from the East. I love the East. I admire the wisdom that has flourished there for thousands of years and likewise the superior intelligence of the Asiatic peoples. The Chinese have to know several hundred pictograms just to be able to read the newspaper says my friend Tilman Spengler (he's also a sinologist). I'm the sort who has trouble with the measly few letters of our alphabet. Of course they were sufficient to produce—among other things—the *Divina commedia* which helps me come to terms with the thought of not being Asian. But I am speaking of the mental training of fresh young brains and mine is old and drilled in the European manner. Easy prey for self-deception. I read my Meister Eckhart and the admirable Mathilde von Magdeburg with the voyeurism of a psychologist savoring the way these people transfigured by faith used the intellectual bag of tools commonly employed in the search for God to measure the depth of experience in their own souls. Reading Sri Aurobindo's letters (I did at least some delving into his work) I was put off by his didactic schoolmaster tone. No doubt a master of remarkable exaltedness and profundity in spiritual matters but schoolmasters intimidate me especially when they're taskmasters. They make me snappish as a cornered rat. The seed of power lies concealed in schoolmasters' bosoms. The Mother coaxed Sri Aurobindo's seed into a most prodigious bloom (or was it the other way around?). Don't forget I arrived in Pondicherry scarcely a month and a half after being in Bucharest. I was still suffering from the phenomenon of the sore thumb that one keeps knocking painfully against things when ordinarily one wouldn't notice. The ubiquitous constant presence everywhere in everything The Mother tormentingly brought back to me the reminders one saw in every Transylvanian village never to forget the greatest man in this country this world this age the Carpathian Genius Conducătorul Ceauşescu. I couldn't help suspecting that here in India I was once more dealing with a master of the public persona just like the greatest protagonists of the cult of personality and using a highly questionable vehicle for the purpose:

religious opportunism. An excellent subject for study. I hadn't foreseen that it would reawaken my senescently slumbering feelings of hate.

We stayed at a hotel that belongs to the Sri Aurobindo Society and is run and maintained by ashram disciples. It is excruciatingly ideological in its militant simplicity on the other hand slightly cleaner (and cheaper) than the usual provincial Indian hotel. ("You could eat right off the floor!" a German housewife might say by way of praise.) It wasn't so much for lack of comfort as it was age that I felt out of place: an old man in a youth hostel. But even as a youth I'd hated everything Spartan. Beds of the sort made for penitentiary inmates or Prussian kings who want to show off their simple castle life. Here a makeshift construction of hollow cement cubes shabby as Ceaușescu's postwar buildings in Bucharest. Functionally economically furnished. Plain metal bed plain metal table plain metal chair— *basta*. A light bulb dangling from its cord. Walls through which you can hear your neighbor breathe. You have to hand over your key each time you leave the building. Keys are not given out after ten at night. That's how strict their customs are. (Quite at odds with The Mother's repeated assurances that her ashram with its liberal convictions disregarded the ascetic puritanical principles of the originally monastic guru-disciples and later groups actually did away with them.) The dining room of course was self-service metal bowls and blunt safety utensils yogurt and lentil dishes. Each table bore a small placard offering tips as to the virtues that should be pursued in an integrally spiritual life: purity faith surrender realization perfection. All of this in English (apparently the lingua franca even here in the former French enclave) though to be sure so suspiciously ideology-tinged that one couldn't help placing a question mark after each word. Each and every one was symbolically expressed with a flower.

The walls were decorated with The Mother's sayings—not all of them formulated by her but cast in words of iron by faithful disciples under the spell of her inspiration as part of their spiritual homework. For example: "Approach the Divine with *loving gratitude* and you will meet the *Divine's Love*." One can always hope. (Let me reiterate: *the Divine* is that which took up position within Sri Aurobindo and was given voice through the mouth of The Mother—in other words slightly second-hand.) "Only to those who have true *humility* will *power* be given." Is that so? (What about comrades Stalin Hitler Pinochet Ceauşescu and consorts?) One maxim in German was voiced by disciple Wilfried as if straight from The Mother's mouth: "He who smiles upon life will be smiled upon in return." Fine. So what. Not all the spiritual messages of this cosmic benevolence were of such impressive carat weight. The Mother seems spontaneously to have thrust her hand into the immense treasury of her own universal insight and pulled out a few jewels to scatter through the city in the form of decorative inscriptions but one can't really appreciate their profundity without having partaken of her supreme consciousness. Monsieur Deloche director of the very serious Institute for Sanskrit Research (this too can be found in Pondicherry) mentioned one such inscribed in The Mother's somewhat prissy handwriting (graphologists would speak of a *Sacré-Coeur* character) across the wall of a restaurant in the old part of town: "This cheese is very good!"

At this point Shahrazad saw the approach of morning and discreetly fell silent; but when the twenty-eighth night *had come she went on.*

𝒲hy we didn't flee Pondicherry right away is beyond me. (B. is in charge of itinerary.) As I remember we stayed there for two and a half days. They felt to me like a whole distasteful epoch. All the sights worth seeing in and around Pondicherry were taken care of by the end of the first day. Nothing special in the way of temples. Textiles only of the sort spat out by factories. Everything else bore the seal of The Mother. It didn't take much introspection for me to realize that the generic designation alone was enough to give me allergies. The sort of maternity inflicted on me by my mother left my psyche scarred with ravines as deep as those carved into the landscape of the Arno Valley. The rod was certainly not spared but the child was spoiled all the same. I steer clear of mothers even when they're good sports. Besides which throughout my stay in Pondicherry I was suffering (as I've already noted) from the sore-thumb syndrome. My Romanian experiences interwove themselves with a thousand threads in the fabric of my daily life in India. Not only because of the Third World squalor (blessed with cement and combustion engines). I had brought along the manuscript of memoirs by a Romanian friend Olympia Zam-firescu. Reading it showed me yet again what an enormous discrepancy can exist between parallel realities. The simultaneity of glaringly contradictory processes in a single present moment: my world different from yours at the same hour the same instant. Even in the same place: my comfortable tourist's shoe beside the leprous hand of a beggar in the dust of the road while a holy cow plunders a vegetable stand unchallenged. Take it or leave it: this is part of everyday life all over the world and not just the Third World. And the evening news on television (happy hour edition) reports fighting in the Cambodian jungle famines in Ethiopia Biafra and Mozambique and glamorous premieres at the New York ballet. Banalities. My three daily four weekly six monthly periodicals bring me nonchalantly up to date on the guest list for Liz Taylor's eighth wedding and the possibility of substituting an AIDS-infected hypodermic needle for a pistol in holdups. In comparison Pia Zamfirescu's descriptions of life under Romanian socialism were disconcertingly personal. The scenes she described were so precisely situated in time that I couldn't help thinking back to the parallel segments of my own history. (Solitary confinement in a cell bristling with icicles versus duck hunting in Denmark; torture at the hands of the Securitate versus sunbathing on the terrace of Hotel Le Sirenuse in Positano.) Now I was experiencing these delightful juxtapositions not second- or thirdhand from my beloved mass media but blood-warm from a first hand I had often held in mine. Everything she had written seemed familiar to me: Romanian in its ultra-reality. For example when the National Communist nomenklatura wanted to get itself some social respectability (typically wholesale half-assed mini-bourgeois endeavor) they couldn't think of any better way to go about it than buying up the elegant cemetery plots of the down-at-heels families of the ci-devants several of the owners of which ornate mausoleums were forced by their situations to give them up in other words to vacate them. So as not to leave the bones of their forebears altogether homeless they called on the hospitality of other members of the former upper crust who had not yet sunk so low as to barter Granny and Grandpa's last resting place and squeeze their dearly departed into closer quarters. The evacuees were taken in. How nice to be in such good company again.

I read this in the dining hall of the ashram hotel over my breakfast of dal and yogurt beneath The Mother's slogans on how to arm oneself spiritually ("Only those who have pure humility blah blah blah") and it really did make me feel better to talk away my irritation with a little speech on the difference between ultra-real supernatural and metaphysical (B. listened with an impatience barely held in check). I said: this direct juxtaposition of the horrific and the absurd lifts my blue yellow red sense of the world above the level of reality and also keeps me from simply rejecting the supernatural. Seeing our existence in this world as a dream state in which the most contradictory things form part of everyday reality makes even the Immaculate Conception seem possible. Why not? A full-blooded Romanian like myself I said (although biologically only my great-grandmother contributed even a drop of watered-down Romanian blood to the sap of our family tree) should therefore be able to tolerate (yawning with ennui) the spiritual tiptoeing of all those who hear the bluebells ringing and sweet little elfin voices chiming away whenever a bird sings. If it makes them happy: no problem. Our contempt however—our hatred and nausea—should be reserved for those who claim to have discovered the source of all light and want to patent the gospel they've scraped together from all the chinks and cracks of other systems of belief under the seal of their chosen personality. Sectarian chieftains and ashram founders. Popular mystics and rock-and-roll metaphysicians. Social climbers (*arrampicatori*) in the salons of gods' sons and prophets. Would-be upwardly mobile who attach themselves to the hierarchy of saints as though tassels on a cosmic cardinal's hat. As a through-and-through Romanian one can appreciate the profitability of such a business—but beyond that . . .

B.'s green eyes are staring into space. She is dreaming of a

101

lovely temple and a *trouvaille* at the bazaar. She knows why she loves India.

And I know why I can't love it the way she'd like me to. It's difficult to explain that my intimate knowledge (going back to my childhood) of lands such as Bessarabia Volhynia Galicia and Lodomeria have toughened my hide against the charms of the Third World (colorful national costumes and cockroaches; women like flowers and syphilis). Besides which India has always been a hotbed of metaphysics. As a young man in the last throes of puberty I spent a great deal of time there in spirit as part of the traditional adolescent religious crisis. This sort of thing leaves scars that last a lifetime. Everything that goes beyond what we can perceive with our senses becomes highly suspect. India is home to too many faith healers for my taste. They come in swarms like the swarms of beggars. It's a nuisance the way they scale the protective wall of my irony. I get impatient and my slumbering hatred is jolted awake. Some of them are outrageously pushy. Take for example The Mother of Pondicherry.

The wondrous tales told of this woman—the tales she causes to be told—are not entirely intelligible (like the gospel of the good cheese). Countless biographies and hagiographies stocked at every newspaper stand in the city (penned by reverent disciples and published and distributed by the Sri Aurobindo Society's own press) report that their subject who was born in Paris to Turkish parents began to complain at the tender age of four that she could feel the weight of the suffering world upon her shoulders and comforted the worried souls around her with the disclosure that "I will have to perform an immense work which nobody knows." When she was twelve an old tree in Fontainebleau asked her to rescue it from the ax and at the age of thirteen "she soothed the afflictions of mankind in dreams pregnant with reality." At nineteen she married a pupil of Gustave Moreau and romped about (an artist herself) in the art scene of the time on an equal footing with Manet Cézanne Matisse et al. Her relationship to abstract art was less intimate ("these horrors!"). At twenty-one she received Krishna the godhead who was never to leave her. Hereupon followed her schooling in occultism in Algeria with a paraphysical couple named Max and Alma Théon. An anecdote from the period of her apprenticeship illustrates how familiar the contact with the forces of nature becomes when one lives in harmony with the supreme powers of the Universe: Madame Théon mistakenly (apparently less well versed in botany than in arcane matters) planted spruce trees in Tlemcen at the edge of the Sahara which in no time began to wither. Madame Théon activated her spiritual powers and that night received a visit from a gnome with a pointed cap dark green shoes and a long white beard who introduced himself as the Lord of the Snow (not Lord Snowdon) come in response to her call to aid the northern trees. But since he was beginning to melt himself and make a puddle on the floor Madame Théon quickly took leave of him. Nevertheless the very next morning the edge of the Sahara was covered with snow—an unprecedented occurrence. (Tellurian functionaries aren't quick to bear a grudge.) With such a teacher it was only natural for Mirra Alfassa as The Mother was still called in those days (only later would she be elevated to the rank of Mater cosmica) to spread her talents around. With a bit of friendly encouragement she persuaded several vital energies to calm a nasty storm in the Mediterranean. She tamed poisonous snakes with a mere glance healed cats that had been stung by scorpions as well as soldiers wounded during the First World War "in her way" that is by projecting her own aura ("to which the poor suffering souls were quite receptive"). When she was still young she'd had visions of Sri Aurobindo and after exchanging her first spouse for a second and spending two years in Japan (where she learned the art of flower arrangement and with pure energies alone put a stop to a fatal epidemic caused by vampires) got in touch with the great yogi. It was to be an uncommonly close and spiritually fruitful liaison. ("She is I and I am she" the supreme guru spoke; as the passionate tennis player she was she returned the shot backhand: "Without him I do not exist; without me he does not manifest himself.")

There is no end to the list of miracles performed in Pondicherry. Except for two instances when the great yogi himself intervened in world history The Mother took responsibility for these miraculous deeds. Meanwhile the great god-seeker displayed his own reality-transcending abilities. His historical interventions were (a) telepathic assistance in evacuating British troops from Dunkirk (curiously in time of war Sri Aurobindo stuck by the tyrants of the Raj whom he had been combating at home as a politician); (b) working this time too by means of states of consciousness transmitted with no physical mediation he shot down seventy-five German aircraft over London on the occasion of his own birthday on 25 August 1940. The above data can be verified in the literature printed and circulated by the Sri Aurobindo Society. Image-building. Someone has to weave the Emperor's clothes. Nothing new (although embarrassingly contemporary: PR). I ought to have realized this earlier. My encounter with Otto von Hapsburg might have taken a friendlier turn.

*When she had finished the beduin approached and bent over her; and since
he felt pity for her, he wiped the tears from her eyes.*

—FROM THE FIFTY-SIXTH OF THE *THOUSAND AND ONE NIGHTS*

$\mathcal{I}$ honestly did set out for India in the spirit of openness one
expects of tourists (and B. expected of me). And it's true I owe
these weeks an overwhelming profusion of images that have
filtered down into my memory banks and mingled there with
all the other treasures from around the world I've collected in
the course of my lifetime. If I were more conscientious I'd sit
down and label the collection with place-names geographical
and historical background dates of viewing and value ratings
and paste it all into an imaginary album where it won't get
mixed up with my impressions of China and Latin America. A
choice assortment of educational fruits. (Bruce Chatwin knew
the literary value of the travelogue. Existence as journey as in
The Songlines.) So March 1990 was India. For the most part
temples as I've already noted. One of them—I can only vaguely
remember a name a practically Gaelic concoction of letters like
a train station somewhere in Wales *Gangakongachilabaram* or
something like that—this temple as I was saying was very beautiful. No longer home to any deity it stood unencumbered and
tranquil in the middle of a large meadow. Chiseled of honey-
hued sandstone the sky above it sea-blue. In the intricate ma-
sonry that gave it the filigree look of Chinese ivory carvings
innumerable birds had built their nests but you couldn't see

them—in the shimmering heat of midday they stayed in their niches—only hear them. They twittered whistled warbled chirped and trilled thousands of them at once and it was as if the temple itself were singing.

In Pondicherry B. must have found me unendurable. I spent one of our days there giving rein to my penchant for terrible puns; on another I was sullen and grumbling; on the day of our departure I laid down my arms. Understandably. I didn't need the help of what colleague Nabokov calls the "Viennese delegation" since psychology without analysis was sufficient: I was frustrated. So much so that I didn't even try to fill B. in on my mental state. She is too well bred to yawn when I treat her to an account of my emotional ups and downs. I supplemented my lecture on the real and ultra-real supernatural and metaphysical with speculations on power and its relationship to all these blah blah blah. B. listens without a word as her thoughts are gliding off into the distance like birds at dusk. I fall silent with the mass of undigested material heavy in my brain. (The feasibility of power in this age of increasing abstraction. *Okay*. Anonymous power money Mafia. Spiritual power—belief. Power of the mass media. *Okay*. Political power and its cosmic manipulation. Acrobatics on the rungs of hierarchies embezzled from past epochs. A wall of exercise bars up which clerks can clamber as they thrust their opponents out of the way. *Okay*. The double bind of threats and promises seen from a psychoanalytic angle. *Okay*. The encroachment on the world of art— *image*-building. The staging of a fabulous career the choreography of showmanship the cult of personality. *Okay okay*.) It's vexing how there's always some indissoluble residue left over. Accursed irrationality. Charisma. Divine grace. That's right: diabolical divine grace. This is what I was unwilling to attribute to The Mother of Pondicherry (though the repercussions of her spiritual power could be felt and not just with regard to cheese) for I found her all too transparently a con woman in the God's

Grace racket. She cast a shadow over sunny Pondicherry and dimmed my brightly cartwheeling thoughts. I realized I wasn't so much interested in power itself as in the people who hungered and thirsted for it: grandchildren of Tantalus whose hunger and thirst could never be stilled. What made them so hungry and thirsty? I was in search of the demonic. (The concept is a make-shift solution, I know. My colleague Jaspers would scold me but for the moment I can't do without it.)

In Bucharest a few weeks before Pondicherry I had been haunted by the satanic state of grace that is power. Why had Party Comrade Ceauşescu been chosen? Why not someone else? What had he had over the others? I had walked through the streets of the ice-gray city pursued by the echoes of the inexplicable. Power exercised despotically can be felt in every corner every glance every word every gesture every sound—even in silence. When it breaks down it separates out from all these and vanishes in the air we breathe like the dust from a collapsed building. Liberated from its own actuality it can still blot out the sunlight. Bucharest had been mercilessly cold. I'm not so foolish as to have expected the city—now liberated from its dictator and (one hoped) the entire Communist system—to burst into blossom overnight and become again what it once had been in my day. But the bone-hard frozen dirty snow in the streets—you could break an ankle in the deeply etched ruts—bore contemptuous witness to the ongoing existence of the same old privation fear oppression hopelessness. There was no sense at all of release or liberation. Not a glimmer of euphoria pride tingle down the spine in the aftermath of the tyrant's murder. The only sign that anything had changed was disorder. Not the usual Romanian disorder which is slipshod in the human-all-too-human manner. Disarmingly innate genetically determined slovenliness. A sort of flea-bitten cosmopolitanism brightened by that loveliest of failings the innocence of being unable to help it. Nothing of this remained. The world was leaden-gray. The city stripped of its last pretense of urbanity was a happenstance conglomerate of rotting half-collapsed not-quite-contemporary petit-bourgeois dwellings and dingy rows of half-contemporary multistoried complexes pieced together out of prefabricated elements with contemporary counterparts still under construction. This gap-toothed assemblage was divided and crisscrossed by roads that with the huge piles of garbage and banks of hardened snow were all but impassable. And the places where this seat of Balkan socialism had been trying to give a big-city impression—in the shiny plate-glass windows of tourist offices and junky state-owned department stores—were pitifully deficient. I saw far less evidence of the so-called revolution than of the deceased Conducător's city planning. His ghost haunted the streets as did the beacons bearing witness to his inglorious ignominious end. Sooty tongues of flame flickered in the window-holes of several shot-up buildings and here and there on traffic islands in the boulevards groups of candles smoldered in beds of frozen floral offerings set there in memory of the slain. All around in between up and down things were restlessly swarming like the frenetic confusion of an anthill kicked by a huge brutal foot. Neither cars nor people seemed to have goals or even know what direction they were heading in. It seemed the agitation of numb panic. The only real signs of life to be seen were among freshly stirred-up dregs of humanity—begging Gypsies. Scruffy half-grown youths hailing taxis in front of run-down hotels. Clinging unsavory money changers. Shady interpreters. Vendors with dubious offers. Hotel lobbies were overrun with the sort of provincials you wouldn't want to meet in a dark alley. Perhaps they'd only come in to warm up for a moment in the naïve belief that under the new democratic system they wouldn't be thrown out. Sinister Western entrepreneurs who'd shown up mere hours after the alleged liberation weren't much more appealing nor the snotty journalists standing around in expectation of a new scoop. (Like what?)

The blindly swarming crowd on the street had the same dead eyes as before the upheaval. Nomads urban hunter-gatherers with gaunt faces beneath mangy fur hats huddled in anemic aniline-dyed mass-produced garments. Except for the roar of motors everything was strangely silent despite vigorous pedestrian activity. Strangely soundless. It was as if these victims of oppression were still rendered dumb by a now nameless and thus formless threat uncannily dissipated in air gray with snow. I wondered whether the air lay as heavily on their chests as on mine. Or did it seem to them a little lighter than yesterday's to whose oppressiveness they had been able to attach the name and image of Conducătorul? Führer. Few of them had breathed air that was truly light and unburdened. Most of them had grown up with the heavy exhalations of unlimited power. Miasmas of unrestrained despotism terror fear compulsions to lie. That's what they were used to. Filled with hatred they'd made their peace with it. Gnashing teeth that had nothing else to chew on anyhow. And if things were now the way their fairy tales described—with one of the three iron rings forged around their chests having burst asunder—they may have felt the remaining two as if all three were still constricting them. It was understandable that they weren't breathing any easier after those few exciting days of flying bullets (exchanged between whom and whom?) those few fires no one quite dared to put out those few dozen dead fallen more by chance than in heroism. I thought I understood: when power no longer has a name it is exercised by Fate and this is what made them so numb so frenetic. They feared that Fate had only horrors in store for them. But there was something they still hadn't realized. They were floundering because they'd lost the concrete object of their old hatred. Hate requires a context to keep it in perspective. A vanishing-point target. Otherwise it turns against the hater. One can hate a dictator but not Fate. Fate is anonymous. As long as it hasn't assumed a particular form you can't rebel against it without putting yourself in question.

Romanians are virtuoso cursers. Their language sprouts tropical blossoms—their powers of invention verge on the ingenious once they start to enhance their curses with variations paraphrases nuances. Well: it's one thing to curse a tyrant. He has a father a mother ancestors brothers sisters children grandchildren who can all be woven into a polonaise of imprecations. Fate is another matter. Fate is abstract. The ultimate abstraction of power. An unassailably absolute despot. From the beginning of time man has been subject to its will. Every individual blindly falls under its control. There's no point leveling accusations or curses at it. The people of Bucharest in those first days of the year 1990 no longer even cursed. They were robbed of their identity because they could no longer say to a tangible opponent: *Bagă-l în pizda mă-si.*

To these words she replied: "O my King, I hear and obey! In my first chapter I will speak of the sovereignty and the duties of kings as well as the good qualities which these must possess."

—FROM THE SIXTIETH OF THE *THOUSAND AND ONE NIGHTS*

*P*ondicherry gave me something to hate again. The nausea that came over me thinking about how the period of crisis in Bucharest coincided with this touristic adventure in India gave me the courage to address The Mother in good Romanian: *c'am s'o bag în pizdele mă-si.* In other words: I was going to send her back to her mother and her mother's mothers. I perked up. Soon I was wide awake and raring to go. Though without humor. I was on the warpath. My hatred had found a new toy for the days of my senescence and I let it have its way. Forcibly imposed leisure—that is idleness—makes me vicious. B. no doubt learned this lesson years ago and now she learned (a further test of her already well-tested patience) how nitpicking my gaze can be when—already queasy from its distant roamings—it concentrates on some loathsome foreground detail.

Sri Aurobindo had been dead for four decades and The Mother for almost three. Nevertheless you couldn't take a breath anywhere in Pondicherry without inhaling them. How long does the dust of expired power hang in the air? In how fine a mist does the departed's personality charisma aura of divine grace continue to infiltrate the consciousness of posterity? Centuries? Millennia? The ashram of Pondicherry is still run in the name of its two founders. Nothing unusual about that for religious teachers and teachings but in Pondicherry the show was lacking in substance. Not so much Sri Aurobindo's theosophy or pure will to redeem the world (neither of which come off too badly compared with other Indian exports in the same genre) as the cheapened, ridiculous personality cult surrounding The Mother. Who if not she herself was responsible for it?

In the numerous publications of the Sri Aurobindo Society constant mention is made of her "celestial" beauty. I'm sorry but I just don't see it. I was unable to discover it in her countless portraits in Pondicherry nor can I discern it today in those I brought home with me. I've returned to these pictures time and again always willing to be convinced. *Approach the Divine with loving gratitude* . . . Mine seems to be a hopeless case and yet somehow I kept coming back to her. Certainly not because of her beauty. More because of the mystery of its revelation (becoming visible becoming real). Why had it not been given to me to see it? What was I lacking? (Faith? Surrender?) Once in the prehistoric days when I worked at the Hamburg radio station one of our British controllers—a German Jew who had emigrated to London—told us in a moment of intimacy that he had spent many hours during the war staring at a picture of Adolf Hitler trying to understand what had made this man so fascinating for millions of people that they were prepared to give their lives for him. "What was the secret of the bastard?" It tormented him that he had been unable to grasp it. He was plagued with guilt at his failure to see and feel what so many other people readily saw and felt. He tried to discover some sense that was missing in him and suspected some sort of spiritual color-blindness that kept him from recognizing the obvious. This is how I feel when I contemplate The Mother's portrait. I reproach myself for being too frivolous (too cynical) to experience the state of transfiguration in which disciples of Pondicherry saw their saints and scold myself for being unreceptive to something that means so much to so many. None of it helps. All I can see is a listless old Turkish woman with her head wrapped in muslin veils like a Madonna and fastened with a clunky diadem. The veil has been artfully embroidered by adoring children so that strings of pearls radiate from the diadem as though her forehead were emitting light. A theater costume: half priestess half fortune-teller; half bride half widow. She looks like a comic actress with getup pieced together out of the inventory of a provincial theater. One cheek of her crafty face is swollen as if from a chronically infected tooth. The protuberant lips are either drawn down and to the sides in a bittersweet grimace or tacked up at the corners in a ghastly smile permitting a good half-dozen prognathous incisors to make their spiky appearance. When she is solemn and sweet-bitter (as though squelched by her own maternal nature) I see a postmenopausal youth-hospice matron gazing at me with unbearably soulful eyes. But most horrible of all is her smile. Unspeakable greed makes her look like a cat lying in wait outside a mousehole. A cat with bared choppers. I don't mean that her piercing eyes are frightening but they are scarcely comforting. Twenty-seven years after the demise of their owner. What does it mean?

Back in 1947 in Hamburg with the pseudo-British controller confessing his human-all-too-human irrational feelings of helplessness in front of Hitler's picture my radio colleague Dr. Kurt Emmerich my writer colleague known under the pen name Peter Bamm was just as moved as I by what we heard. But unlike me Emmerich was a highly decorated World War participant twice over and would hardly have denied that battle was among other things a personal experience even when forced on one by a tyrant (or by Fate). No one was better qualified than he to describe the mysterious effect the Führer Adolf Hitler had even on those who had been hardened in storms of steel like himself and his comrades and he was a spokesman for all who had fallen between this satanic despot's demonic millstones. And now—to offer us a crisis of conscience comparable to the one that had befallen the poor Jew luckily so far from the line of fire (nothing brings people together like calamity)— he recounted a few wartime anecdotes. He spoke vividly graphically as one might expect of a skillful writer and even more accomplished tongue-wagger warming to his subject. In the course of impassioned and ever more distressing descriptions of tank battles attacks on bunkers guerrilla warfare executions of hostages the fellow from London sank deeper and deeper into the collar of his British "battle dress" (which was a few sizes too large and identified him as a civilian and non-Englishman at a hundred paces) aging visibly before our eyes; and when we said goodbye to him he stood up heavily, gave an intimidated nod and—without a trace of irony but purely mechanically under the spell of this uncanny sharing of experience this vicarious ordeal (in other words out of emotion)—he lifted his hand in the Nazi salute. The powers of the demonic can transcend time.

And Mohammed said: "He who is moderate in his ways in this world will receive not only this world but the next as well."

—FROM THE SEVENTY-EIGHTH OF THE *THOUSAND AND ONE NIGHTS*

I am a writer whose books have appeared in most languages of the so-called civilized world. As such I owe it not only to the public but also to myself to explain in the name of what beliefs what convictions what views what intent I think myself entitled to exacerbate the hubristic paper epidemic that plagues modern man by adding the products of my own navel-gazing. This summation is my reply to these charges.

As you'll have realized I'm a dyed-in-the-wool cynic (my only line of defense against a cynical world). My attitude with regard to the conditions in this world is Romanian: I believe in nothing (which means: in everything). I'd be lying if I claimed not to be superstitious. Quite the contrary. My day passes in a succession of blurted prayers and childish invocations. *Scaramanzia* is my soul's daily bread. I turn the success or failure of the most insignificant operations into oracles. I wouldn't go as far as B. who shrieks when she sees a hat on a bed or forces me to stop the car and turn around when a black cat crosses the road. Peacock feathers in the house do not fill me with panic nor do funeral processions terrify me with the thought that my time has come. I'm not afraid of ghosts but don't plan to stop believing they exist. I firmly believe in telepathy clairvoyance and soothsaying. Also in curses. Not in dreams (and certainly not in their explication by the "Viennese delegation"). From every religious standpoint I am a heretic. An ignoramus out of (no doubt genetically determined) lack of interest. Cosmologies and mythologies I can admire as aesthetic constructs. Also the choreographic masterpieces of rites. Nor would I want to deny their magical efficacy. Above all I believe in the demonic. And in its antidote: laughter.

It bothered not only me but also B. that in Pondicherry I lost my ability to laugh. For the most part I'm almost pathologically quick to start chuckling over something or other. Laughter driven largely by impotent hate—i.e. nausea—yet also a release from nausea satisfying a physical need. *Ce monde me fait chier*— this world makes me shit (as my friend Brigitte Bardot used to say). And alas there is no other world. (I don't believe in worlds sung into existence even though I enjoy visiting them.) My laughter must always be lying in wait in all possible nuances from divinely liberating hilarity to the braying of malicious wrath. Despite the drawbacks—notably that it makes me seem like a person who doesn't take anything seriously (least of all himself and therefore he isn't taken seriously by others)—it has one invaluable advantage in serving as a buffer between me and everything I don't have to take seriously. It saves energy. (Hating is a strenuous activity. Nausea is paralyzing.) At the same time I am choleric melancholy in other words a moralist (perhaps a prize example for colleague Klages: the mind an antagonist of the soul).

Even in Bucharest I was far from tempted to laugh but in Pondicherry things were different. I didn't have to approach Sri Aurobindo and The Mother with the same blood-drenched seriousness as I did Ceauşescu the Carpathian Genius. The stench of corpses did not hang in the Pondicherry air. Something quite different had me in a stranglehold. The kitsch of travesty. The unintentional parody of power. A farce of power barely concealed in religious robes. It wouldn't have helped much if I had tried to penetrate Sri Aurobindo's gospel. I'm sure the path he showed us leading out of the murderous reality of the world is pure and leads theoretically to a desirable goal. (Like all gospels it leads us out of the world.) Whether it offers practical solutions within this world is questionable. The Mother had her own decisive answer to this quandary and on this point I agree with her: the union of spiritual and material dining halls. The world may well be improved by saints at a snail's pace for which I like most of my contemporaries lack the patience. In the meantime even those who steal off to take refuge in some blessed hole-in-the-wall must be fed not only with the bread of spiritual nourishment but also with some of the chewable sort and it is noble kind and good to procure this for them. But must this be done with the blackmailer's imposture of doing so in the name of the metaphysical? Is it necessary to enslave if not their bodies then their minds in the process? (Not exactly a new line of questioning but one justified by current events as CNN shows us.)

I know it was thoughtless of me. After all B. and I were on vacation. The point of vacations as everyone knows is to exchange one's same old workaday reality for a lighter breezier one. What was the ashram of Pondicherry to me? Sri Aurobindo and The Mother? At worst I had the troublesome juxtaposition of post-Ceaușescu Romania and the ashram of Pondicherry in a single point of time. But when you get started on something like this you wind up dead-ended in pure hypothesis. As far as power was concerned there was a distinct parallel between the two but in terms of ends and means the Pondicherry enterprise was ethically morally and even aesthetically head and shoulders above the leader whose work had been interrupted in Bucharest.

Indeed the two were in direct contradiction. Opposite poles. Almost an act of heresy to name them in one breath. Yet somehow I felt the urge to do so. Perhaps because of my loathing of all manifestations of effusive soulfulness. Any kind of enthusiasm. Any kind of exaltation. (One of my father's lessons: Beware of soulfulness! It has no form.) The Mother's inscriptions in the ashram hotel were a difficult trial. Something about the whole place put my teeth on edge.

I was beset with doubts even about the purity of this gospel. Too businesslike. Too well versed in commercial matters. The moderation that was preached verged on asceticism and the boniness of the besandaled inhabitants suggested that the bread they ate was meager indeed. I wanted to know whether it was satisfactorily supplemented by their spiritual diet. I immersed myself in the literature issued by disciples who had found the road to salvation there. But their retrospective view seemed to have effaced their undelivered past so completely that the transition from one to the other was imperceptible. It was not readily apparent what had been renounced for the sake of a higher good. Sociological speculations are difficult here since the disciples are recruited from many nations and social backgrounds. Perhaps their common denominator is naïveté. In any case they are soon reduced to the lowest common denominator of religious addiction.

In a booklet with the promising title *At the Feet of The Mother and Sri Aurobindo* a senior disciple writes of joining the ashram in 1928 (two years after it was founded) because he was "suffering from an internal feud" between his thoughts and feelings. (Apparently a condition similar to my own in the intensive-care unit after the heart attack I suffered as a side effect of my first operation.) The moment he crossed the ashram threshold the novice felt his mind "become free of fear and anxiety" (presumably in a different way from mine). This transformation he writes can be attributed to the ashram's "soothed" atmosphere (not as in my case to a drug from the medicine chest). He calls it a realm of "concentratedly muted processes." One moves quietly walks on soundless feet (bare of course) maintains silence whenever possible eyes downcast to be lifted—if at all—in a gaze transfigured by divine harmony to the visage of The Mother. Naturally the new resident had heard breathtakingly remarkable things about Sri Aurobindo and The Mother. As in the first act of my collegue Goethe's *Egmont* the main characters were the constant focus of anticipatory attention without actually being on the scene. But then came the grand moment of their entrance all the more splendid for the suspense preceding it: high priests and priestesses in full regalia surrounded by the throng of disciples "at their feet" (presumably on all fours). An encounter so overwhelming that the author is at a loss for words. But all the more vividly does he recall the "indescribable joy" that fills him when a hand is placed in blessing atop his head. Two photographic portraits are given him and he tells a brief anecdote to illustrate the all-encompassing fervor with which ashram residents devote themselves to the transcendent superreality of their two saints: he has in his possession two handsome frames one of which is just the right size for the picture of The Mother and the other slightly too small for that of Sri Aurobindo. In his naïve innocence he trims the photo to size thereby sawing off the feet of the vessel and provider of divine grace. An ashram disciple a girl of fourteen discovers this desecration and runs off shrieking: such sacrilege is the sign of a mind that must work its way through many stages of purification before it achieves a higher consciousness of the divine. The guilty party willingly submits to the process of disinfection which takes the form of a series of lessons that bring our protagonist "indescribable" mental and spiritual benefit and above all prepare him for the Descending of the Overmind (in other words to be its eager receptacle): work in the ashram. (The fourteen-year-old who indefatigably embroiders saris for The Mother says "It isn't work it's adoration of the Divine." In exchange a pair of glasses is procured for her at ashram expense.) The narrator's own worship is performed at a sewing machine which at first—a relapse into impurity—he tries to conceal but then finds himself compelled to turn over to the ashram.

His spiritual development is meanwhile taking a steep uphill course. Outside the classroom sessions (mostly silent meditation in which the spirit communicates itself wordlessly from teacher to pupils) disciples are free to engage in spiritual exchange with the guru and The Mother—though from a distance. Sri Aurobindo does not often appear (in later years he will retire altogether) and contact with him takes place in written form: in an exchange of little notes the soul struggling to attain consciousness of the Divine receives reassuring answers to its apprehensive inquiries (sometimes crisscrossing with The Mother who either answers as the guru's mouthpiece or has him answer in her place). The tone of the questions is dithyrambic and the answers Orphic or laconic. ("Mother this time it was given to me despite severe temptations to keep my consciousness pure to receive the Overmind! What must I do to sustain this condition?" Sri Aurobindo's answer: "In this you may behold the Overmind! It shows great progress that you were able to keep your consciousness pure despite severe temptations!" Or to Sri Aurobindo: "Yes I have understood that he who is mute has no enemies. So I shall be mute from now on. But will I not become a burden?" The Mother's reply: "In any case *Silence!* is the best motto.") Gauging the ability to fathom the depth of wisdom in these statements is how the recipient's spiritual progress is measured.

External circumstances are decisive. As each disciple is given a new name (for example Philippe Barbier de Saint-Hilaire becomes Pavrita) they are hatched into a new existence. Practical worries are lifted from their shoulders. They receive three meals a day. Strictly vegetarian fare: in the morning a bowl of Phoscao

("Tastes like cocoa only better"). For lunch rice curry or dal a bowl of soured milk and two bananas. For dinner soup bread curry or dal and a mug of milk. Two or three times a week the menu is spiced up with a bowl of payesh ("a kind of pudding"). But partaking of this fare isn't so simple. First thing in the morning The Mother's blessing must be obtained. ("She came to us and took her seat on the cushions of a platform covered in velvet. Beside her was a tray with different kinds of flowers. We waited outside the door until she had taken her seat then entered one at a time and sank down at her feet. She placed her right hand upon the head of each of us and gave him a flower. All this giving and receiving took place in a silence that was all the more eloquent for being so complete.") Only after this may the ashramites enjoy their morning treat (Phoscao).

In the evening too a solemn rite is performed: the "soup-serving ceremony." This time The Mother is seated on a throne. Her costume is particularly festive: the veil that falls from her head over her richly embroidered sari (one of the many works of adoration executed by bespectacled ashram children) is held in place by a broad headband of gold. The lights are all extinguished except for one dim lamp. ("The room was filled with an atmosphere that was as pure as it was profound and suspenseful.") The suspense reaches its climax when The Mother holds her hands above a large soup vessel set on a stool at her feet. For a moment she pauses in the utmost concentration while the spirit of Sri Aurobindo enters the soup. After this the soup is served. Disciple after disciple rises from contemplative meditation at the place The Mother has assigned to him and approaches with soup bowl in hand. She fills the bowl takes a tiny sip herself and returns it to him. He slowly leaves the room with a feeling of spiritual enrichment which the author of this report (for once not at a loss for words) describes: "It was as if the reflection of a higher being were glimmering in the muted light. In my consciousness an influence that was not an earthly one became manifest. Inside and outside crystallized in the concentrated silence in which all identity dissolved so as to be incorporated in it. I did not know who I was or where I was or where I had come from. Inconceivable perceptions of the inner world appeared in my mind with great clarity. The Mother radiated a divine aura. Her eyes were no longer of this world. They pierced through the armor of the corporeal and penetrated my interior. Her smile too was otherworldly. Often she paused with the soup bowl in her hand as if experiencing a state of rapture and only after a short while returned to her physical consciousness so as to go on distributing the soup quite naturally." The ceremony lasts more than an hour "in an intense inner glow." The recipe for the soup is not included.

And Shahrazad said: "These, O my master, were the words of the wise man."
—FROM THE HUNDRED AND TWENTIETH OF THE *THOUSAND AND ONE NIGHTS*

My father was a passionate hunter. As a self-declared woodsman he felt obliged to develop a philosophy of his own in woodcut-like simplicity whose spruce-needle-fresh apodictic statements would brook no retort. Explaining the female psyche by comparing it to the behavior of difficult horses was one gentlemanly example. He was in the habit of saying: Man is a stepchild of Nature and if he didn't stand up to her with his own make-believe superiority she'd have devoured him long ago with his pitiful naked skin and rudimentary hair growth. For millions of years now they've played the game of who'll-outwit-whom. The way it works is that he has to pay for every advantage over her with a disadvantage of equal if not greater measure. But he can't let go of the fiction of his own active participation in this game. If he doesn't want to be devoured he has to keep coming up with new fictions to enlist against her. Watch out! If these fictions become too fictional he may provoke her wrath and the wrath of Nature knows no mercy. On the other hand if he too eagerly serves her wishes she'll be grinding his bones in no time. To survive on this planet man must find an equilibrium between these fictions and his devotion to Nature.

It's obvious why Pondicherry brought back these memories. I was of two minds whether—The Mother and all her tra-la-la notwithstanding—I wasn't doing an injustice to the basic concept of the ashram and all the ashrams operating in Pondicherry and the rest of India (and California). Were they not visible manifestations of the age-old fiction of possible escape from the horrors of earthly existence through spirituality? Wasn't an ashram as it were a monastery without walls? A monastic order of free and unrepentant affirmers of life not death?

I tried to estimate the total carat weight of the fictions governing the ashramites' daily routine. In their affirmation of life they were diametrically opposed to crude Nature the Universal Devourer. In a word: art. But the flatfootedness of this rejection of Nature as wicked spirit got on my nerves.

I read: Once a week—not according to Schedule—The Mother visits the disciples in their quarters. (She "consecrates them with the touch of her feet.") "On such days we were permitted to speak with her about questions of spiritual development or our work. Often her opinions were expressed more clearly in glances than in words. At times when a question was troublesome she would immerse herself in meditation together with the disciple she was visiting her hand on his head: soon the question was completely forgotten and his being filled with a supernatural reward." Earthly items were also in evidence. On the first of each month The Mother distributes "necessities of life"—"a bar of soap a clean towel and similar items"—and gives each disciple two rupees for pocket money. These alms are distributed with much ceremony and flower symbolism. The "divine aura" comes back into the picture when The Mother invites a few favorites to share in the daily cross-country drives she takes in her car in the cool evening hours. Pavrita (formerly Monsieur de Saint-Hilaire) is the chauffeur. Without knowing the region he drives—under her spiritual direction— to the loveliest remote places. She is the first to alight from the car: the disciples follow. She appears to know the region like the back of her hand. Finally she chooses a seat. To sit around her in the lap of Mother Nature (with whom she is One) is so divine a pleasure that the narrator is once more at a loss for *le mot juste*. He's been falling back on "indescribable" again (on occasion also "unimaginable"). The Mother has brought along some sweet French cookies and gives one to each of her companions. Suffer the little children to come unto me.

And come they did. They're still coming today. Whole herds and hordes of them. They cluster in clumps and umbels about the ashrams of India (many of which pull far more questionable metaphysical wool over their eyes). They cast off the fictions they've grown up with along with their so-called identities and trade them in for the freshly refurbished boutique-exotic fiction of pure spiritual life on this filthiest of planets. *Beati loro!* Unless they notice that Kali is sitting right behind them laughing up her sleeve.

As he saw him standing there with the drawn sword in his hand and the blood running from his nose from the severity of his rage, he asked him what had happened.

—FROM THE TWO HUNDRED AND TWENTIETH
OF THE *THOUSAND AND ONE NIGHTS*

$\mathcal{M}$y profligate (and for the most part profane) laughter lies in wait for me as well. Nothing frightens me more than the thought of being ridiculous though I know it's inescapable (as is stupidity; of which I'm almost equally frightened). Fear of my own ridiculousness (and stupidity) has caused my attack dog of a superego to develop the musculature of a Schwarze-negger. In Pondicherry it failed me. It couldn't stop me from whetting and rewhetting my hatred until the blade was notched. I could see nothing but the object of this hate. After all what was this Mother but a self-infatuated comedienne? Admittedly one of the last great figures in an art form that's been plummeting downhill since the end of feudalism. With the exception of rock stars there's hardly a soul left in our middle-class world who understands it. Hollywood has done away with divas. Today's politicos are hopeless failures. Of course there are the occasional costume pageants staged by the Vatican with a hundred bishops humbly spread-eagled on the ground awaiting consecration: museum-class epoch-embezzling popularized by regular appearance of department-store Santa Clauses straight out of Disneyland. But the great spectacle of power belongs to an earlier stylistic epoch. After the end of feudalism it blossomed only in the geometrical mass choreography of the wonderful 1920s and '30s. On the small scale of homespun handicrafts The Mother of Pondicherry managed to coax one last anemic bloom from its branches. To be sure the field—or rather compost heap—on which she raised this orchid has a vile odor indeed: the pseudo-religious—

and my superego put aside its laughter and abandoned me ignominiously. I stropped my hatred not only on The Mother herself but on all the naïve fools who'd fallen into her theatrical trap. The belief in the metaphysical (*faith*) as manna for the poor—above all the poor in spirit—what's the point of denouncing it? It feeds on the worldwide demand of everyone who has tripped over his own crooked existence and tumbled down into the uncertain zones between realities. Addiction to miracles and craving for religious devotion go hand in hand. Thus "every despot rides the magic carpet of some myth or other at the head of his pack of followers" (I quote myself). What bears him along are venerable impulses: the instinct to flee from oneself toward some unreachable Other—from I to we and soon to the Unreachable itself—the unquenchable longing for the Absolute. In secular terms this is a desire for oblivion and guidance. A latent willingness to be enslaved. (*Surrender.*) Effacement of consciousness. Once someone gains control of this mechanism and sets it working to his own ends the rest is child's play. He—or she—doesn't even have to resort to the standard alternating threats and promises. Even today there's scarcely a child who isn't asked where he wants to end up: heaven or hell. Utterly superfluous in the Age of Neuroses. By itself the promise of heaven fulfills the household needs of those to whom intimidation comes naturally. No need for threats since these hordes of eager sycophants supply their own hell. Nothing spooks them so badly as their own hopeless selves and all you have to do is offer them the prospect of trading these latter for a better higher nobler more beautiful and above all different mode of being. With strict guidance of course.

But to make this promise plausible I said to B. (who was only half listening) it has to be given concrete form. You have to say the Messiah is not on his way but already here. He—or She—must be manifest in a constant epiphany day after day. It isn't easy to stage such a thing. Making a good show of it requires—well damn it! something along the lines of artistic sense. (Adolf Hitler originally wanted to be a painter.) Even the demonic needs support. Some hint no matter how trivial of divine grace. I assured B. (who was keeping a sharp eye out for textiles) that of course I saw the difference between The Mother and Nicolae Ceauşescu. They had in common the nauseating smell of cheap charisma. Ready-to-wear shoddiness of the demonic. (My colleague Hannah Arendt would love it.)

And then something utterly unexpected happened: to my consternation I found myself in the position of a sword-bearing archangel defending God's name against The Mother of Pondicherry. I would not permit these false prophets to abuse it. They seemed to me even more worthy of nausea and hate than the despicable minor and major power-besotted dictators who deny Him. I said that their power was ephemeral and we had weapons against it. The viscous adhesive power of con men of the divine produced from the residues of decomposing religions. The arguments against them keep slipping out of your hand. (Who wants to turn to theologians for help?) The charismatic washouts would never Lord knows touch a hair on the head of Holy Values: no one clings more fervently to the Great Fetishes Faith Love Human Dignity Human Rights Democracy Culture Art blah blah blah and so forth. They use them to blend the mother liquid of all power: *stupidity*. Archenemy of all upright men and dangerous ally of the humorless.

Thus did I spend my days in Pondicherry in a listless funk. Not at all my sweet hilarious self. To stimulate my foul spirits I occupied myself with everything that might be cited as evidence against The Mother. I took arguments from as far afield as I could manage for example from economics. When you read the disciples' dithyrambs in the pamphlets of the Sri Aurobindo Society you note that they often speak of the early beginnings of the ashram when a total of perhaps sixty disciples had banded together and go on to say that when The Mother passed away in 1973 there were a good two thousand of them (men women children). When you consider that according to the principles of the ashram "the radical transformation of human nature *which is the basic prerequisite for all spiritual development* can be reached in no other way *than through work*" more favorable conditions for the economic prosperity of an enterprise are indeed "unimaginable." ("Our only path is work" stood above the ghetto of Lodz in 1944; above Auschwitz "Work makes you free": *"Arbeit macht frei."*) It's enough to make any manager turn pale with envy: the effortlessness with which this potential workforce was kept in harness: the economy of it—I'm tempted to say the elegance of means. The feeling among company members of belonging to an elite entity. *We.* Yet with no share in the profits. Instead celebrations of the we-ness feeling in a ritual festive atmosphere. Cheap lighting effects for the manger ceremony (magically muted). The silent cult of the work process (work as prayer). The symbolic use of flowers to raise production levels. Entertainment (*dopolavoro*) in musical form. All possible sorts of uplifting artistic activity: painting pottery embroidery. Unlimited sojourns in the depths of the soul twenty-four hours out of twenty-four. The Mother plays the organ in the evenings (improvisations). The father (Sri Aurobindo) is shielded from profane eyes: he receives the Divine and The Mother passes it down. The only thought either of them has is to help their disciples partake of this grace. Perfect parents: a feat of image-building on management's part that would make any self-respecting PR agent gnaw his knuckles in envy. As a workshop—a home office as it were—for lucrative soul-squeezing the ashram of Pondicherry is exemplary. A textbook example. That the business continues to flourish after the death of its founders speaks for the solidity of the enterprise. Unfortunately only imitable on a small scale. Yet there are certainly enough spin-offs. Not all of them equally kosher. But they all have one thing in common: the spiritual exercise of power. Domination is carried out without physical force. That alone is enough to coax dithyrambs from art enthusiasts. This is how pyramids and Mayan temples were built: as a form of worship. Worship of terrible deities.

Please forgive me: after Bucharest I found all this confusing. I had just come from a place where the (apparent) cessation of physical violence (supplemented by a certain degree of spiritual brutality) had given way to a situation almost more hopeless than the preceding one. Over my lunch of dal and soured milk in the ashram hotel in Pondicherry I was tempted to admit (reddening with vexation at The Mother's epigrams affixed to every wall every object around me) that in this case possibly the end did justify the questionable means. To be sure spiritual violence perhaps more than any other sort—the compulsion to lie and to live a lie—is traumatic for those violated by it. But here in Pondicherry I repeated to myself it was being done to subjects in need of religious devotion for whom it was not compulsion at all but their very salvation. (The true nature of this salvation can be seen in a pathetic exchange of letters between a disciple suffering a spiritual crisis and his stern providers of guidance: "My Mother! I am tormented by desire: do you know what for? For eggs lobster and canned sardines. I crave them, Mother. Take this desire from me or allow me to satisfy it under your protection." The suggestion appears to have been so shocking that The Mother forwarded it to the highest authority. Sri Aurobindo responded promptly: "Never! What you can consume is your own desire. This alone shall be meat and fish to you. It is the temptation that comes from the subconscious. Do not give in to it. It forces itself on you in order to be overcome.") Especially a craving for canned sardines.

I honestly did make an effort to enter into the pure spirit of Pondicherry without putting out my claws. But the limits of my goodwill were reached when I read this passage in the confessions of the happy disciple: "I preferred meditation. I was not convinced by the gospel of work. But gradually I came to realize the spiritual meaning of work [at the sewing machine?] and enjoyed performing it. But precisely this contentment seduced me into meditative contemplation. I sank so deeply into myself that I forgot my work. That couldn't be right and so I appealed to The Mother. She wrote: '. . . when you work it is always better that you are in full consciousness of your body and the skill of your hands. With love and my blessing!' " *Ora et labora*. (That certainly sounds familiar.)

They say that in Pondicherry not so much as a betel nut goes on the market without the organization of The Mother being somehow involved. No doubt true. I wandered all over the city. Where the buildings of the former French colonial administration end the settlement is overrun with the war-sustained undergrowth of Western civilization. Cement and corrugated iron. Tangles of electrical wires. Shop after shop filled with cheap shoddy goods. Neither sewer system nor garbage collection. Rust and crumbling mortar. Occidental mange imported to the Orient. Interspersed with cascades of bougainvilleas and the colorful palettes of spice stands. And chewing gum and Pepsi-Cola. Motor vehicles rattling out their last breaths and freely roaming cattle. A bitter disappointment for B.: no bazaar. Nothing handwoven hand-embroidered hand-carved hand-hammered. A shantytown. Whether the human compost fermenting there was being maintained or exploited by an alleged Sri Aurobindo Mafia or by ABC or CDE or DEF or one of the other standard multi-polyps was a matter of complete indifference to me. Just as incommensurable as the charitable character of the enterprise. Even if you could calculate how many orphans had been given housing courtesy of The Mother (learned to read and write pluck string instruments pump the pedals of bicycles and sewing machines sing idiotic songs play soccer and volleyball throw pots weave paint religious monstrosities and practice other fine arts) or how many were guided by the spiritual fallout of psychopompous Aurobindo to find and follow the road of salvation and purify their formerly unclean souls to the highest transcendence—even if these things could be extolled before God's throne on Judgment Day it would not in my own heathen perceptions acquit The Mother and the guru of the charge of enslaving spiritually defenseless people. Even if these slaves served an Order of God. I would—assuming I were there—raise my voice and address this question to the Creator: Lord! Have I understood You aright that You promote order only so as to produce more perfect chaos?

The ashram is situated outside Pondicherry. Extensive grounds that in The Mother's heyday witnessed processions of world youth world reformers world renewers the consolidators of world religion fighters for world peace advocates of world brotherhood world spiritualism and similar globally relevant standards about which great hearts can rally. (Postcards are available for cash purchase from the Sri Aurobindo Society: geometrically flawless cadres of adolescents in white blouses and neckerchiefs brought into neat ideological line: the geometry of the military parade. Art Deco choreography. The ornamentalism prized in the early 1930s along the future-crazed axis of Rome–Berlin–Moscow.) On a platform The Mother surrounded by a group of obscure dignitaries and draped in white veils from her king's-widow head to the rhinestone-glittery sandals: Mater cosmica. Or: The Mother in tennis whites and a sporty headband amid a throng of young handi-capped athletes. Or: The Mother at the ceremonial unveiling of a memorial of high-voltage symbolic power in the middle of Motherville (Sri Aurobindo nowhere to be seen). Today this field lies as barren as the grounds in Nuremberg designed for similar purposes though more straitlaced: like a checkerboard of garden allotments. (Anselm Kiefer wouldn't be interested.) It's hard to imagine the place as a parade ground for ideologically inflamed mobs or for any assembly bigger than your average Boy Scout meeting.

Even more difficult to conjure up is the image of the monklike intimacy among the first ashram disciples that is so often stam-mered about in rapturous admiration in the many publications of the Sri Aurobindo Society. I drove up and down the muddy roads of a desolate colony of one-family bungalows whose great variety of styles bespoke considerable tolerance in matters of taste; not a single inhabitant was in evidence. Far off a tractor clanked into the distance leaving behind a mile-long ribbon of dust that gently descended upon the sparse vegetation of agaves privet shrubs and rachitic eucalyptus. (Desert Storm.) Other-wise no signs of life. I felt as if I was not in the lap of The Mother's ashram but on a sheep station in deepest Australia. I felt Bruce Chatwin's presence along with the black dandelion stamen balls framing the flat-nosed wrinkled heads of his Ab-origines who sing the world into existence. But they were no consolation. I couldn't escape the notion that Bruce would have smiled indulgently at the way I was carrying on. Gregor the Crusader on the warpath against all self-appointed curates. I remembered the irony with which he recounted his experiences among the monks of the mountaintop monastery at Athos. I pronounce my own acquittal because I know he died piously repentant as an orthodox Christian.

"My son," she replied, "I know very well that you had an uncle, but he has been dead for many years; I do not know since when you have had another."
—FROM THE TWO HUNDRED AND SIXTIETH OF THE *THOUSAND AND ONE NIGHTS*

They say the need for the otherworldly comes from fear of death. I've never felt anything of the sort. I'm a flat-out coward when it comes to physical injury yet I've always thought of my own death (and still do) without perturbation. They also say (according I believe to colleague Vico) that the concept of humanity comes from the word *humare*—to bury. The reverential interment of forefathers as a way of preparing cultural humus. (The grave purchasers in Bucharest must have been thinking this.)

When my erstwhile friend Ernst Schnabel put together his memorable radio program based on that day picked from the transitional years of ice and hunger—1946 and 1947—in Hamburg-on-the-Elbe he didn't want to risk in the many letters he was certain to receive not getting some about the experiences of holders of certain key social positions (important even then): midwives undertakers and whores. This was in the sunniest heyday of our friendship and so we set out together to fill these possible holes prophylactically. It was the bitter-cold January of 1947: Age of the Reichsmark.

132

The midwife was overworked. "Too many" she said. "Far too many. Makes you wonder: where do they get the strength on that kind of grub? Every two farts—if you'll pardon the expression—there's another one knocked up. On a bellyful of frozen turnips. And then the mothers are surprised when you can't squeeze a drop of milk out of them. How they get a drop out of their fellows in the first place is the real question. They're all swollen up with hunger bloat too. And then the miserable little buggers want to live. Too many. Far too many . . ."

But the whores on brothel lane near the Davidswache were brimming with confidence. It was toasty warm in their cramped rooms. Cognac and the smell of Cuprex in the parlor. "Why don't you stay awhile, boys?" they asked. "This is the high life. Who's going to bother us? The Russkies? If they come piling over the Elbe as everyone's so afraid—what of it? Let them come. They're customers like everyone else. Probably have loads of canned goods and vodka on them. Just the thing to warm a girl's heart. We don't have to be afraid like everyone else out there. Just imagine me having the shits that someone's going to rape me—hee hee!"

The undertaker had found an even cozier niche in the Ice Age. His "institute" (as he called it) lay in the cellar of a divided house in Altona. (The other half was a pile of debris: the house next to it had taken a direct hit.) From the sidewalk you could see into a ground-level window where on display (to attract customers?) was a simple coffin of wooden boards unfinished on the outside and the interior painted black. We descended half a dozen steps to the door which was locked. It was 9 p.m.— which in those days meant the middle of the night. The only illumination was the far-off streetlights of the Reeperbahn. Our visit had been announced so we groped about until we found a doorbell and rang it. Nothing. Minutes passed in the deep silence of the icy night. We rang again. More minutes went by torpid as the current of the black Elbe behind the fields of ruins. We rang a third time. There: gradually approaching slap-slap of house-slippered steps and a snuffling sound that slowly increased in volume. It stopped along with the footsteps and terminated at the door in a long deep breath. A lock rattled. The door opened. A pointy shark-head shape appeared at testicle height. A black truffle two black eyes two pointy ears. Above and behind this set off against a gloom in which four coffins were positioned (two rows of two) a fat short man dressed in a bathrobe stood silhouetted in the yellow rectangle of the door to a second room. On a short chain pulled taut to iron-bar rigidity he held a nearly hairless mutt whose pointy snout was aimed like a torpedo at our family jewels. With one more deep snuffle it inhaled their odors and exploded in the cloudburst of a violent sneeze. Before either we or the dog's owner could say anything a massive female silhouette darkened the yellow rectangle of the door to the other room and a rich throaty voice called "Come right on in, gentlemen! Santa's little elves have brought us some treats." (The tail at the other end of the dog began to wag.)

"Right this way" the undertaker said. "My old lady's made us a little snack. It's not every day you have gentlemen from the radio." I raised one hand to pat the dog's sharky head between its (hybrid) pointy ears. "Don't touch!" the undertaker cautioned. "He's trained to attack." He rotated the dog on its stiffened chain and shuffled (he was indeed wearing floppy felt slippers) between the rows of coffins to the door at which his wife was awaiting us. She was a full head taller than he: a motherly figure in a flowered housedress. On her head a plaid scarf wound into a turban. (The wartime garb of air-raid-cellar inhabitants.) With a curtsy-like gesture she ushered us into the living room.

It was the very model of a German parlor: a black oilcloth sofa with white buttons and above it a photo portrait of ancestors in a gilt frame; a glass knickknack case (containing among other things a vase made of seashells and a porcelain flamenco dancer wearing a bolero). On the mirror-bright polished surface of the oval dining table a whole battery of schnapps and beer and two slender bottles of white wine. On tiny little doilies in the shape of flowers with neatly stitched edges lay the snack: bowls containing blutwurst and soapy liverwurst bread butter mustard horseradish cigarettes and two bars of chocolate (black-market goods from the British PX). "Dig in, gentlemen!" the undertaker's wife said knowingly with a maternal nod. "There's more where that came from."

We didn't wait to be asked twice. We'd been tightening our belts for six years along with everyone else and the whorehouse cognac burned in our empty stomachs. While his wife assembled a few open-faced sandwiches the undertaker chatted with us about the challenges of his profession. There wasn't nearly enough material available for the proper burial of all the corpses. "Too many. Far too many." (The cycle of life was completed.) He'd at least found a substitute for the shrouds in such short supply: "Paper dickies. They make these elegant ones with patterns stamped on them. Of course it only covers the chest and down below. But it's good enough. His back isn't going to get cold anymore and at least it's decent." There was even a way out of the pinch of coffin shortages: a coffin with a removable bottom. It's worked out in advance with the gravedigger that he will only cover the coffin loosely with dirt. Then the bottom can be removed by means of a string. ("Naturally only once the mourners have taken off.") The coffin is lifted from around the corpse and recycled. "C'me're: I'll show you how it works." (Santa's little elves in reverse.) The undertaker put his naked dog back on the leash and led us into the first room to the row of coffins. "This one here has already been prepared."

We gazed into the empty coffin. On the black-painted bottom the shape of a human body was traced in pale white: a round spot where the back of the head had lain spade-shaped prints of the shoulder blades accompanied by two streaks to the right and left (upper arms down to the elbow) butterfly of the pelvis ending in two long lines interrupted by the spheres of the knees. A sketch of a human body drawn in the life juices that had seeped out of it. "Corpses leak!" the undertaker explained. "C'mon back. Have another bite of liverwurst and a drop of kümmel. It's nippy out there."

Sri Aurobindo died in 1950. "He left his body" as his disciples so nicely put it. (It pleases me less when they add: ". . . so as to continue his work metaphysically while The Mother realized it in earthly form.") She survived him by twenty-three years. The two of them share a grave in the courtyard garden of a house in the colonial style that combines the openness of a bungalow with the stateliness of a public building. The courtyard is paved. The effect of a garden is achieved by means of a wall overgrown with flowered vines and a flower-bed-like arrangement of potted plants. The branches of a handsome tree extend to shade a rectangular block of light gray darkly be-ribboned marble: elongated table-shaped table-high solemn. An altar. Garish-bright flowers bedeck its surface in ornamental patterns. They no doubt have profound symbolic meaning (which I am too dim-witted to see). In any case it's pretty. A soulful paraphrase of the cheery vegetable stands in exotic mar-kets (or Leila's and Aisha's colorful salads). A spread of sacrificial offerings: a pineapple as centerpiece. The courtyard isn't very large but a few dozen worshippers can squeeze into it. I say worshippers because most of the visitors who arrive quietly and on spiritual tiptoe—in an almost silent and openly emotional coming and going which itself consecrates the site—sink down before the gravestone and rest their foreheads against it as though drinking their fill at a spiritual trough. For the most part these visitors are Europeans and North Americans. But I also saw a few Indians ecstatically melting. Whether they had been contracted to participate in this ritual was not my place to ask. In any case they lent credibility to the scene.

Anywhere else I would have looked on respectfully. I value religious rituals and customs. The more exotic the more interesting. Holy places after all always head the list of touristic sights-to-see: they come even before museums. (Both strongholds of antiquity.) The soles of my feet are calloused from walking barefoot over the stone floors of temples and the tiles of mosques. I remove my hat with the Christians and replace it with the Jews. Here I felt oddly irritable and stiff. These devotions seemed to me embarrassingly exaggerated. Not appropriate to their object. Such idolization was more debasement than exaltation of a scholar like Sri Aurobindo. Regardless of what rank he might have attained for his insights into the nature of God: this here could not possibly have been what he'd wanted. I was positive he would not have approved. Here too the hand of The Mother could be seen: her talent for theatrical stagings. I could sense her almost physical presence. I could feel her gaze (the cat in front of the mousehole). It wasn't only the overdone spectacle that provoked me. It was she—that's right: she personally—who lured me away from equanimity. I felt an urge to do something that would be perceived as sacrilegious —for instance pull out a pocket knife and carve in the bark of the tree "This cheese is very good!" A girl standing in front of me (her pseudo-Indian getup so complete she could only have been an American) gazed up rapturously at the crown of the tree and I was tempted to pluck at her sari and ask whether she was engaged in metaphysical bird-watching: in anticipation of a dove presumably ascending heavenward from a monstrance of sunbeams. For B.'s sake I resisted. She stood beside me graceful and untroubled and I felt great love for her in her composure. My moral yardstick.

I ought to have followed her example. On a stone bench along the courtyard wall a group of white-haired Indians hunkered. Local color. Although this shrine was clearly an Occidental stage production it seemed nonetheless to have been integrated into

137

the ritualistic experience of a number of natives. The shiny parted silver hair along with the silver beards shawls loincloths and shepherd's crooks of the old Indians gave them a priestly aspect. One of them got up and walked—no: glided to the building. His movements had inimitable dignity and grace: slender as a long stalk of bamboo light and lissome in an aura of physical purity that could come only from a spiritually purer race. The beauty of this graveside watchman elevated the site above the cheapness of a tourist attraction and the shabbiness of exaggerated (therefore fake-seeming) religious exaltation. That he himself with his shoulder-length snow-white hair stood on the threshold of the Beyond made him a herald of the transcendental. Death—which had gnawed its way into my thoughts in the form of various memories and in my recent experience of the rotting gasping lives of survivors in Bucharest—appeared here in all its majesty. I saw that the reverence of the worshippers went beyond the two people buried here. Its real object was the sublimity of death. Kali the blood-dripping Universal Devourer was present here not as the frenzied goddess of destruction but as universally receptive. Soothing. The most truly maternal of beings. In a last sly coup de theatre The Mother of Pondicherry had cast herself in this role. It wouldn't have been surprising if—given all the parroted metaphysical phrases she'd spouted in her lifetime—she'd slipped up and uttered slogans of worldly optimism like those you hear on public tribunals and from usurpers of power: glorification of life youth the future and everything else that denies death (unless it serves the cause). But she was clever enough not to have done this and now she lay in peaceful repose beside the religious patriarch beneath a marble slab opulently adorned with flowers. A witness to his sovereignty. Mater cosmica indeed. Sri Aurobindo for better or for worse had endured her joining him (twenty-three years later) in his grave and giving the quintessence of his doctrine (of all religious doctrines) one last illustration—Death soothes all—and endured this with the same magnanimity expressed when he'd let himself be henpecked in life. I felt a brotherly bond between us.

This is presumably what gave me the idea of asking the beautiful graveside watchman to show me where the library was. What I meant was Sri Aurobindo's private reference library: it had been promised in the brochure. (Yes even the gravestone for the society's founder had its own tourism-promoting brochure.) What I wanted to see was whether there weren't also a few Occidental God-seekers who'd influenced this greatest of God-seekers. (It's not true that all light comes from the East.) Meister Eckhart? Cobbler Böhme? Thomas à Kempis? Certainly Thomas More. Definitely Swedenborg. Assuredly William James. (After all Sri Aurobindo had studied in England.) The beautiful watchman apparently did not know. The word "library" took a while to filter into his consciousness. But then he shook his head vigorously and said: "Yes. Yes. Library. Yes." With the lissome step of a desert prophet he led the way. (I imagined how clumsy and barbaric I must have looked beside him.) He led me around the building and pointed to a rear entrance: "Library." There beside the door stood his double with loincloth shawl and sandals though more earthly and robust-looking. I am not familiar with India's caste system but that this was no Brahman navel-gazer soon became quite clear.

From my Romanian homeland I know the procedure by which country shopkeepers lie in wait for passing peasants before the doors of their shops and steer them inside with a crude show of chummy sincerity. Here the sincerity was missing. Before I knew what was happening I found myself in the first of two narrow adjoining rooms wallpapered floor to ceiling with shelves of books in gray paper covers. These consisted exclusively of publications of the Sri Aurobindo Society: writings of the guru and studies of his thought but the vast majority of them written by or devoted to The Mother. I was not permitted to immerse myself in the contents of any of these volumes. My loinclothed retailer breathed down my neck nearly snorting with impatience. Meanwhile other customers had been similarly netted and were pushing to get in. I skimmed the titles as best I could: *Sri Aurobindo's Teachings. Sri Aurobindo's Thought. Sri Aurobindo's Letters. Sri Aurobindo's Life. Sri Aurobindo's Ashram.* (Motherville.) *Sri Aurobindo and the Mother. The Life of the Mother. The Work of the Mother. The Sayings of the Mother.* ("This cheese is very good!") *The Thought of the Mother.* In several instances the title was simply *The Mother* (various tributes by various authors). I was suffering from an *embarras du choix.* So as not to spend too long in irresolute paralysis I chose the biographies of the ashram's founders supplemented by *At the Feet of Sri Aurobindo and the Mother* as well as *Sri Aurobindo's Letters on Art and Literature* (the contents of which were to prove to be of negligible intellectual originality). One last glance allowed me to snatch up a brochure that unlike all the others promised to speak not of Sri Aurobindo and The Mother but of traditional Indian medicine. (Out of personal interest; though as it turned out even traditional Indian medicine had been able to boast of successful cures only after it had incorporated the philosophy of Sri Aurobindo.)

I found myself in the second room devoted to visual materials documenting the process of spiritual education. Photographs and postcards. The Mother in full regalia. The Mother in a simple sari (and king's-widow veil). The Mother on her throne. The Mother on the tennis court. The Mother as a simple mother. Sri Aurobindo on his deathbed (side view). The Mother receiving flowers fondling orphans giving a benediction organizing youth gatherings presiding over world congresses she herself has organized. Again Sri Aurobindo on his deathbed (bird's-eye view). I selected the picture of Sri Aurobindo's feet on his deathbed (close-up) as well as the feet of The Mother on a taboret (apparently the footstool before her throne). Reparations for the desecration of two holy feet sawed off by a not-yet-initiated disciple. The cashbox where I was to pay for my purchases was manned by the beautiful watchman. I handed over sixty rupees (thirty weeks' worth of pocket money for ashramites) and tried to draw him into a conversation about foot deformations: was it possible to determine whether they were caused by wearing overly tight shoes at too young an age (The Mother's syndrome) or whether the toes suffer more grievous indignities when they are stuffed into solid footgear after years of going barefoot (Sri Aurobindo's)? But my noble companion's knowledge of English was insufficient. B. took me by the hand and led me back outside.

Then he took several long breaths and told his mother the whole story. When he had finished, he undid his belt and let the marvellous provision of transparent fruit fall upon the mattress, and the lamp tumbled out also.

—FROM THE TWO HUNDRED AND SIXTY-NINTH
OF THE *THOUSAND AND ONE NIGHTS*

*W*hat I love about B. is her uprightness. Her character is as clear as glass (and just as brittle). As the Bible demands her words are Yea, yea; Nay, nay. More often the latter than the former but usually this is when you confront her head on: she lives her zodiac sign: the ram. (I don't believe in astrology but know there's something to it; especially when one lives by it consciously.) B. is sociable and extroverted takes a lively interest

141

in everything and is surprisingly warm-hearted in interpersonal matters (while unforgiving in her rejection of what displeases her). You just have to give her complete control over whatever decisions are to be made. A person to be reckoned with. Fair in her judgments (unyielding in her prejudices). Utterly sure of herself in moral principles (not the Victorian sort) as though they had not been handed down to all of us from time immemorial as universally valid but were native to her: part of her own individual structure. Even if these rules were not universal she'd be incapable of breaking them. Physiologically—not to say genetically—of the highest ethical caliber. Worlds removed from my own constant relativizing. I admire her for this. (Once I enraged one of her rivals by saying "She is my moral yardstick.")

I owed her an explanation for my inappropriate behavior in Pondicherry. She knows me well enough to realize it is irritation that makes me act silly crack stupid jokes make horrible puns and provoke everyone. There—in India where she'll accept anything as though it were a gift of God—my irritability seemed to her uncalled for. I had to explain how deep its roots were. They reached back in time to the most confused epoch of my adolescence. I had just turned eighteen and was anything but mature for my age. The death of my sister (the quintessential O.W.A.) had brought me closer to one of my aunts: a prominent theosophist and spiritualist who had great psychic influence on my mother's side of the family (which consisted mainly of female fools and a few black-sheep men). This sister of my mother's had offered me my first glimpse of India at an early age.

At the time I really was a child: barely seven or eight and my aunt was a friend of that Mrs. Annie Besant whom everyone talked about. She had come to Vienna with a young Indian lad whom she presented as the reborn Saviour. It had been announced that she was to visit us along with him and they brushed my hair and subjected my fingernails to humiliating scrutiny so that I too might show my face before the reincarnation of Christ. Since Mrs. Besant was English all conversations about her and her activities were conducted in English as well. The familiarity with this language that I enjoyed thanks to my pseudo-English governesses was just sufficient to allow me to catch the "carnation" in "reincarnation" and so at first I imagined our reborn Saviour as a sort of lapel flower. And indeed the Indian lad whom I then bashfully approached was of extraordinary beauty and choice elegance. I studied the deep shine of his shoes the blossomy freshness of his linens the flawless fit of his suit the gracefulness of his necktie with an attentiveness that I was to devote to gentlemen's fashions throughout my later life—I admit a shabby way to encounter a spirit of the rank of Krishnamurti though it had the advantage of immunizing me against the mythmaking and mystification of all things Indian that eventually infected my generation (our children and grandchildren even more so). A decade later it did not prevent me from listening with a mind wide open to metaphysics (a result of my sister's death) as my aunt elucidated for me her Neoplatonic-theosophic-spiritualist worldview—its core Indian and its sugarcoating Christian—and I was ready to swallow it.

For a while I lived in the blissful contentment of the believer. My aunt's worldview in its multidimensional plasticity convinced me completely. Even my Christian beliefs revolved around concrete images. Not for nothing had I gone with my father on his visits to monasteries in the Bukovina on whose church walls human fate is depicted in illuminating beauty at the moment when the decision between heaven and hell is being made in the sight of God. But that was as far as things went there. All the glorious colors were put to the service of monotheistic simplification. What wasn't shown—or taught in any picture—was what a late adolescent brought up in a rational spirit is most likely to ask about with ever greater impatience: what goes on behind the scenes of world events? Of course everyone knows the name of the play's great Author-Director but you don't find out who engaged him and why and no one may peek over his shoulder into the master script. You're supposed to be respectful of authority and content with the text of your own role. Now this arrangement was so to speak theogonically exploded thanks to my aunt's Indian dowry. I witnessed the birth of dramaturgically functional gods; I was given an overview of their manifold spheres of influence and the logistics of their ensemble work. This magnificent play—with its insane alternation of procreation and destruction (and monotonous reprocreation and redestruction)—still did not add up convincingly (too much trouble for the preparation of Rama Mehta and Jane Doe for Nirvana) but I saw it with the eyes of a theatergoer finally sated with images: not a hackneyed old classic but a lively new musical production. The wonderfully poetic sophistry of the holy texts enthralled me. I managed not to get tangled up in karma and dharma. I accepted that here too higher powers were at work giving order to chaos in the name of an even higher authority—which brought things back full circle to the great One but gave my imagination all sorts of trellises to climb on. It was nice to be able to say to a young sweetheart "Definitely: in an earlier life you were my sister" or "my wife." My sister was dead but she lived on within me in a closeness we'd never known and I took comfort in the thought that she had already begun her various reincarnations and was setting the stage where—after finishing my own tour—I would meet her again in her utterly unreal reality and all the things we'd done to each other when we were alive would be reconciled. I had found myself in the world. Brahma's universe fit in well with my own youth with my naïve expectations of life and with the salvation that so many were expecting at that time. My initiation took place in a climate of European chiliasm in the years following the Great War when everyone expectantly awaited a new and better world.

I didn't have to make B. a list of everything that happened in the world between 1932 and 1990. Or tell her that the thought of mankind allowing these things to happen (still doing so) erodes my belief in its positive development through industrious reincarnation and purified karmas. B. is cautiously reticent in matters of faith (in her heart of hearts she's unquestionably Catholic). She doesn't want to lose faith in the intrinsic goodness of man which is the will of God. Naturally she erupts in spontaneous indignation when she hears someone say there weren't six million Jews killed in the Holocaust but only four million or when I tell her that in Romania children are kidnapped—ten- eleven- twelve-year-olds (little Vasili from the Bucharest artists' studio might have become one of them) not to be trained as pickpockets or anything like that but (the rumors go so far as to suggest) to be killed and their bodies plundered for salable donor organs—livers kidneys hearts—to keep up with the demands of the latest headlong forward developments in scientific medicine. Still even my journalistic fox terrier of a friend Tilman Spengler could not confirm this rumor. But as the saying goes where there's no fire there's no smoke. The mere suggestion fills B. with outrage but it stops at the outrage of a Dickens reader. She's one of those fortunate individuals who can surrender with a sigh of resignation before an iron *That's how the world is that's life and that's how it is because that's how it is and because God has willed it and still wills it to be so.* But behind these immutable letters the silver lining of hope transfigures the dark clouds: *God is good and can will only good even when He admits evil.* The Christian world of God. The Buddhist's road to salvation: Nirvana. Sri Aurobindo's religious doctrine. The alibi of The Mother and all those like her who exercise power. Power makes use of God the same way God makes use of power.

That's what stopped me. When I had to realize that the Creator of all this splendor (the *Overmind* that lords it over the rest of the brutal deities) has been riding roughshod over us. He helps along our forward development until it turns into Treblinka and Cambodia and the scientific discovery that we are nothing more than cannibalistic monkeys come down from the trees but doesn't give us the wits to stop behaving like them. Resourceful monkeys who have forward-developed the hand ax into weapons capable of destroying the planet (my father's theory of the supposedly cunning fictions). My belief in God began to wobble as my questions about *Why?* and *To what end?* of this monkey theater could no longer be drowned out with mythological poetry. I wasn't the first to bruise my brain over the nothingness these thoughts opened at my feet.

Ever since (I said to B.) religious ideologies have irritated me all out of proportion. I don't want to have anything to do with them (I said). I don't want to hear about them (I said). Don't even get me started on our compulsive temple-sightseeing. Heresy in the name of broadening one's mind. Idolatrous worship of the Great Fetish Culture. At my age you learn to accept this sort of thing with humanistic obedience. Anthropological interest. Barnum's gallery of gods. But please don't make me ever go see anything else that will send me up the wall like The Mother of Pondicherry.

We left town on the third day. No regrets. In the end no resentment on my part either. No need to begrudge the old fraud her myths. After all don't we all have myths of our own? (The worthless live out collective mythologies: ideologies.) B. is privileged to have her own private mythology which she lives out physically. More than just her sense of herself along with the curious history of her origins. It is the beauty born of her transfiguration by her own romantic past. Perhaps it is not so rare for a beautiful woman graced with the attributes of the *haut monde* (whatever that means these days: noble birth or the nimbus of professional success or jet-set membership) to feel a sort of tribal kinship deep inside as though she came from a Kurd village. But it is rare indeed for this feeling to be so gracefully expressed in physical form. B.'s spirituality can be read in her face: the cathedral figure. Her features are strong but there is something about them very very delicate even fragile. Symbolizing the transitoriness of happiness delight and sorrow. She speaks of her mother who died young and her peace-loving Armenian family driven from the court of the Sultan into exile; of the fairy-tale riches they left behind; of the poignantly light-hearted dignity of these emigrants; and of an Italian stepmother the Brothers Grimm might rub their hands over. But this is more than mere biographical material that lends itself to literary use and more than mere psychology. It has been made flesh touched by a long-vanished sorrow as by the finger of God.

I love her very much for this. If she loves me then at least in part because she too loves my mythology. Which is far more robust than hers and more banal. Disorder and early sorrow depersonified by the purely historical: born into a gap between ages. Geographically suspect as well. Teetering on the border of East and West. No tears shed over a lost world seen as lost long before it really was. An eventful past impinging unnostalgically on the here and now (bringing with it the sentimental values of bygone days). No-strings-attached metamorphoses: fictions of my own being. As much a part of me as my books. I am all this—and am not. My mythology has not coalesced in unified form as B.'s has in her. I keep my Everyman face chameleon-style attuned to each new setting that the vicissitudes bring. But my mythology does have its own explanatory heraldic code. Two banners fly above it—one black red gold the other blue yellow red; the first my love for the German language the second my love for the land of my birth. The language allows me to sing myself into existence. Like Antaeus I draw the strength I need for singing from my native soil the earth the grass the grainfields forests mountains the clouds in the Bukovina sky. Unlosable losses. This is not nostalgia (though if I tune my mood properly I can howl for my lost treasures like a watchdog at full moon). It is a mood I nurture in perpetual lightheartedness with just that tiny dash of melancholy from which folk music is born. (Heartfelt sentiment can avoid becoming kitsch by not denying the horrific: the tear gleaming among eyelashes does not hide Kali's leer.) During my childhood terror was more ordinary than joy. Both of them I received with the same prescient curiosity. The beggars in the Bukovina ("like a medieval curse") the rabbis bowed beneath the weight of their wisdom the Romanian operetta officers the beautiful women the humble peasants in their eternal wedding garb (bridegrooms and brides of the earth) the scoundrels and fools the dreamers and dullards the far too many witty tongues of the legendary city of Czernopol all helped to weave the fabric of a durable life that I carry within me and love and sometimes even more deeply hate. Even today after another life—two three even more—spent in other places I can feel that all the fibers of my being are interwoven in this cloth. All my images come from it. The dowry placed in the cradle of the enchanted princess B. lacked such a source of fortitude. If her personal composition might be compared with a Persian miniature then mine by contrast would resemble the canvas of a Sunday painter from some Balkan land. The problem with Sunday painters is that they know they're Sunday painters and sooner or later comes a point where they fake their naïveté. I know my own private mythologies are myths. If I don't keep working on them they'll cease to exist. I am writing my own mythology. Its two banners fly above the temple of the Great Fetish Art. B. loves me for this: the artist in me.

In Bucharest too a once mythically exalted couple lies buried. Not side by side like the Pondicherry saints but separated by a distance of twenty yards. Without the hospitality of affluent mausoleum owners. On two different levels in two separate sections of a (this is a mocking touch) upper-class cemetery. The graves are quite fresh and—in stark contrast to those around them—have no gravestones let alone monuments. Only insiders know who is buried there: the Conducător Ceauşescu and his wife Elena. The Carpathian Genius and the scientist. Slaughtered in cold blood like so many of their victims. Modest bouquets are strewn over the still-black earth. But the city does boast a monument to the memory of their crimes. It stands on a low man-made hill in front of an enormous plaza at the end of a grand avenue nearly four miles long (unfinished). Buildings were razed specifically to create this barren round expanse where the monstrosity stands. The largest building in Europe and the second-largest of the modern world after the Pentagon (or so was said). An abomination that combines the classicism of a Speer with turn-of-the-century Americana to arrive at the megalomaniac postmodern Stalinist style. (Like-minded Hitler would have nodded appreciatively.) How many thousands of halls rooms cabinets vestibules staircases corridors this architectural changeling contains beneath the flat-roof terraces; how many megatons of marble jasper onyx precious woods bronze gold Cyclopean furniture crystal chandeliers soccer-field-sized carpets in the design of its interior; how deep beneath the earth the atom-bomb-proof bunkers guards' quarters armories munitions depots garages soldiers' dormitories reach—we'll be able to read these statistics in the next guidebook to the Romanian capital. (No doubt set off contrapuntally against mention of the notoriously arctic temperatures and few hours of electricity permitted per day in the dim-lit households of the citizens whose hunger and privation made possible this atrocious monument to megalomania. My three daily four weekly six monthly periodicals have been delighting for years in the graphic description of this misery. And there's nothing like the portrayal of human suffering to buck up a sluggish tourist industry.) The plaza before which this mammoth edifice towers once lay in the heart of Bucharest: winding little streets of low-set petit-bourgeois dwellings from the late nineteenth and early twentieth centuries laid out village-style with courtyards running alongside and garden plots around interspersed with intimate chapel-churches wedged in between buildings left over from the days of the Wallachian princes in the era of Turkish rule and the Louis Philippe villas of picturesque boyars. Around the corner was a more plebeian part of the city with vendors selling handicrafts junk shops carpet merchants barbecue stands carnival-gay red-light districts and lively Jewish neighborhoods. That's where the Conducător Ceauşescu sent his hungriest bulldozers not being satisfied with having torn down a good two-thirds of the city and planted it with ranks of prefabricated houses bare as gravestones in a military cemetery. He needed space. He had to erect a monument to his own megalomania and—I have to say—the megalomania of his nation. The great monument to the Carpathian Genius—mockingly named Casa Po-porului: House of the People—blocks the view of the horizon and quite a bit of sky on top. Now it stands empty and unfinished like the dead avenue that was to lead up to it like the Via della Conciliazione to St. Peter's in Rome: nearly four miles of boulevard palaces for the nomenklatura of a Greater Romania. The world would have been too small for such a nation. A central row of fountains sporting elves and water sprites in a Romanian folkloric style with modernist touches—a chiseled-stone Balkan Disneyland—runs down the middle (an artistic contribution from Madame Professor Elena; the Conducător's daughter-in-law was responsible for the architectural creations).

It's a well-known phenomenon that the self-understanding of despots tends at the height of their careers to slip into the realm of art. We owe pretty much all the great art that's come down to us over the ages to this syndrome. That the will of despots to eternalize their own circumstances tends to be ejaculated into architecture has been conspicuously demonstrated by pharaohs Roman emperors Renaissance popes and all the Louis from XIII to XVI and Ludwigs (also Hitler in a rudimentary way) even the bourgeois Monsieur Pompidou. Not to mention the Conducător Ceauşescu. I approached the product of his architectural self-fulfillment on tiptoe with bated breath. Not out of awe or fear. There was nothing to be afraid of in this unfinished colossus from whose many thousand glassless windows the emptiness gazes out at a larger emptiness. An unimaginably isolated sentry in a pea-green uniform stood beside a bunker entrance by the terraced grassy banks ascending the mound. He looked like a termite who had gotten lost among the Pyramids. Before him lay the clean-swept round of the enormous plaza with the double row of huge dead palaces leading up to it. Except for the cadaver of a flattened rat (trophy for a driver with a good eye) there were no signs of life. This might have been fear-inspiring but wasn't. Fear wasn't the right word for the feeling I had standing before this negative of what might have been threatening.

Once in Moscow on the equally long equally barren stretch of road that leads to the heart of the Kremlin I dared for the sake of a better view to step off the sidewalk into the street. Immediately a policeman sprang out of nowhere intimidating in ankle-length black coat and black Kirghiz cap and shooed me back onto the sidewalk with shrill whistle shrieks and peremptory hand gestures. That was perfectly understandable: the road was to remain clear in case some VIP vehicle came shooting past or I would have wound up like the Bucharest rat. Here in Bucharest there was no danger of VIPs showing up. I might have unloaded a truckful of garbage in front of Ceauşescu's grave or pitched a tent and had a cookout: no one would have minded. And nevertheless just looking at this insane building in the middle of its eerily magnificent grounds was enough to drain me of fortitude. I stood there as if bewitched. Paralyzed.

Not simply ill at ease at my aesthetic sensibilities being offended (or martyred rather). I was reminded of the torments I had suffered a few years before in the intensive-care unit. But this seemed too personal an association and I rejected it. What remained was—yes—something objective. I've since had it confirmed by various eye- and nerve-witnesses: Ceaușescu's mammoth palace is more than just unspeakably ugly more than just monstrous more than just deranged in its fantastic size. As a spectacle of power it is so utterly immoderate that it is a tangible embodiment of power liberated from power's manipulations means paths goals circumstances. Liberated even from those who once exercised power there and will soon do so again. Liberated from the barbarity of the man who built it. Power itself created this monstrosity of a memorial to itself. Two fetishes locked in an eternal reciprocal kowtow: Power bows to Art; Art bows to Power. For even this palace in Bucharest was supposed to have been a work of art.

Further it has been reported to me, O greatest King of time, that the Sultan, upon hearing the words of the wazir, was certain that this speech had been inspired in him by jealousy alone.

—FROM THE TWO HUNDRED AND SEVENTIETH
OF THE *THOUSAND AND ONE NIGHTS*

$\mathcal{B}$. ran an art gallery in Milan for twenty-five years. An internationally respected sanctuary for the swiftest front-runners of the avant-garde. (William Rubin when a director at the Museum of Modern Art in New York expressed his admiration: "Beatrice, you have a kosher gallery.") She doesn't like to talk with me about art especially not contemporary art. We both agree that in these matters our chemical makeup differs too greatly. In what way is hard to specify and therefore hard to analyze as well. (Efforts end in a total breakdown of understanding.) Nevertheless I am permitted to say that her erotic relationship to all things visual is much more physical than my own. Like everything else about her it is immediate. My own appreciation hobbles behind broken in a prism of reflections. Occasional exchanges of jabs are unavoidable.

To spare the nerves of both spouses it is therefore advisable to avoid the subject altogether. Even peripheral zones can be dangerous. I have to creep through a minefield of nervous reactions just to get tidbits of information in her area of expertise. There's scarcely a person alive who could give me any better: dewdrop-fresh straight from the epicenter of the contemporary (though ever hurtling into the past) art world. It's not as if I want to delve into matters of general principle (for example by raising a simpleton's questions which I hope she no longer half expects of me: What do artists today define as Art? Or is the fact that every kind of sorry effort is being vastly overrated as a work of art a conspiracy on the part of dealers?). All I want is evidence to support a claim that is so self-evident as to be commonplace: the relationship between power and art has been reversed. Nowadays only the crudest epoch-embezzlers like the Conducător Ceaușescu and his kind (or manicured drawing-room heads of state like Monsieur Pompidou and consorts) use art to leave flyspecks of their own on the monstrosity of world history (in this resembling artists in their will to immortalize themselves). While since the days of Renaissance patronage (I say to B. with my innocent look) art has achieved autonomy and thanks to its vivid fetish-like nature has become an instrument of power. A reliable slat in the trellis of

epoch–embezzled traditional prestige hierarchies. (Image cultivation: the bourgeoisie somersaults into bohemianism and the
artist becomes a cult figure and the clerks clamber on his shoulders and museum directors become kingmakers and auction
house managers make crucial adjustments in the climate that
determines cultural trends thereby influencing weather across
the globe.)

B. quickly admits that all this does indeed have to do with
the interrelation between art and money. (Money: power's
mightiest vehicle.) But she begins to get suspicious when I try
to fix a precise date. Was the climax of this phenomenon reached
during the American era? With the epiphany of Action Painting?
When Ugo Mulas (for whom she opened many a studio door)
was photographing his beautiful book on the New York art
scene? (She remembers in the early 1960s reading in a newspaper
for the first time that contemporary art was being recommended
as a profitable investment.) In other words did the populari-
zation of art—formerly so very unpopular (even "degener-
ate")—begin only once art had found its place in the market?
Or had it taken the Zeitgeist a century to penetrate into the
wooden heads of these uncontemporary souls and open their
eyes? Or to put it much more mysteriously: did the Great Fetish
Art develop fully only once it had changed its form to that of
perfect abstraction? (Only children believe God has a patriarch's
face and a mane of white hair.)

For B. these reflections are neither here nor there. What matters to her are the works themselves (and only secondarily their
value in lucre). What she admires loves respects—because for
her they represent the highest form of human existence—are
artists: those so possessed by the spirit of art that they devote
their existence and their passion to the single goal and purpose of producing objects of the highest possible perfection:
pure artists. Standard-bearers of the aesthetic. Self-forgetting
(though not necessarily self-repudiating) unconditionally ex-

acting furiously zealous servant-priests of the Great Fetish Art. She has a role in their cult: vestal virgin. And even when I cling to my crazy notions—for example that it's the world spirit getting into the game and living our lives when we suppose it is we who control it—I'm allowed a whiff of the temple's incense. B. forgives me because she considers me an artist though admittedly in an inferior field.

That I never became a visual artist can be put down to a stroke of good fortune. Thanks to my and my guardians' indolence I missed the chance to become a great master. Not a painter but more likely a draftsman (possibly a sculptor). I spent my youth in the dream that I already was one. By the time the ferments of puberty had died down it was all over. I turned to the lower art of writing as if sleepwalking. At some point (in the summer of 1938 in Berlin to be precise) I started writing something (a ridiculous story to be precise). Someone or other (an all-too-maternal friend to be precise) sent it to a publisher. The result: my first book. Completed in the winter of 1938–39 in a Tyrolean ski lodge and first appearing in the fashion magazine *Die Dame* in September of that fateful year and in 1940 published by Propyläen. A committee of booksellers (editors manufacturers sales directors: the culture-promoting brain trusts of major publishing houses!) dubbed it *Flame That Consumes Itself.* The book itself was entirely in keeping with the pretentious stupid kitsch threatened by its title (as with my life at the time: a sentimental testosterone-glutted hunter's son). Exemplary popular fiction: the story of a young man (guess who) who falls in love with a virtuoso violinist. He wins the love of this mature woman then abandons her with stereotypical contempt as she trembles on the threshold of menopause. It would have made a terrific television movie. Sung blithely into existence with no consideration for the historical events of the years 1938–40. That I returned to these events after this excursion rather than con-

tenting myself with a world sung into existence in pure autonomy was not only a literary mistake but a metaphysical failing.
But that is another story. Whichever way you want to see it
this was my real birth: the birth of the writer. With this began
the existence that elevated me from my own private everyday
reality to a more generalized reality that carried obligations with
it. But it too could do no more than parallel the course of
historical events. I dreamed myself in its context. A first-person
dream in the lap of a nightmare of world history.

The year 1938—and I as well—saw the annexation of Austria
to the Third Reich. Soon afterward the Führer and Chancellor
of the Reich brought home our brothers and sisters from the
Sudetenland. The year 1939 was not yet over and already Poland
was overrun Warsaw in ruins armies stood face-to-face on the
Western Front all set to attack one another and reduce the continent to a heap of debris and ashes. Nevertheless it was possible
(in the Germany of the apotheosis of Adolf Hitler and the imminent end of the European world!) for a rosy-cheeked bit of
idiocy like *Flame That Consumes Itself* to be written printed
published and—strangest of all!—read. To be sure this only
confirms the truism that at any given moment several realities
are going on at once all tangled up together often glaringly
contradictory or (even more confusing) variously juxtaposed
side by side or in alternation or so tightly interwoven as to be
indistinguishable. Quotidian paradoxes. No one notices. If
someone does notice he shrugs his shoulders: *"That's how things
are in this crazy world!"* Everyone lives in the ongoing present
—in one or the other (presumably all) of the intertwined simultaneously occurring realities and thinks they are a single
reality—complex yes but singular. Just unfold a copy of *The
New York Times* whenever you like: the report that China is
testing the hydrogen bomb above a foot and a half of advertising
for a department store clearance sale offers a mirror image of

the newspaper's readers. This too is old hat: you can be the camp commander of Mauthausen your thumb sore from turning the gas on and off for the Final Solution of the Jewish problem and yet celebrate Mozart and Bach in private concerts consider Edgar Guest the greatest of all poets and believe in forward development through reincarnation. You can be born in Czernowitz ("where people and books lived" my colleague Celan once said though in reality they were pranksters and gallows birds) and have experienced the annexation of Austria to the Third Reich and the expulsion of Jews from Vienna and thus also the death of the soul of the Occident and the world's great leap into the second dress rehearsal for the fulfillment of the mission of the zoological species human being—and at the same time write *Flame That Consumes Itself.* The pursuit of art. The chinks between the strands of interwoven realities allow us to engage in all sorts of "secondary occupations" (as my colleague Thomas Mann called it in sublime sophomoric irony). For example sing worlds into existence. Be enthralled by the sound of your own voice. In the sleepwalking steps of the blind bard. Groping the strings of your harp for the core of reality—although to do this you must remain blind. If you try it with your eyes open good luck keeping your wits about you (whatever that means).

If I hadn't had to go to Cologne for Carnival in the spring of 1990 (right after Romania and just before India) I'd have hardly been tempted to dig out and dust off that old hat about reality's many forms and try it on in the mirror: does it fit? The question may have to remain open. Though it's a shame that in 1990 I couldn't manage to preserve my innocence as I had before 12 March 1938 and even beneath the rain of bombs beginning to fall on Berlin (though by then my innocence was cut with the black-humor cynicism of the reluctant witness). I might have stuck with popular fiction after *Flame That Consumes Itself* (and similar masterworks) and become rich admired well known and respected and it probably wouldn't have occurred to me fifty-four years later to write this summation. The impulse to do so can be traced back to Cologne where my black red gold mythology (the myth of my identity as an artist) was put to a difficult test. It would have fared better had I fastened the banner to the flagpole of popular fiction. At the time—when I was wearing out the soles of my literary baby shoes while around me fire and sulfur rained down—I took up the flag with the noble intention of joining the team of world-singers. Or so I thought. Today I have the impression I was clinging to it so as not to be separated from myself in the current. As if I might conjure back into existence the intact world from the days before 12 March 1938 with a bittersweet love story and lots of nice descriptions of meadows and woods (and lose my identity, man).

I carry the date 12 March 1938 around with me like a literary watch fob like a monogram seal dangling from the watch chain of some coxcomb. Indeed I have capitalized in more than one novel (*Death of My Brother Abel* and *Memoirs of an Anti-Semite*) quite nicely on the events of that icy glass-clear sky-blue but in world-historical terms darkest of days. Not with pop-fictional intentions but because on that day something happened to me in me that has preoccupied me to this day. I indeed lost my identity and had to look for a new one. But that's just chicken feed. I saw the world losing its identity—several times in rapid succession. Gaining new ones at the drop of a hat (ye olde hat of "reality").

I have to explain that my innocence (not only literary but as to the ways of the world not to mention politics) was unusually large. I was a babe in arms of twenty-four. I had just returned—in December 1937—from four reality-packed years as an apprentice and journeyman in Romania (military service youthful whore-wrassling farewells to my painting and graphic-arts artistic dreams stereotypical love affair with girl from good family equally stereotypical love drama with married woman not exactly a virtuoso violinist but the spiritual model for one) and tumbled naïvely right into the political scuffles over Austria's future. Vienna—the setting of my adolescence and my pitiful schooling: once a Golden Jerusalem in my expectations for the future—Vienna was churning. Still in the prewar manner with an Art Deco flair. The stylistic model was Fritz Lang's *Metropolis*: the rich and powerful revel in the light of day while down below in the cellar darkness the dispossessed insulted and suppressed brew up a cataclysm. The brave myth of an age of new departures (where to?). In Vienna of 1938 this was stylistically translated into an Alpine idiom of folksy dirndl skirts and lederhosen but for an Alpine population paradoxically tilted from vertical to horizontal. Not mountain-peak world and underworld but a leveled-out plain with on the left side of the road red proletarians milling about shaking their fists and on the right lower- middle- and upper-class bourgeois bawling out "Heil!" and giving the imperial German salute. On the night of March 11 the waves topped the floodwalls and everything got swirled together. (Anyway that's how things looked after the next election: everyone had had exactly the same idea.) I have described the Walpurgisnacht orgies that marked this grand wedding by flickering torchlight in the novels named above. Along with my awakening the morning after. Inadequate. Fifty-four years later I am still searching for what might convincingly depict what happened to me in me that night. I cannot manage better than this implausible and undocumentable claim: when dawn came I lay down feverish exhausted my skull bubbling over with apocalyptic images my thoughts buffeted by the most contradictory emotions and woke up on another star where the world of yesterday no longer existed. My own past had been amputated and no longer belonged to me but had become a legend (on its way to becoming a myth).

Yet the present too was unreal. Things manifested themselves in different aggregations. Less dense. Airier. (From the icy air of those March days: arctic emptiness beneath a heartlessly sky-blue sky.) Events lacked their former weighty significance. They seemed distant and free-floating. From that point on I lived as though half-anesthetized. I perceived what was happening to me with me in me around me with greater clarity more sharply vivid than ever before. But none of it had anything to do with me. The world had attained a higher degree of abstraction overnight. . . .

Who's going to believe that? (Perhaps I should ask a young citizen of East Berlin how he felt when the Wall was breached.)

Perhaps people today are more likely to believe such things. The educational benefits of television. One accepts the irreal side of reality as part of normal experience. The present exists as a series of colorful images flickering on a screen and in these images events become real with their various strands joining in . an ostensibly uniform singular reality all of which occurs— thanks to the media's fabulous speed—at the very moment one sees it hears it and then it is lost from sight vanishes instantly. Reality happens just as we are about to perceive it and then it's gone. Transformed into a piece of the unreal past the instant it's delivered conveniently packaged to our homes. Occurring without allowing us anything but passive participation. Then someone turns off the set. The good citizen now richer for his newly acquired experience returns to his evening beer. What has occurred has no bearing on his here and now and has happened to him with him in him without his having perceived it. Like a procedure under anesthesia.

I've experienced such things. I check into the hospital to have a side effect of my previous operations corrected. Though I know it will be a harmless procedure *I am prepared* and I know no matter how it turns out something is about to happen that will change my life decisively. They wheel me on a gurney into the vestibule of the operating room. Naked beneath the green smock that ties in the back like shit-proof baby wear. (They have to humiliate you to keep you humble.) The intern approaches with the syringe. The needle points heavenward: thread-thin scepter of all-powerful Fate subtle ensign of an event progressing on its own authority magic wand of the shaman who will remove me from one present and (while I drift to a no-man's-land between times) transport me—*Insh'allah!*—to a new better more auspicious future. In the half minute between the injection and the extinction of consciousness I observe myself closely. In vain. As I have done for decades when I go to bed now too I lie in wait for the moment of effacement. This time not finally slipping off after sleepless hours but in a quickly beginning whirl of all my senses that will centrifuge my self away from me—

and this induces a specific sort of wakefulness: I sharpen my consciousness to the point of despair. I want to draw a tiny advance on my experience of death: to experience consciously the effacement of consciousness. Nothing doing. I'm out before I have time to wonder how and when. What was my last thought? In what images did language dissolve? What was their semantic content? What was their reality like? One thing I know for certain: when at the left edge of my field of vision in the depths of the sightless and lightless independent of my thought and my knowledge of my thought precise images begin to appear—no matter of what: a face an iron a housefly a hackney cab the Eiffel Tower an egg a doll a bit of Sufi calligraphy (and each with its own semantics laden with meaning) in a word surrealistic images in a mishmash of heterogeneous realities— at this moment I am on the threshold. I have never been conscious of crossing it. The black hole swallows me unawares.

Then all at once I am back. All around me is daylight. I lie in my hospital bed (too high for the *pappagallo* out of reach beneath it). B. is beside me and kisses me on the forehead. The operation was successful. *N'y avait pas de problème.* They say I felt everything that was done to me while under anesthesia but that all memory of it has been erased. I trustingly acquiesce to everything. The past is past. Swallowed up by the present. I am still living in the same old strand of reality. No problem. A few days of recuperation under clinical supervision. A few weeks of convalescence at home (under B.'s lovingly strict supervision). Everything seems to be back to normal. But this is definitely not the case.

Everything is back to normal under a new set of circumstances. Ungraspable changes since nothing has changed but everything has become abstract. As if the light of day had been precipitated into bright new difference. More transparent. More irreal. Something magical has taken place. (An operation? A revolution? A household or world-historical event?) Nothing in the external world has changed and yet its new circumstances lack all connection to the old ones. The past has been transformed into a fairy tale as though it had never really existed (only literarily). One more step in time has been taken (toward the last days of the world)

and it took place in me to me with me unawares. Some procedure was performed upon me. Somehow something in me to me with me was altered lessened cut away attached rerouted displaced sewn up and abducted from the flow of time that is trickling away to the realm of fables sagas legends and myths. And I—tormented by a silence that seems to be waiting for a word that will release it as with Otto von Hapsburg not long ago—I feel called upon *to say so.*

And the younger sister spoke: "In Allah's name, O my sister, recite for us a tale to while away the sleepless hours of this long night."

—FROM THE THREE HUNDREDTH OF THE *THOUSAND AND ONE NIGHTS*

The year is progressing. Summer arrived without my really even noticing (though B.'s been working in the garden and I must have realized I was being less strictly monitored). We are preparing to leave the tower and move back to the big house. The revamping of its interiors has been completed but now there are problems with the domestics. Leila has been sent back to Morocco for lack of residence and work permits. There's been an alarming increase in hostility toward dark-skinned foreigners lately. In Florence (the Golden Jerusalem of my hallucinations in the intensive-care unit) people attack North African street vendors with bicycle chains and screwdrivers. Turn them out of their wretched shelters. Set their trailers on fire. I fear the day is coming when even Aisha and Ibrahim will leave this Promised Land of welfare and television and return to their goat udders at the stony foot of the Atlas Mountains. In Ibrahim's case I have no regrets: he's a frivolous ne'er-do-well. But I will miss the two women with their robustly supple light-footed skirt-swaying physicality; their cinnamony smell; their flat strong-jawed Mongolian faces; their white-toothed smiles with eyes cast down as if in modesty (the most chaste most subtle form of flirtation); their peppermint tea at all hours of the day;

and the folkloric delight in bright colors that comes out when they set the table. Together these three Moroccans brought a sense of luxury to our household: a poetically vivid expansion of our world into the exotic realm of a courtly tapestry. Anna and Fedora have remained faithful to us but can come only now and then. They are good Tuscan housewives of the sort you see on television praising the virtues of this or that laundry detergent. They bring us back to prosaic everyday reality.

In strict accordance with my blue yellow red mythology I could turn this into a second watch fob. The calendar announces the month of June. It will go down in the history of an ostensibly liberated Romania as the date of the scornful unmasking of a coup d'etat treacherously camouflaged as a revolution: when the replacement dictators (and ostensible liberators) ordered the workers from the Jiu mines to march on Bucharest and—in the name of the newly established "democracy"—club down intellectuals and students protesting there in the name of the very same thing. This too I partake of glued to the television screen (with ice-cube-clinking gin and tonic in hand) contrapuntally playing the news report of these events against the violence-free rule of The Mother in Pondicherry. It's good for my aging circulatory system when I get riled up over these problematic juxtapositions: can order be established without violence on a large scale? Or on only a small one? Are there quantitative limits (family clan ethnic group religious community nation)? An idle pastime for which I the eager viewer have the graphic vividness of events flickering on the screen to thank (South Africa Nicaragua Afghanistan). I am taking part in current events around the world and am more closely interwoven with them than ever before. Instructed with more detail and accuracy on the course of events than mankind was ever asked to endure—but at a comfortable remove. Acquitted of responsibility. It's called being informed. Up to one's ears in information in a no-man's-land of reality. This shows us most distressingly that *it is not we who live our lives: we are being lived* (God alone knows by what powers and what divine authority).

Why can't I reconcile myself to this state of affairs? I'm an old man. I've witnessed the better part of a century. The tales I can tell of it are as futile as my lament for the frogs of Băneasa. What I the chronicler might pass on as a warning to posterity would be as pointless as the transformation of that Bucharest intellectual (or my erstwhile friend Ernst Schnabel) into a bureaucratic mini-despot. (But what of it? And I feel obliged to say so.) Should I really go back to singing the world into pop-fictional existence at so advanced an age? It isn't easy to come up with anything more dramatic than Adolf Hitler's attempted Final Solution of the Jewish problem. Or more surrealistic than the Ceauşescus. Or more soulful than The Mother of Pondicherry. And as for love the Carnival in Cologne made me realize I have nothing exciting to add on the subject.

A rule of thumb for the manufacture of marketable popular fiction (what's the point if you can't sell it?) is that it must have a hero (or antihero and recently lots of heroines) involved in the battle of Good and Evil. He—or she—must have qualities that will make the reader identify willy-nilly with him—or her. This assumes some level of shared experience. In what does this consist? Broken hearts that psychiatrists can't patch up? Marital conflicts that competent divorce lawyers can't solve? *Scherziamo!* On the other hand the rat race for success money fame power is a subject that offers interesting material though unfortunately it's well picked over. The rest of our shared experience is made up by the abstract events on the television screen (and in our daily weekly monthly periodicals). A present moment lined with contemporary history. A journalist's Eldorado. The nature of its reality (even when experienced on the spot live) was revealed to me in Vienna on 12 March 1938 (and thereafter repeatedly elsewhere).

. . .

165

I don't want to claim that my situation and my behavior on that memorable day were in any way typical. Anything but. In fact the uncanny magic trick of the so-called Anschluss had no direct effect on me. I was as politically aware as a carp. As far as the future of Austria was concerned—that miserable Alpine republic of Karl Renner (and his not much more laudable successors) left over after the breakup of the Hapsburg Dual Monarchy—I simply didn't give a hoot. We—my forefathers that is since I alas was born too late—had been proud to belong to and serve this glorious empire. But its time had passed leaving it to become a legend saga myth. My homeland was the Bukovina (which at the time had not yet become legend saga myth but existed concretely and was far from events in Vienna). I was a Romanian citizen: the subject of a Balkan king whose German blood had long since been repudiated. My own blood was only one-quarter German. I could watch the events unfolding like some spectacular performance. (Television wasn't yet on the scene.) Ideologically (as one says) I had nothing against the homecoming of Austria to the Third Reich. With much more dramatic furor than that of the recent reunification of West and East Germany I saw my father's ardent youthful dreams of a Greater Germany come true before my very eyes: the (at any rate geographical) restoration of the Holy Roman Empire of German Nations. My black red gold mythology (the act of Providence that was the German language under whose spell I was soon to fall) made me welcome this development but with as little emotional involvement as I'd have felt at a championship soccer match. My party loyalties were determined by my milieu: likes and dislikes preprogrammed by inherited prejudices. Among members of our circle anything left-wing or red was rejected out of hand; anything conservative was automatically acceptable even when it was so far right as to look red. Of course the horrible little jumping jack of a man with the villainous forelock and stinky little tuft beneath his aardvark's nose playing sorcerer's apprentice was utterly ridiculous. But you had to admit he did a good job of maintaining order. His brown masses arranged in geometrically precise marching units were aesthetically in keeping with the style of the epoch. The idea was straight out of *Metropolis*: better to have the dispossessed insulted humiliated and stiflingly oppressed run around in the open air and fresh spring breezes brandishing cudgels in Art Deco–style cadres than to let them brood in dark cellars about how they ought to be using these cudgels to bash in their oppressors' skulls. A sort of Bauhaus functionalism could be observed even with regard to the Jewish question. The need for an answer to it had weighed heavily on people's minds in good epoch-embezzling fashion since the Dreyfus Affair and the *Protocols of the Elders of Zion*. I myself—pampered by my many Jewish friends—was a steadfast anti-Semite.

Admittedly: much of what happened around 12 March 1938 might well have prompted one to revise certain perceptions and views. All sorts of things happened that were hard to reconcile with the promised vision of a German people brandishing blond wheat stalks and finally united by a network of Autobahns. Dark rumors circulated. People were allegedly being humiliated incarcerated without cause tortured perhaps even killed. If this was your idea of fun you could go to the Leopoldstadt district and watch elderly lawyers doctors literature professors and so on being forced to clean the pavement with toothbrushes. (Even more dreadful was the sight of the delighted bystanders.) Meanwhile the bright blue (if arctic) spring air was filled with the promise that had seemed imminent since the end of the last bloodbath. The euphoria of a newly awakened will to live had the chestnut trees in the Viennese Stadtpark bursting into resplendent bud before they froze. You felt as if new possibilities had opened up: at long last dreams were coming true that would stop the clocks of world history. To weigh this splendor against the horrid violence boots kicking away at human dignity victims dripping blood was so to speak moral hairsplitting. Going on about human rights at this auspicious moment of history seemed a lame gesture of self-righteous sentimental humanitarianism. (How many women children elderly lost their lives to the Desert Storm bombs?) I did not feel called upon to catch the coattails of the Apostle of Humanity and block the path of the goose-stepping SS. I was thinking the same thing as everyone else around me: *Il faut casser des oeufs pour faire une omelette.* And anyway what was it to me? I was fully occupied with the true mission of testosterone-glutted youth: love. Love removes us from the events of this world. It is the sweetest diversion a troubled consciousness can find. I loved the model for my violinist in *Flame That Consumes Itself.* (She had not yet achieved her true reality on the page.) What did I care about the historical context of so sweet a present?

In colleague Musil's *Man without Qualities* a naïve historian comes up with an image of history that takes shape before our backward-gazing eyes like the landscape in the eyes of a man standing on the rear platform of the caboose: he does not know the train's destination or the region that lies before him; meanwhile his view to the rear fills with mountains hills fields woods streams brooks hamlets uniting in a living flux to form one single landscape all the way to the pigeon-blue horizon. Allow me to augment this exquisite metaphor by noting that traditionally railroad-car windows are furnished with little signs warning the passenger in the various languages of the civilized world: *Aus dem Fenster lehnen verboten. Ne pas se pencher en dehors. E pericoloso sporgersi.* Don't lean out: with a single glance you might see in advance where the journey is taking you. Though in a sort of reverse prophecy you might also predict the topography of the next few hundred miles from the rear platform. Accounting for possible changes in the character of the landscape. Meanwhile the final destination is hurtling toward you.

In the days following 12 March 1938 one would have had to be even blinder than I was not to see how the measured swaying mountain dwellers' gait of the former Austrians was taking on a more and more rhythmically accelerated march tempo to which even the outdoor-sport cadres brandishing their cudgels to the dance-floor rhythms of Grete Wiesenthal's school soon adjusted. But this was not just part of a passionate leap into the utopia of a golden future my generation was preparing for; it was also taking place on an abstract level like everything else that followed the blackout of that memorable night. It happened with us to us—unawares. And I could not seem to grasp how and when this raptness came over us. When I thought back to the event that descended on my existence and sliced it into the two halves of before and after I can picture only a whirlwind of barely glimpsed images coming just before a plunge into a black hole of incomprehensible procedures carried out on me in a state of unconsciousness: a churning dough of human beings; thousands upon thousands of pale spots faces each rent by the hole of a bellowing mouth; smoldering twitching torchlight; red demons' tongues of flags a billowing chaos licking at their white poison tablets marked with black swastikas; childish men drunk with enthusiasm; screeching twirling staggering women limp with pleasure—and so on. When I look back today (from the last car of a train that is swiftly bearing me toward my final destination) this occurred only a few miles away from similarly fragmented images I carry within me from the Age of Bombs in Berlin—but directly linked to one in particular:

And indeed it had a railroad setting: a platform at a station on the local Berlin–Potsdam line. I don't remember whether it was spring summer or fall 1943 or 1944. The weather didn't change: it was a steady rain of bombs over Berlin. This was yet another morning after a night of heavy bombing. Along this stretch outside the exploding carpets lay acres of garden allotments and the train discharged a number of housewives who having escaped with their lives one more time wanted (before or after or in between whatever obligatory war-effort work) to have a quick look at their garden sheds and their four square meters of beets chard potatoes. They had taken off the most obvious insignia of their air-raid-cellar uniforms: plaid scarves sometimes twisted into turbans sometimes gathered into Phrygian caps. The moment they came out from under the shower of bombs they donned hats: precisely the sort of hats in which second-rate milliner's shops then specialized and still do: hats that cooks wore on their days off in the time of my childhood: ingeniously crumpled elevated or flattened lobed lapped tabbed pleated constructions of various materials with various embellishments little bouquets of flowers bunches of cherries clusters of grapes stuffed birds feathers rhinestone stickpins Bakelite buckles glass brooches. Constructions of felt velvet taffeta silk rep oilcloth. Beneath them the housewives' faces were sooty from nearby fires in the wreckage of the city; their cheeks were hollow with starvation their thoughts somber their eyes red from crying for all their loved ones who had not escaped with their lives one more time and from worrying about those who had. They made this journey to their garden plots to harvest a few miserable roots that in the city's lunar landscape were priceless life-preserving treasures: the food of survival: a backpack of cabbage potatoes beets. And in honor of this journey they wore hats.

They wore hats because outside their housewifely sphere of influence they were reluctant to give up their claim to respectability. And with these hats they have helped me to a sudden flash of realization: they wore these hats in victory. It's true that from their massive arched bosoms in housedresses down to sportily clad legs in sweatpants they were prepared for their

170

war duty. All around them cities were crumbling into their own cellars. Their native soil was pocked with bomb craters. Villages were on fire. Entire harvests lay crushed beneath the treads of tanks. Cadavers of livestock lay rotting in ponds. They and their children were bloated with hunger edema and their men were dying their bodies torn to shreds. It still remained to be seen who would prevail. But one thing was certain: the victor would be like them. In a horrible misunderstanding people were fighting: one national group against the other. But no matter how the battle turned out they would rise from its ashes. Wearing their hats. (Even Her Majesty the Queen favors headgear of this sort.)

A belated insight. It wouldn't have done me much good in the spring of 1938 (not that it does today—though it has since been consolidated in an ideological credo). At the time I was far from being able to understand such a thing. I was in love and my love wholly preoccupied me. The more so as even this cathedral of my early spiritual development began to crumble. The historic events impinging on my life contributed to my general confusion. I rambled blindly through a present that was no longer mine. A Kaspar Hauser amid the hubbub of national renewal. Since I am not spiritually intrepid I soon took flight. Not home to the womb of the Bukovina: that would have been too natural. An artistic temperament will reject what comes naturally (so as to find the things that are the most truly natural of all). I fled full steam ahead: right into the epicenter of the historic events. To the city that throughout the years of my childhood had been the epitome of a metropolis seething with intellectualism and that now in a different light had become the site of the drama and glory of world-historical processes: Berlin capital of the Third Reich. That is where I went in the summer of 1938. To write a book that might have come from the pen of a giggly adolescent girl.

I shouldn't be unfair to *Flame That Consumes Itself.* Writing it allowed me a hunter's son to scrape a layer of fir-needle-green sugarcoating off my soul. I might even be acquitted to a degree of my disgraceful lack of political engagement. Atmospheric changes in the state of the world cannot stop epoch-embezzling. In popular fiction the theme of love is as perennial as the hats of petit-bourgeois ladies and ideologically my book was in keeping with contemporary neo-German sentiment: no objection could be made to the tale of a young man valiantly overcoming his hopeless love for a black-haired Hungarian. Besides which the violin strains in *Flame That Consumes Itself* are the musical accompaniment for a quite different sort of love theme: "to my father." One might say an Aryan revolt against feelings of Oedipal guilt imposed by Jews. Subconscious impulse to commit homoerotic incest being a piquant interlude in the forward progress of the line of succession. At the time my father was deep in his Bukovina woods; had he been close enough to me to see me suspended there between realities he—ever the great hunter—would have applied a woodland metaphor: one person walking through the forest sees only trees—not recognizing the forest as a forest; the other thinking only of the forest bumps his nose on every tree—he doesn't recognize the reality of the trees. But at the time I was still so caught up in my own present moment I couldn't have made sense of this image.

I suspect I must translate my condition at that time into contemporary terms. I'm not sure how successful this can be. The new generations that wash up on the world-historical tide are refreshingly inclined to simplification. Though—or perhaps because—the threat of loss of identity (and of center) is generally acknowledged to be part of everyday experience and unduly complicates life in this remote-control age people have developed the habit of dismissing it with a quick wiping motion. The guardian spirit of language has produced a trope for this that is used in all idioms to remove spiritual and intellectual unease: *Kein Problem. Pas de problème. Non c'è problema. Njema problema.* No problem. The Carnival in Cologne showed me how deeply my old perplexity of 1938 still affected me today —in 1992.

And he cried out: "Why is it that I do not see the Holy One, he who has cast off his earthly cares?"

—FROM THE THREE HUNDRED AND THIRTIETH
OF THE *THOUSAND AND ONE NIGHTS*

$\mathcal{M}$y trip to Cologne in 1990 was undertaken not for pleasure (as with India) or out of curiosity (as with Bucharest) but rather—to fall back on the technical term—"for professional reasons." I had recently returned to the line of work I once practiced at the prehistoric broadcasting station in Hamburg: this time working for Vienna's troglodyte television as a free-lance collaborator on a cabaret-like series of commentaries highlighting selected contemporary issues. Light fare: easily digestible entertainment. Mass-media lubricant. My German image stands me in good stead: man of the world with a satyrical bent. Connoisseur of life and social critic. Rooted literarily in the culture industry with just the right dose of disreputability to qualify me for membership in the mass-media intelligentsia. In this capacity I interview prominent personalities (such as *feu le baron* Philippe de Rothschild) and other sorts of interesting figures (such as the staff of Lower Austria's livestock-fattening units). Or I stroll through thoroughbred stud farms and factory

173

cafeterias leaving a trail of commentary in my wake. A whimsical grab bag for slippered patrons propped in front of their screens of an evening. Offering a few morsels of food for thought.

B. follows these activities with bristly distrust. She worries about my image (a lost cause in any case). I find that taking part in television reality has a number of advantages. (a) Salary: the happy clink of coinage. (If I had to live on what my books brought in I'd have starved to death long ago.) (b) Travel around the world at the station's expense (not as a tourist trotting from one monument to the next but in the good honest role of the workingman). I use these trips to collect valuable information anecdotes dramatic scenes—in short stories to tell (not in black notebooks like Bruce but in the Lord be praised still-functional memory cells in my brain). (c) Fieldwork with a small crew (production manager cameraman sound man assistant) brings me into contact with young people. The most fundamental honest sort of contact: the camaraderie of shared work. These crew members could be my grandchildren. That I never invoke the privilege of age when dealing with them has earned me a sort of affectionate respect that would make me the envy of a tough-minded boss. We potter around together perspire together freeze together eat together drink together get angry together feel happy together laugh together sleep in the same cheap lodgings luxuriate in the same high-class hotels and don't give a damn about much of anything except whether the project's going to turn out well. This time our task was to report on the activities of Prince Carnival.

It's not just an old man's hardheadedness and soft-in-the-headedness if I suggest (falsely) that I went to Cologne for Carnival *after* India. In reality Cologne came first: directly after Bucharest. But my literary existence has its own chronology according to which Cologne was the icing on the cake of my experiences in Bucharest and Pondicherry.

174

Carnival in Cologne lasts from November 11 until Ash Wednesday of the new year; it was mid-January when I arrived. The weather was wintry. A snowless winter lacking all winterly criteria save the cold discomfort in the air asphalt cement and mortared surfaces more barren than usual and the ugliness of my fellow mortals' seasonal garb. A department-store winter. With a thin gloss of sunshine in a sort of immortalized holiday cheer (it was after all Carnival time). The hotel in which the Viennese production headquarters had registered us (long-distance and with complete indifference) was in keeping with everything else. A family-run pension no doubt recommended by the local tourist bureau. Agreeably hygienic after the filthy Balkan pomp of the Art Deco cliché that was the Bucharest caravansary (Grand Hotel Monopol Savoy Excelsior Metropolsk). Utterly sterile. Vaguely familial atmosphere in prefab-eat-in-kitchen-style abstraction. Director of the establishment a horsey matron with nicotine-cured fingers and short-cropped yolk-yellow hair. Each of us was assigned a cubicle. Everything virginally bright and simple. ("Come little Swedish table dance with me!") The washable wallpaper displaying the same pattern of daisies as the mini-curtains in the window. (View of the air shaft.) Glaringly clean. ("You could eat right off the floor.") If you reduced this pretty-posy-sweetness to its essence it was nothing more than a soulful variant of the asceticism of the ashram hotel in Pondicherry (which I was to check into only a month later: unless I maintain the strictest precision in temporal matters I'll slide out of "reality" altogether—an embarrassing sign of schizophrenia). In Cologne the influence of the Maternal could be seen in the breakfast room. Although this time not in edifying inscriptions—Sri Aurobindo's *Overmind* be praised!—but in an overwhelming cornucopia-like profusion of the buffet. A heraldic emblem for New Germany: the overflowing display case of a delicatessen. Fusion of historical materialism and consumer capitalism incarnate. Salami splendor socialized according to the principles of free-market economy. With subtle echoes of the fairy-tale resplendence of a never-never land. A medley of oatmeals and porridges as a starter. Muesli with dried fruit without dried fruit. Cornflakes and Crunchies galore. Then the heartier fare. An artist's palette of bite-sized cold cuts. Baked ham raw ham smoked ham Westphalian ham Prague ham. Hard-boiled eggs soft-boiled eggs sunny-side-up eggs scrambled eggs eggs with ham with bacon with smoked eel with grilled tomatoes. Sardines. Smoked herring. Compotes. Milk and fruit juice. Yogurt soured milk buttermilk. Coffee Nescafé Kaffee Hag. Hot cocoa. Russian tea Chinese tea chamomile tea peppermint tea herb tea. Little baskets full of pumpernickel bread white bread crispbread whole-wheat bread graham-flour bread raisin bread. Little baskets full of iron-hard molded-plastic tubs of butter honey jam. Rosettes of cheese. ("This cheese is very good!") Fruit: apples pears grapes plums peaches passion fruit oranges bananas kiwis mangoes. Dried plums dried apricots dried figs raisins walnuts peanuts brazil nuts cashews almonds. Bonbons. Chocolate cookies. In prewar years such plenty was to be found only aboard luxury ocean liners. Breakfast from seven-thirty until nine-thirty. Please no smoking in the breakfast room. Sorry no dogs allowed. The waitress wore orthopedic shoes and her thin hair in a skimpy knot on the crown of her head. I asked her whether she did pottery on the side. Ceramics? She denied this with uterine embarrassment. The horsey director observed this ostensible effort to start a flirtation with a basilisk's gaze. My young co-workers (thinking the same thing) grinned. Old bastard's at it again.

All around us lay the city of Cologne. As noted before: weather clear as glass. Since it was dusk when we arrived most drivers had already dutifully turned on their headlights. They hurt my eyes: red and white asters in the metal lava of vehicles streaming toward and ahead of us and bearing us along with them into the heart of the city. The sky above was stony.

Translucent stone. Transparent turquoise dusted with the soot of dusk. Cut into it with hard-chiseled lines—and soon transversely striped with the sudden gleam of lit windows—the steles of the skyscrapers: Manhattan export. This was no longer Cologne but a stereotypical cityscape for our turn of the century. Product of world-historical events in my lifetime. It could have been anywhere on the planet: in Alaska as easily as Greece; in Sweden as easily as Brazil. An abstracted world. Cologne city of elves and St. Ursula's eleven thousand virgins pierced with arrows it was not. That Cologne was destroyed in 1944.

I had seen the city's destruction. In the winter of 1945 I had found myself wandering through its ruins. All alone. Far and wide no sign of life. (Colleague Böll had presumably not come home yet.) It was around Christmastime and the rubble still preserved something of the solidity of its long-gone status as a free city (no matter whether real or perceived: whether truly medieval or a late-nineteenth-century imitation of Old German). Demolished walls and piles of debris somehow more venerable than those elsewhere. More Catholic. Witnesses to a more solid past. Not the usual mix of crumbled mortar cement and crushed brick. (Germany at the time offered the student of ruins a rare opportunity for excellent fieldwork.) Cologne city of ruins was so to speak more tellurian than other urban rubble heaps: more stonily collapsed into its own soil. More romantic: rudera beneath racing clouds sliced by the moon's sickle; I expected to hear an owl hooting. It was midnight as I hurried through these ruins my head pulled down between my shoulders with cold and fear. Every nook and cranny behind what was left of the walls might harbor a band of wayfarers ready to leap out and attack . . .

and in four short decades (each flashing by more quickly than the last) this ruinous landscape was transformed into a metropolis of assiduously circulating traffic like any other major city in the world. A miracle of German reconstruction in the style

177

of American hyperrealism. It shared with Berlin of the summer of 1938 that transparency characteristic not only of the excessively real but of the unreal as well.

Our assignment (that is: my film crew's and mine) entailed showing the three Carnival luminaries in the full range of their official activities: the triumvirate Prince Virgin Peasant. Days ago they had checked into their headquarters at a (logically) three-star hotel. Compared to our family hostel there were a few stylistic differences. Here everything was given a masculine sybaritic touch. A la three stars of course. A gentleman's world right out of advertisements in the glossies for champagne and fancy after-shaves. High-society refinement with Rhineland culture. (Hunting gentlemen in pink coats with worldwide banking connections; tails in the evenings and the silvery laughter of women washed down with a glass of Töchterlein Trocken bubbly.) Behind the mahogany reception desk (green marble surface baroque room keys in patinated bronze) stood the head porter in a Stresemann suit: striped trousers gray vest silver tie the sharp eye of a good judge of character. Coolly he gave us television riffraff from the half-Balkan East the once-over. Yes indeed. Prince Carnival and his retinue were staying here. It was still early in the morning and Their Madnesses were resting from their exertions of the night before.

We waited in the lobby. Club atmosphere. Armchairs of honest-to-God Russia leather. Garish red-and-black Oriental rugs. On the walls fox-hunting scenes. On the end tables lampshades painted with old English landscapes. Malachite and alabaster ashtrays. I could just about hear golf clubs clinking. In an adjoining room was the bar. Muted lights. In niches cozy seats covered in black leather. Diminutive brass lamps with green gold-lined patent-leather shadelets. All sorts of mirror reflections. Pressed glass posing as crystal. Everything brandnew. Everything right out of the catalogue of the best furnishings store in town. Behind the bar (and in front of an amber-glimmering array of bottles) a blonde with the breasts of a wet nurse. They were invitingly arranged in a sort of tight bodice like fruit in a basket: help yourself! Among the faded odors of yesterday's cigar ash one could pick out a discreet hint of disinfectant.

It was eleven in the morning and we waited. The simultaneity of all past events in the present moment came back again to haunt me. Keeping people waiting is one of the favorite tricks used in staging the entrances of despots. Even today I can still feel in my old bones the feverish expectation of the good million eager zealots who that long-distant March day in the year 1938 (I can't seem to break free of it) gathered together in a sort of human gruel on Vienna's Heldenplatz and soon kneaded themselves into a sturdy human dough—a rippling fermenting dirty-gray dough—to see with their own eyes Austria's greatest son who had brought them home to the Reich. And he kept them waiting. He let the dough ferment and swell until bubbles broke on its surface: bubbles of noise made by the shouts of many thousands of voices. They rose out of the horde of thousands and thousands of black mouth holes in blotchy gray faces and for the moment popped and vanished. There was still some churning on the surface. But still muffled for the time being. The moans of the monster of the populace were still being held back. Not yet released. Still before the great roar of orgasm. Always and everywhere the Germans' greatest (at the time) son let the masses awaiting him stew at higher and higher temperatures until the last faint traces of recalcitrance had been leached from their impassioned zeal—

so that finally—*finally*—with the appearance of the divine focus of their hopes the pure spirit of rapturous submission is precipitated out of them: the essence of ecstasy in the communion of thousands upon thousands of oblivious souls. Euphoric surrender of ego in the frenzied mass. Individual consciousness at last extinguished. Blissfully assimilated in the collective zeal.

Individual fulfillment in the submission of thousands of ecstatically emptied-out souls: I was to see this again and again in Cologne over the next few days: in each of the gigantic halls each of the packed ballrooms where we followed Prince Virgin Peasant to capture them on our videotape. For four days and nights I witnessed the magical process: kneading individuals into dough whose libidinous fermentation culminated in epiphany. My heart was in my mouth at the sight of these Carnival enthusiasts in lecherous anticipation of their fetish figures: squeezed in around long beer tables flank to flank back to back beneath the tumultuous janglings of a brass band. A human dough heated to the point of bubbling fermentation. (What they call "atmosphere.") This atmosphere washed over us in a flood of sensuality. Embarrassingly erotic. We entered it like high-school boys venturing into the patchouli-and-vagina effluvia of a whorehouse. Gutter concupiscence. Billows of beer vapors and rotgut from half-empty glasses sausage spices meat juices leftover dabs of mustard on empty plates herring liquid sweat-impregnated clothes cigar and cigarette smoke and a constant low growl of voices from sweaty heads . . .

and just as once (in the Year of *Our Lord*-who's-been-riding-roughshod-over-us 1943) at a station of the Berlin–Potsdam local I recognized in the hats of the garden-allotment tenders the object of my smoldering misanthropy the Carnival atmosphere in Cologne showed me the true source of my hatred: I got in my own way far too much to love this human dough. I hated the floury faces with their wide-open mouth holes and what I hated in them was something in myself: feelings of guilt—any bloody kind of guilt from the crucifixion of Christ to the protracted use of a *pappagallo*. Guilt for being an I an individual opposed to the They of the crowd. But above all guilt for feeling hatred. I hated them for something they could do nothing about: their susceptibility to mindless zeal. Their eagerness to turn I into WE under pressure of suppressed guilt. Wanton desire of individuals presumably conscious of their own worth (wearing their petit-bourgeois insignia) to surrender and abandon themselves (in a collective dough that absolved them of personal guilt). Collective hatred excuses individual rancor. The herd redeems. Participating in the fermentation of a unified throng has a soothing effect—except when one of the haters churns it up in an explosion of mass hate. The women in the packed ballrooms factory buildings beer palaces of Cologne and environs were not hatted, but I was certain that on more solemn occasions (ladies' teas churchgoing weddings baptisms funerals department-store clearance sales subscription concerts) they would take their variously crumpled bebowed and beribboned fabric creations (trademark of their solid middle-class convictions and militant defense of propriety and political correctness) from their closets and plop them onto their hair-curler-ringleted heads—as an emblem of their willingness at all times to devote themselves with unstinting application of their personal resources to a worthy cause (the national movement of the hour puritanism witch-hunts women's rights the celebration of a diva national soccer team Pope President Bush's Desert War the condemnation of molesters fiends and other sex offenders) and to give of themselves ecstatically. Provided that everyone else was doing the same thing (for which they had an unfailing instinct). Their men had left off wearing armbands with swastikas or hammers-and-sickles (not to mention visored caps battle-uniform shirts steel helmets clean-shaven skulls) and yet you could hear in their beer-happy rowdiness see in their arm-in-arm rhythmic carousing perceive with awful clarity in their consciousness-buffeting head-splitting eardrum-rupturing outbursts of enthusiasm when their Carnival idols made an entrance that they too desired nothing more fervently than *to adopt a cause as their own.* (To be German means: to give oneself to a cause for its own sake!) They looked for (and found) oblivion in this. They gave themselves up so unquestioningly and unconditionally that they were released from the constraints of individual existence. Liberated from the worries burdens afflictions torments of the guilt-ridden ego. This was presumably the diametrical opposite of the barefoot humility of the ashram disciples in Pondicherry but a product of like impulses that produced a similar result: one of their number seized by the demon of Power could see his chance and take the opportunity to consecrate their zeal. For this I could not hate them. It was happening to them unawares.

In the lobby pregnant with high tea of the luxury hotel in the bank-studded heart of Cologne (where we waited for our three luminaries Prince Virgin Peasant) the sterilized club atmosphere acquired an electrical charge that intensified the longer we waited. It crackled in the fidgetiness of the elevator boys and lobby personnel and in the occasional absentmindedness of the head porter who after a moment of vacancy replied distractedly to a question like a man being woken from a light sleep. The event was imminent. This imminence became all the more suspenseful when various picturesque figures trickled in: strapping Teutons of solid middle-class appearance dressed in Frederick-the-Great-style uniforms: braided powdered wigs red jackets silver epaulets white breeches and high-buttoned gaiters. Their beer drinker's breasts crisscrossed with wide white sword straps and ammunition-pouch belts. The Prince's Guard. Perfunctorily drilled. Home-reserve sloppy. Biedermeier domesticity with saber and gun. Other arrivals were more coquettish: uniformed maidens in miniskirts ankle boots and tit-stuffed red jerkins with three-cornered hats on their curly heads. (Each of them was called "Little Mary of the Sparks.") The lobby of this smart three-star hotel was swiftly being transformed into the backstage wings of an operetta. The extras patiently settled in to wait along with us. Also waiting were several policemen of the quotidian non-Carnivalesque peace-keeping type discreetly lingering beside a row of cars at the hotel entrance. A particularly warriorlike philistine's head in a braided wig— apparently the commander of the Guard (a balloon glass of cognac in his right hand cigar in the left after all it was nearly noon)—wore spurred boots in which he sauntered up and down rattling his saber in front of the elevators. Fired by the spirits and Cuban leaf his impatience was soon conveyed to everyone else.

And then it happened: the elevator doors rolled back revealing the leather-lined box that had just alighted. From it issued the trio whose arrival had been so fervently awaited: Prince Virgin and Peasant. "Their Madnesses" in full regalia.

He said to her: "I have a second house in addition to this one here; it is meant as a gathering-place for my friends and companions."
—FROM THE THREE HUNDRED AND SIXTIETH
OF THE *THOUSAND AND ONE NIGHTS*

*I*n my youth a second banner flapped alongside the blue yellow red one of my love of my Romanian homeland: the black red gold banner of my love of all things German. It was my father who had unfurled it. It flew above the myth of a Reich that even then in the first decades of this century had long since been as unreal as the Bukovina is today. The Holy Roman Empire of German Nations. Its reestablishment: a youthful dream of the nationalistically inflamed nineteenth century. My father had loyally passed it on to me a hundred years later without first subjecting it to scrutiny. Blind epoch-embezzler. In his day the dream had been a progressive one shared by enthusiastic liberals. Even in the early years of my childhood it implied the vision of a nation united in freedom and dignity. Bismarck's Second Reich had been a parody of this vision. The breast-beating weapon-rattling nation that collapsed in 1918. Hitler's Third Reich was its monstrous offspring: engendered in the womb of this once beautiful vision by the underdogs' hate. And hate was what was taught in the name of the old illusion. In Austria's questionable school system this national hatred haunted the classrooms (and the teachers' brains). A black-red-gold-dyed hatred for everything that wasn't German. (In later years this was replaced in my case by hatred for everything associated with this German sentiment.) The old First Reich and the Second too had shriveled up and disintegrated because of this hatred. The double-headed eagle (for a century it hovered over Austria alone and then lost a head there too) no longer spread its wings over a multitude of regions and peoples. One-headed and expressionistically plucked it crouched here upon an Alpine residue of imperial Austria there upon the carcass of Bismarck's Reich and what separated these two amputees went deeper than what they had in common. Only the language was left to hold this black red gold myth together (and to fan the flames of the shared black red gold hate).

In fact the empire embracing all German-speaking peoples as it was originally dreamed up had nothing to do with the First Holy Roman variant or Bismarck's Second let alone Hitler's Third. It was a purely philological dream. The pure myth of linguistic unity. It had never existed in any recognizable form.

The empire of all Germans had no fixed boundaries and even in a fantasy future was not a real nation. It was a fairy tale through and through. Its mythology included Theodor Fontane as well as General Moltke; Sauerbruch as well as Schiller; Walther von der Vogelweide as well as Richard Wagner; Andreas Hofer as well as Alaric; Schubert as well as Nietzsche; Frederick the Great of Prussia as well as Empress Maria Theresa; Dürer as well as Daimler; the Edda as well as the zeppelin. Enthroned above all of these was the Hohenstaufer Emperor Frederick Barbarossa. For the time being he was slumbering along with his Reich. Had sat for so many years encircled by ravens deep in the Kyffhäuser that his beard (no longer red but now white as snow) had grown through the stone table in front of him. Nevertheless one day he would awake. A German Messiah who would put an end to the discord envy malice hate among Germans and toward the rest of the world. Old and new wounds would heal. No Austrian would perceive the insidious use of the needle gun in the Battle of Königgrätz as a brotherly stab in the ribs. No Catholic raised this side of the Limes Germanicus would quarrel with a Protestant across the way. Though Prussians with their cheese-knife-sharp idiom might find the Saxons' mushy-squishy speech ridiculous and both might sound like Slavs to a Bavarian they would all confidently declare themselves German-speakers. In its dialect-rich diversity this black red gold empire was a fatherland of language and I was wholeheartedly its citizen.

I am still its wholehearted citizen today though I realize I too have become part of its mythical heritage. (The voice that praises me for the German I write is tremulous with memories of a bygone age.) This dream of a holy empire promises freedom even from hate.

The three figures who emerged from the elevator in the clubby swank of the three-star hotel in high-rise-studded Cologne

—as if descending from heaven—epitomized the spirit of Germany. The strong-calved barrel-chested Prince was encased in knee-length trousers and jerkin so thickly encrusted with silver and gold embroidery that they looked like the German version of a torero's costume. Siegfried the Dragon Slayer as matador. A short little cloak stiff with embroidery was tossed over a shoulder with a hussar's aplomb. He was armed for militant festivity. Hilarity and pranks would not catch him off guard. On the contrary: he was prepared to extrude boisterous merriment from his own person. His shopkeeper's face glowed with exertion. He laughed with bared teeth. His tread was heavy but elastic. To be sure: he did not seem at ease. The bell-jingling fool's cap on his head called him into question being as inappropriate to his rank as a baseball cap placed in jest on a police dog's head. Fun was fun—but at whose expense? He was not ready to tolerate fun paid out of his own pocket. Yes he was the Prince of Fools but that didn't mean his princely dignity could be assailed. This made his joviality all the more insistent. He clutched his fool's scepter—an instrument resembling a folded fan—as though he meant to wield the wit of an Eulenspiegel like a cudgel. He would hit his people over the head with the purifying ecstasy of these saturnalia.

This imposing pageant was reinforced by the weighty Virgin at the Prince's side. She was a tower. That her beribboned puff-sleeved black white blood-red gold lobed slashed tasseled damsel-of-the-castle's gown with its landsknecht's panache concealed a man—a hulk of a man at that: nearly a full head taller than the strapping Prince—was part of the Carnival fun. But it was melancholy fun. The spirit of travesty had given way to brutal caricature: yellow braids thick as arms dangling down on breasts like pumpkins butcher's cheeks painted fiery red lewd whorish lips; atop the beer belly two huge paws lay folded in hypocritical chasteness. I should note that I was probably the only one who found this getup offensive and everyone else no doubt thought it irresistibly hilarious. To me it was horrifying. It was not a lived disguise as with transvestites nor a scornful repudiation of masculinity through feminine attributes adopted in irony. It was a mockery of Woman achieved by maliciously having the huge masculine hunk show through. On the fellow's yellow head sat a crest—heraldic symbol grotesquely inflated —such as might top a city's coat of arms. To me it was a cruel parody of my own black red gold mythology: Germania.

The Peasant too was more an unmasked type than a comic exaggeration. A burrowing rooting sod-shifter—I involuntarily dubbed him Eberhard—the Boar. The aggression one expects from such a creature was held well in check. He wore a sort of chain mail over his sagging loam-brown costume that lent him a warlike air but his hunched-over carriage revealed the vassal in him. This was no warrior but at best a blindly enraged flail-swinging marauder in a peasant uprising. A personification of the vassal's wrath: impotent for all eternity. Strapped beneath the yoke even in the frenzy of ostensible liberation (which always ends up being suffocated in blood and flame and ashes). I caught a whiff of the German late Middle Ages in all their ruinous desolation. And German malice. Here too the ridiculous figure of the country bumpkin was portrayed not through comic exaggeration of forgivable weaknesses but in contemptuous denunciation of its negative core (which ruined the parody's chances of being amusing). The head of this doltish peasant was graced with another abstruse piece of headgear: a scourge of peacock feathers like the headdress of an exotic chieftain. This was shockingly self-revelatory; upstart arrogance standing in the shadow of princely glory. The hand of the *genius loci* was visible in the costume's design. The Peasant was presented to the people not as a simpleton to poke fun at but as a brutal cretin. A half-tamed savage. Deeply unsophisticated outrageously presumptuous unpredictably dangerous. City humiliating country. Good citizens venting their frustrations on hayseeds. Petits bourgeois taking revenge on the source of their secret fears.

So there stood the triumvirate in front of us and I had no time to linger over the notion of how delightfully clever a half-mask is with its elegant concealment of eye area and nose (the latter according to my colleague Proust being an unmistakable sign of intelligence or stupidity: for which reason it is turned into a fool's beak at the Carnival in Venice). Here there were no masks to create with their temporary erasure of identity an anonymity that makes every playful transgression permissible and gives free rein to boisterousness frenzy surrender to secret fears in ecstatic oblivion.

Cologne is not Venice. But even in Cologne people were promised the blessing of a temporary escape from their own identities: that happened on Shrove Monday the day before Mardi Gras. This was the day everyone ran around in masks. Every man woman and child was invited to indulge in delicious foolishness. Egos were cast aside to be purified while their owners assumed new identities. But Shrove Monday was still far off. For the moment anticipation was everything.

Here in the lobby of the three-star hotel preparations were under way. Prince Virgin Peasant—or rather the three men dressed as these (in costumes that embarrassingly emphasized their identities rather than erasing them)—didn't just stand there in front of the elevators inhaling the incense of satisfied expectation. With vigorous strides they crossed the hotel lobby giving their Guard of Honor not so much as a sideways glance. They had a cast-iron sense of the importance of their roles. In front of the hotel a cordon of white Mercedes limousines had been waiting for hours under police supervision. In a twinkling they swallowed up Prince Virgin Peasant along with Guards Spark-ettes and police. A green-and-white police car lights gaily flashing took the lead. We followed heavily laden with film equipment in a rented Volkswagen bus.

• • •

Four days and four nights we followed these stars filming our way through the all-out paradox of a meticulously organized chaos. The preparations were systematic for this respite from the principles of order this anticipated catharsis. Alas: the futility level rose at each stage of fermentation. It wasn't just Cologne where fools were on holiday. World-historical disturbances were occurring all over. This particular Cologne Carnival had been preceded by the breaking down of the Berlin Wall which had certainly given people something to think about. Unfortunately food for thought kept coming. Shrove Monday was now being canceled because bad storms were expected. A year later the Gulf War was to keep the revels from reaching their natural climax and thus obstruct the traditional purification process. At a time of such momentous world-historical events German propriety deemed it improper to sanction the frivolity of an orgy of release. Only the foreplay leading up to it.

This amounted to emasculating the promise whose fulfillment had been so ardently anticipated. For not until Shrove Monday—we were told—do the expectations systematically aroused over several weeks explode in an apotheosis of release. Under cover of masks everyone's rattled-loose boozed-loose bellowed-loose individuality is finally cast off. The ordinarily fearful isolated intimidated man or woman hides behind the disguise (clown geisha domino Pierrot dancing girl gangster wet nurse—anything but oneself). The demonic is released in a sense-baffling make-believe. Shrove Monday exists for the therapeutic deception of demons. The human dough has hatched them out during its fermentation and now it turns them over to the mocking public. Shrove Monday represents not the triumph of Prince Virgin Peasant but their heroic demise. The human dough that has been building up pressure over weeks of fermentation has now risen hugely and is beginning to overflow. Spilling from countless beer halls festival halls assembly halls into the streets and alleys of the old (now hyperrealistically Americanized) free city of Cologne and filling it up with Germanness like casings on a sausage machine. There's room left only for a Rabelaisian display of the cast-off rationality: a narrow passage for the procession. Fancy cars full of fools. Idiotic jalopies. Past a riotous gantlet of delirious maskers (the history of whose mummery is recounted in German schoolbooks) trundles a parade of gigantic papier-mâché caricatures. Figures that might ordinarily inspire fear magnified to the point of absurdity. Satirical likenesses of fetishistic cult figures swaying back and forth at rooftop height amid flurries of confetti: Kohl Bush Gorbachev Mitterrand Mickey Mouse Batman Superman Marilyn Monroe Dracula. All these deities mere glue and paper. All this reality mere illusion. Cheap flaking paint. Dross and rubbish. The jubilant gloating pleasure of revelers freed from their own egos rises in a frenzy of mass ecstasy. Everyone is sobbing with joy kissing one another whacking their folded-fan–cudgel scepters over one another's heads bellowing themselves hoarse with the traditional shouted greetings: "Alaaf!" "Helau!" boozing and vomiting. (What the tourist brochure calls "festive Carnival spirit.")

But unfortunately—as I've noted—given the precarious ecological and world-political situations that might have precipitated into full-blown catastrophes at any moment such gaiety would clearly have been too much for the good citizens of Cologne (not to mention the global audience taking part in these ceremonies via television screens and photojournalistic reports in their daily weekly monthly periodicals). (Especially since the local chemical industry was hard at work on new potential catastrophes.) For this or that reason with this or that excuse Shrove Monday was canceled. All we could do was film the anticipatory fermentation. Thousands of meters of tape for a report barely thirteen minutes long during which the triumvirate stayed firmly in the spotlight.

In a tiny telecast this might well have been tolerable but we were already finding it intolerable by the day after our first night. The three men costumed as Carnival royalty had to hold out for weeks more which made their ability to produce a steady stream of joviality downright admirable. But that was all that was demanded of them. It was their job to be effervescent vivacious ebullient spirited effusive merry irrepressible humorous. That was it. Sizzling sparklers of enthusiasm. Incarnated prophecies: heralds of the frenzy that according to protocol was to govern the city's mood. What marvelous talent lay concealed in these dignified citizens! How wondrously receptive were their neighbors! Whether in a factory packed to bursting or a mammoth beer hall brimming over with human dough a mobbed assembly hall in an upper-class Carnival club (where the fermenting agent came not from beer but from Rhine wine) overflowing rooms in an old folks' home a hospital a cripples' asylum (unfortunately not a real asylum for clinically certified fools: the comparison would have been interesting)—everywhere the anticipation of our trio was at fever pitch. The citizenry was lusting for anarchy. And this anarchy was meticulously organized. Our itinerary from one bubbling-over site to the next was planned with general-staff efficiency. As was the anticipation of the sacrificial victims offered up for the public's mirth. Decorations— paper lanterns and scrawny crepe-paper garlands—made people's hearts beat faster their spirits rise in ever more heated merriment. Brass bands droned away deafeningly. Traditional Carnival soapbox orators or *Büttenredner* whose inanities set off salvos of laughter wild cabaret acts dance performances solos duets trios groups folkloristic choirs the presence of prominent individuals from politics business theater film and broadcasting—all this enabled the revelers to take gratifying leave of their senses and give the stoked-to-a-boil insanity something of the solemnity of Advent. And precisely when the expectation

191

had reached its highest pitch we appeared—Prince Virgin Peasant Guards Sparkettes and bringing up the rear (for the record as it were) my television crew and me. Importantly loaded with lamps cameras microphones cables. And always received with licentious zeal. Thousands of individuals had been kneaded into one. From thousands of black mouth orifices in the mass of human dough came a single cry: roaring raging bellowing ear-battering eardrum-shattering consciousness-obliterating. Our sound mixer clung to the controls of his instruments like a skipper in a storm.

An intoxicated crowd divested almost entirely of individual identity was Prince Carnival's true element. He swam in it. He let it buoy him up. Hovering erect above his heavily tramping feet as if walking on water in somebody's dream his arms raised spread in universal salutation his fool's scepter whirling as if in an upcurrent his face glowing with merriment gum-flashing benevolence-fizzing turning now to the right now to the left like a windup toy—thus he entered the festive melee and stomped his way to the stage where whichever committee it was this time waited for him. Every moment promised to have him levitating. His two satellites seemed more firmly anchored: the Virgin a broadly grinning mischievous accomplice in hilarity ready to lend a hand in nonsense of every sort; the Peasant trudging dully gamely along behind. The uproar subsided when Their Madnesses reached the dignitaries' podium but after a few words of welcome spoken in such immaculate Cologne dialect that we German-speaking foreigners couldn't catch a word (beyond the oft-repeated cries of "Alaaf!" and "Helau!" which we'd gotten used to) the tumult would break out again with renewed fury—and Prince Virgin Peasant and their retinue of Guards and Sparkette Marys (and we television bondsmen in tow) would be swept up and borne off again. Flashing red gums faces flushed with benevolence frothing with high spirits and encircled by police the sovereigns of calendrically regulated ego erasure sped off to their next appointment.

The exclusive duty of putting in epiphanic appearances kept Their Madnesses busy every day from late afternoon until well past midnight. The sites of public merriment associated with Carnival clubs employee-celebration leagues old-folks'-home senility supervisors invalids' social-schedule planners lay scattered throughout the greater metropolitan area. A good part of each day was spent in transit half an hour to several hours at a time between one place and the next with interludes to fill the gaps: brief stops for beer and bockwurst in various cheap restaurants (whose owners knew how to show their appreciation for this blessing) or for coffee and crullers in some respectable middle-class pastry shop (look-alikes of the Virgin waiting on us with beaming smiles cops loitering by the front door). Then the green-and-white police car would flick on its lights and take its place at the head of the line of white limousines and the convoy would zip off through the wintry city thinly glazed with sun—often all the way to the outskirts through loops of futuristically spacious cloverleafs to smooth multilane highways that whisked us to some spruced-up idyllic little village harboring a monstrous industrial complex behind its rustic façade whose employees wanted to partake in the sanctification of the Holy Days of Carnival by our three luminaries. After bathing briefly but deeply in their jubilation we returned to the city center where the lava of vehicles halted then parted like the biblical Red Sea for the flashing green-and-white head of the white snake of cars until the very tip of its tail (us in the television bus) had slipped through. Prince Virgin Peasant and entourage zooming off to the next step of their itinerary.

Thus did morning noon afternoon and evening coalesce in day after identical day lasting deep into the night. Only on the morning of the last day was I granted permission to interview Their Madnesses. This took place in the elegant hotel suite that served as their headquarters. The leather-padded elevator bore us up to their suite where they were in the process of harnessing up for work and received us in a state of half-undress: the Prince already wearing his fool's cap and jerkin but without his breeches; from the hips down his sturdy-calved legs were encased in wool long johns (the January days were cold). The Virgin was blond-braided but clad in a nightshirt and lacking the melon globes on her chest which was visible in its furred glory. The Peasant wore his saggy brown robes but was bareheaded and had not yet donned chain mail and peasant's boots (he was in slippers). On a low table half-encircled by the sofa ensemble in the antechamber the remains of a hearty breakfast of fried eggs rolls with sausage ham and cheese and empty beer glasses offered a still life that joined these three strapping half-costumed figures in a Germanic parody of one of Picasso's acrobat paintings.

As an interviewer I am easily distracted. I devote too much attention to what interests me personally and forget to ask the things the general public wants to know. As in Pondicherry (where the figure of The Mother diverted me from no doubt more significant questions as to the intellectual content of the teachings of Sri Aurobindo and the ashram's economic prosperity) I forgot the important journalistic issues here in Cologne. What fascinated me were the psychological motives that could bring upright citizens to spend weeks on end blithely playacting a comically exalted cross between feudal lords and country-fair buffoons. By concentrating on this I neglected far more interesting aspects of the Cologne Carnival.

The Prince especially showed extraordinary skill in dodging ticklish questions. He acknowledged that his princely robes encrusted with gold and silver rhinestones and pearls had cost him seventy thousand marks in hard cash. Whether and how he hoped (and planned) to amortize this expenditure was unclear. He had apparently forked over this juicy sum out of pure idealism. "Can't you understand that? But you're not from Cologne. A real Cologner dreams of becoming Prince Carnival from the time he's this high. For a few weeks you rule the world. You've seen what it's like. Nothing like it. Memories like these will last you a lifetime. You're king of your hometown Cologne." I ventured the objection: "But only in make-believe, right?" His Madness flipped off his slippers and pulled on his embroidery-bristling dragon-matador's pants: "You've been following us around for a few days now. You've seen the kind of reception we get. How everyone cheers us. How everyone longs to be in our shoes. You call that make-believe? Sure, we know it's not forever. But what lasts forever in this world?" I was dumbstruck.

I turned to the Virgin. "Do you share this opinion?" The Virgin shared it unreservedly. She or rather *he* is no longer a Cologner—he's lived abroad for several decades—"But I too was born in Cologne. And you get it in your bones, the tradition. Carnival comes from the Middle Ages. When Cologne was one of the most important cities in the Empire. I mean the old German Empire: the Roman one. We're building on Roman foundations. But at heart we're Germans. No German worth his salt would pass up the chance to march at the head of his people—even if only for a little while." —"In drag?" I ask. "That's just for laughs. Humor is important. There's something buried inside every man that wants to get out and play." (My colleague Nietzsche slightly misquoted.)

The Peasant had nothing of substance to add to the above. I told my crew to stop filming. We couldn't use more than three minutes of interview in a program barely thirteen minutes long. Besides which Their Madnesses had requested that they not be filmed half-dressed so we had restricted ourselves to head shots. (The Maiden had demurely held her nightshirt closed over her hairy thorax.)

When Shahrazad paused, King Shahryar said to her: "The moral of your story is an excellent one." "It is, O auspicious King, yet the tale is not to be compared with one which I have in reserve to tell you."

—FROM THE THREE HUNDRED AND EIGHTY-FIRST

OF THE *THOUSAND AND ONE NIGHTS*

$\mathscr{I}$n the mornings when I was waiting for the appearance of Their Madnesses in the club-chaired lobby of the three-star hotel the simultaneous existence of all past moments in the present offered me various parallels to my own present situation. The hotel I'd stayed at in Bucharest a few weeks before had also laid claim to these quality-confirming stars. I couldn't help thinking them better deserved there than here. The Bucharest hotel was dirty and besieged by money changers shady wheelers and dealers probable pickpockets. The lobby a hangout for whores and unsavory characters engaged in nonstop haggling duping cheating. A horrifying industry that was later to thrive was getting started: the sale of children. Mothers offered up their brood like market women selling bunches of radishes. Lawyers were present to wrap up the unavoidable paperwork on the spot. Customers came from prosperous countries—mostly Americans. Every so often there was a parroty shriek: "Gee isn't he sweet! Look at those eyes!" (No doubt a Gypsy baby: their eyes are renowned; nevertheless blond children were more expensive. There were rumors that a sort of Fountain of Life National

Socialist style had been set up for the production of blond blue-eyed babies.) End-of-season sell-out of practical socialism. Down-at-heels hotel employees were either insolent or fawning depending on your tip; the doorman was a thief. (There were others.) Nevertheless this den of iniquity was more grand-hotel-like more cosmopolitan had a more worldly air than this Russia-leather imitation of a golf and country club in skyscraper-bristling Cologne. Its questionable refinement plastered-on respectability and inept elegance were deeply provincial. I imagined a lady with a hat seated in each of the armchairs: enchanting triumphs of millinery designed to coordinate beautifully with that most essential accessory of every woman of the world: the folding umbrella. A traumatic vision. An unmistakable sign of paranoia. But I had trouble finding ways to keep amused in Cologne.

Except of course for my chats with the leader of the Mercedes convoy in which Prince Virgin Peasant and retinue sped about stoking up excitement for a Carnival that wasn't supposed to take place. (Shrove Monday canceled: what a quandary!) I soon got out of the habit of immersing myself in the noise bath at the sites we visited. While Prince Virgin Peasant were making their triumphal entrances into the roaring assemblies escorted by their Guards and ringed by dancing Sparkettes (and my crew was scurrying after them camera running) I sat with the owner of the car-rental agency to whom the white limousines belonged in the Prince's luxury limo listening to the monologues of a man exactly as old as I—to the day—though much more robust and energetic.

"It's all just theater. Nice money though. Don't ask me how it works. It's not so easy to follow. Connections. Set something up here build on something there. Nothing wrong with it either. Can't be much pleasure in driving back and forth all the time and people going crazy wherever you go. Hard work if you ask me. Costs a bundle. I personally couldn't afford it. Couldn't go through with it anyway not with my liver. When you think about what these people have to get down sixteen hours a day. Better be worth it. Still. Let me tell you: there's something more to it. They make people happy. It's nice to make people happy. That's what everyone gets so excited about. That's nice—right? Makes you feel good just to see it. Not much else you have to feel good about these days. Folks like us have been running around all our lives. You say you were born in 'fourteen too. So you know what I'm talking about. The minute you were old enough to take some pleasure in life you had to stand up and get shot at. Four years of it. On foot from Liegnitz to the Pyrenees and from there to Russia and back to Mount Athos. And the air had a high iron content if you know what I mean. You know what I'm talking about. And then three years prisoner of war in Scotland. It's a way to see the world. No denying it. The army—a tourist enterprise. Just like travel agencies nowadays. But not as comfy. Riding shank's mare all the way. And what for? You're one of the last to be sent home and then you can throw yourself right into the spokes of the reconstruction miracle. All well and good: I have nothing to complain about. When I think back to what I started out with I have to say: Oskar you've shown them what you're made of.

"And then reunification is coming along. Now everything's going to hell in a hand basket. I'm not even thinking about the taxes they're going to slap on us to pay for it all. But with a few million out of work over there and pretty soon over here too—you think they're going to want to be driven around in a Mercedes? I've been feeling it for a while now. Any time other than Carnival half the fleet never leaves the garage. Don't think I'm not sympathetic. I'm from over there myself. From Upper Silesia. But I came here right after the P.O.W. camp. Who wanted to go back to the East then? If I'd gone home I'd have been in Poland. So I stayed here in Cologne once the Brits let me loose in an old army overcoat dyed brown and thirty Reichsmarks in my pocket. I can understand when my brothers and sisters over there want to drive a decent car for once in their lives and go to Majorca for vacation. They haven't had such an easy forty-five years of it with the Russkies breathing down their necks. But now they don't remember what it means to work. All the same: when things started happening all at once and they tore down that sad joke of a Wall and so forth I couldn't help feeling something in here. It's no disgrace. There you are sitting in front of the tube one evening and someone jumps in there with a pickax where they'd have shot him dead just the day before and now he's hacking away at the thing with bits of brick flying all over the place and everyone cheering their heads off on both sides. A thing like that it makes you really wish you could be there. It's like when someone shoots a goal in the world championships. And then all the celebrations at the Brandenburg Gate: at least as much emotion in the air as here at Carnival time. But more dignity. More decency. Not just bare tits everywhere you look like on Shrove Monday. You know what? I couldn't be happier they've canceled Shrove Monday this year if only because it means they can't disparage Kohl in public. The man has not deserved such treatment. Would you have thought him capable of reunifying the German people in a single fatherland? I say the man has earned his rank in history just like Bismarck or Frederick the Great. A great German. You can see it perfectly well for yourself when you look on TV or in magazines what they did to their country over there in the East. Everything crapped up and full of poison. Everything left to decay just like down where you live in Italy. All that's going to have to be rebuilt. And that's what's going to happen. Only problem is we're paying for it. You know what it feels like? Like you're a pack mule and someone's just scooped the sweetest half of the oats out of your food trough and then they strap twice the load on your back. We're already overrun with guest workers brown as a cup of coffee and now all the Ossies are showing up and want us to hand over what we've earned all these years by the sweat of our brow . . ."

Timeless palaver. The simultaneous occurrence of all happenings in the present moment. World history fermenting in each individual. Even the future has been stuffed into the present. I can still hear him saying: "And on top of everything else that criminal in Kuwait goes and lights a match to our oil wells. You think you're not going to notice at the gas pump? It stands to reason the Yanks had to step in. Even at the risk of the man using his poison gas. Probably already has his own atomic bomb. Of course the West has to move in and stop him. It's God's job to see to it trees don't grow taller than the sky. But it's better when you take things like that into your own hands. The man is a lunatic. No consideration at all for ecological balance. It makes sense you're not going to want to celebrate Shrove Monday with something like that going on. Still it's a shame. Personally I have nothing to complain about. My cars are booked up even without Shrove Monday. I mean with the Prince and all. But that's only for Carnival. What comes next remains to be seen. And even so it's a good way for all the others to work off steam. You can see it yourself when you go in there and watch the celebration. It's a real festival. Okay, it's not the same thing as a real Shrove Monday. You should see that some time. It's like Schiller: 'How the crowd cheers, with what swift feet it rolls in waves all down the street.' [He slightly misquoted.] The people are good Germans. They want to have their fun. Don't get a chance often. Life is like a baby's nightshirt: short and shitty. And who knows what else this Saddam Hussein (or whatever XYZ) has up his sleeve . . . ?"

No letup from my friend at the head of the Prince's convoy. As he sees it he and I are brothers. He says: "Well I don't know what you think about it but at our age you learn to be patient with time and what it brings you. As for me personally . . ."

Personally he is a ferment acting on time and its dowry of reality. History is a by-product of this process. He churns it out along with others like him. A fission fungus. It happens to him with him in him and those like him unawares. History lives him while he thinks it is he who is living it. Yet all this time he is living in the world. Not always in festive spirits as at Carnival time. Not always is he allowed a release in these harmless eruptions when Their Madnesses Prince Virgin Peasant appear in foaming beer halls factories gymnasiums festival halls. Or even in the exorcistic ecstasy of Shrove Monday (when it isn't canceled). Sometimes history brings out nastier sides of him as for example in 1938 in Vienna. But always in full confidence that he lives his life in a respectable and upright fashion. (There's no doubt in my mind: his wife wears a hat.)

The nights in Cologne were icy. Even more quickly than during the day our convoy raced through empty streets. From time to time above the flickering shadows of housefronts flashing by in the car window I caught a glimpse of the moon. From time to time the bone-pale unreal-looking towers of Cologne Cathedral emerged bathed in moonlight. I saw them with mixed feelings. In its Wilhelminian patched-up Gothic style this cathedral once epitomized a Germany I had loved as a child and felt a wholehearted part of. A youthful dream (and old man's longing) of my father's. For me in the Bukovina an unreal reality. My father had tried to anchor it in me which wasn't hard for him. He was his own witness. He himself possessed a hard-as-nails reality: the great hunter. Phenotype of an age-old mode of existence. Doing and existing in seamless unity. It was irony on the part of the world spirit on a small individual scale that he—sovereign in his deeds lord over life and death in his woods his heart filled with Greater German longings—rooted me with my every fiber to the soil of my Romanian homeland.

At his side in his care under his strict supervision I experienced myself as though I had grown up there with the creatures of the woods. Probing the earth to gauge its value as a browsing or hiding place. Gazing with the eyes of deer. Listening sniffing tasting with animal senses. Woodland air in my nostrils: black earth fermenting spring growth rotting autumn leaves mushroomy scents and the spice of herbs. The alphabet of tracks inscribed in the first snowfall. The experience of woodland creatures: springwater-moist moss on the stones of the stream bed rustling wind in treetops woodpeckers' hammering measuring out the breadth of the forests. Each nearby sound sets off an alarm system: squirrels swishing in the branches make you catch your breath. The titmouse's warning call electrifies you. A jay shrieks: escalates your pulse in trembling expectation. Then the slain deer. Growing cold beneath the hands that turn it over. Ruby-red drops on green foliage and black earth. Crumbs of humus drinking the dew of life. Life becomes experience through death. Blood-pounding presence. Existence liberated from time. Full presence in the now and here. My father the great hunter is the high priest of this reality and I the boy gaze up at him in worship: he has given me these hours outside of time. Given me the wonderful oblivion of this present moment. In it the golden autumn countryside and the myth of my own highborn status within it: I the son of the hunter. Nothing will ever place me so intimately in the world again. Nothing will have this sense of presence. Everything else will be weightless compared to the purity of this sense of my own ego in a selfless present. My father has given this to me from the wealth of his utterly unified doing and being—

and I know that his sovereignty is a fully aware self-deception. This world of immediately graspable things and elemental actions is a fiction an escape to which his loneliness drives him. His secularized loneliness: he is alone; and so he creates for himself a world in which he is sovereignly alone as lord over life and death. He must kill in order to confirm his position in his world. Unless he tracks his prey and brings it death his world—he himself—will have no reality. His death-bringing presence rescues him from time. Time is the presentness of an experience of a world of which he partakes as the others do. He is separated from them by his loneliness. He removes himself from time by taking on the form of an ancient figure. And he is great because he sees through this fiction. His sovereignty is the consciousness he has preserved of his own self-deception. He makes the exterior world the world of his interior because he alone exists in both the one and the other. Thus he folds his interior out to face the outside world. Gives himself reality outside the world. In a process of doing in which he himself is effaced. Gives himself being as himself in a vision of himself. Singing *himself* into existence.

Allah bless him who has spoken the words: "The man of honor dies, his riches are scattered and the most base of men seize his wives."

—FROM THE FOUR HUNDRED AND FOURTH
OF THE THOUSAND AND ONE NIGHTS

No one expected me to write about the Carnival in Cologne (not even me). The part of it available to journalism had been (with the superficiality proper to the medium) immortalized on videotape. The need to say what happened within me during my encounters with Prince Virgin Peasant manifested itself only as I became aware—with increasing distress—of the simultaneity of my life phases. I the present moment for all time. Here in Cologne I was filming three mummers disguised in the costumes of archetypes each with his own misleading role in the identity-erasing chaos of Carnival. Their purpose to bring the fermenting human dough release through laughter. Who they were in private—businessmen maybe import-export merchants if not detergent or cardboard manufacturers fur designers PR men—was theoretically relevant to journalism but wouldn't have made sense in the context of our report (thirteen minutes of Cologne festivities). I had to confine myself to the picturesque façade. But as it happened this façade pointed me to something most astonishing: the pleasure these highly placed good citizens took in having the power to bring this fermenting human dough to ecstatic eruption—

and I was filled with the presentness of 12 March 1938 and the manikin with the tuft beneath his piglet nose whom all the fuss was about: a microscopically tiny manikin on a balcony above Vienna's Heldenplatz a single churning mass of human dough (go read—oh do go read—the relevant scenes in my books! Not *Flame That Consumes Itself* but the later ones). Up on the balcony the brown-shirted manikin wriggling about with the artistic forelock dancing on its brow was so moved by its own greatness that it could utter no other syllable but "I— I— I—" repeated over and over cut off over and over by tumultuous applause . . .

this manikin had imbibed the I the ego of a good million individuals in the human dough on Heldenplatz. No point in asking *Why? How? By what means?* The demonic? The word is a crutch. (Like *God*.) Certainly this manikin epitomized the idea of masculinity that the good citizens' wives carried around in their fashionably hatted heads. (If they knew anything different it was from movies or similar dream institutions: not reality. At any rate not *their* reality.) This manikin solidly planted in trousers and bulky boots with his fanatic's gaze beneath artistically dancing bangs was *their* reality. He was the sort of man they opened their legs to the sort they gave birth to the sort who was father uncle brother to their husbands fathers brothers sons. So when he said "I" he was speaking as one of them. And what pulsated in their ears in the heartbeats of his helplessly inarticulate "I— I— I—" was their own egos now dissolved and erased for their own pleasure. And the manikin reveled in it. Fed on it. Swelled to monstrous proportions—

and in me at the same time was the paralyzing present of a rainy day in a P.O.W. camp in Scotland. March 1948: still in the days when I was dreaming of contributing to the renewal of Germany (and thus Europe and indeed the whole world) from my niche in the on-the-air culture industry. Since I had a clean political bill of health—my Romanian citizenship kept me from being classed with the collectively guilty Germans—our British controller had chosen me for a so-called resettlement tour: a proud task. I was to visit P.O.W. camps and gently break the news to the men who had been languishing there for nearly three years what would be awaiting them at home when they were released in the—"let's hope!"—very near future.

What was awaiting them was none too agreeable: ruined cities hunger missing families desolate graves. I was armed with a large repertoire of encouraging moralistic catchphrases. But the dough of gray faces before me in the corrugated-iron assembly halls with the rain drumming down made the words stick in my throat. The gray puppets these faces belonged to had not been ordered to come hear me; they were here of their own free will insofar as the dull stupor of their existence admitted of free will. This did not make them less sullen. They were driven to the meetings by boredom emptiness of the days rigid mindless routine. They trotted from their Nissen huts to the corrugated-iron assembly halls to fill the gaping holes in their lives regardless of whether it meant being made queasy confirmed in their hatreds driven to impotent despair by films showing the

horrors of Buchenwald and Bergen-Belsen by political reha-
bilitation lectures by palaver from the resettlement teams. I too
had nothing but palaver to offer them.

I told them this right from the start. I said: Everything I have
to tell you is about hopelessness. I can try to answer direct
questions as honestly as possible. ("What happens if I go home
and my wife is having an affair with a Yankee a Brit a Russki?")
But even if I could put myself in the shoes of every one of you
my answers would be pretty useless. (Colleague La Rochefoucauld: *"Les conseils ne servent qu'à ceux qui les donnent."*) They
sent me here to make your lives easier. That's horseshit. It's
you who make *my* life easier if you're willing to believe I mean
well. That's all—

and the more often I used this trick and the better I became
at it (controlling my voice for effect: from the slight hesitation
of soul-searching honesty to the chest tones of self-conviction;
from time to time an unexpected dash of humor; painting a
picture as reassuringly simple as it was deceptive) the more
clearly I could feel the threads being spun between my listeners
and me: stronger and stronger threads with which I pulled the
dough of gray faces and could entice lure lead and mislead. I
never wanted to be an actor and have hordes of spectators delirious at my feet. Quite the contrary. I've always despised actors
a little: their vanity their licentious self-effacement their vain-
glorious identification with their roles. But now I realized what
they craved: the relinquished egos of spectators starved for experience. They imbibed the egos of their admirers. Fed on them.
Fed on what turns rock stars into contemptuous gods. The here-
today-gone-tomorrow happiness of Carnival princes. The devilish seduction of demagogues.

Having gotten an inkling of all this in the drumming of rain
on the corrugated-iron roofs of P.O.W. camps in England
Wales and Scotland I returned with my own homemade gospel:
steer clear of the overly soulful! Hate your neighbor as you hate

yourself—that is: until you're ready to dismiss him with a shrug. Beware of his soul and yours. Don't be seduced into loving him. Love of your neighbor will make you lie and perhaps even commit more serious offenses.

During my tenure as free-lance contributor to the evening program at the North West German Radio Network one of my major short-lived accomplishments was a seven-part series of eighty-minute segments devoted to National Socialism. I owed the assignment to the intervention of Jürgen Schüddekopf whom I'd taken by storm with my enthusiasm. I'd declared that now—now and not a moment later! (it was 1947)—we would take the past by the horns: soon it would be too late to get it to yield up that atmosphere you get in the interstices between realities which are home to the irrational. Those underlying strands of reality that disintegrate so quickly that historians can't register them but that nonetheless contain precisely what makes actual occurrences "real." It was beginning to be too late for such undertakings. Nearly two years had passed since the end of the nightmare. A general unease could still be felt. Hanging in the air as the echoes of Ceauşescu's dictatorship in Romania did so many decades later: the present moment appropriating the horrors of the past. The situation in Germany was worse than ever. And the reasons for it were in danger of being misidentified. Someone had to say what bad reality had preceded the present bad dream.

Speaking in favor of the project was my first choice as a collaborator. Herbert Blank had (as he himself toothlessly put it) "experienced the thing from its first beginnings": starting with the days when the germ cell of the movement had met in a petit-bourgeois apartment in Munich and a handful of Party-minded conspirators proclaimed Adolf Hitler—installed on the black white-buttoned oilcloth parlor sofa—"drummer of the movement." (Not without an ironic exchange of glances among the schemers who had made him their spokesman because of his "idiotic fanaticism" and whom he a few years later as Führer of eighty million Party members and fellow travelers was to keep under his black leather thumb.) The second pillar on which I propped my plan was Dr. Elef Sossidi: historian military scientist cosmopolitan and—as a Germanized Greek— a man who enjoyed a profound knowledge of the German psyche. (Self-knowledge is rare.) An incomparably thorough digger and a rare exponent of the ups and downs in the Zeitgeist he brought a quality of transparency to Blank's lively anecdotal descriptions and took the edge off their furious bias with his scientifically skeptical distance. Backed by these two along with a horde of eyewitnesses I set about feeding the eternally ravenous dragon's brood of microphones with scraps plucked from the chaos of world-historical developments. These were eventually broadcast to no noticeable effect (predictably): sent out into the void of rubble-strewn lots and Nissen huts where the inhabitants in a half-stupor steeped in the miasma of hunger edema were much less likely to be moved by these events of the past than today's television viewers are by live broadcasts of up-to-the-minute world history. (Though ever since colleague Proust everyone knows that vicarious experience of the past moves the soul more deeply than direct experiences in the here and now.)

We wrapped up our first six programs—on Nazi ideology and its origins; promise and seduction; the rise and perversion of the nationalist movement and its influence on German history—successfully (or so we thought; in truth they were amateurish and botched). Nothing was shown tendentiously. Level-headed presentation of corroborated facts. Antiseptic analyses. *Sine ira et studio.* No commentary—whenever possible. (What we were presenting was horrible enough in its own right.) The last program was devoted to Adolf Hitler himself. And of course this time too we set about our work with the utmost conscientiousness. Utterly without prejudice. (Hee hee!)

Fair. ("Let's give the bastard the benefit of the doubt.") Nothing that might have spoken in his favor was omitted. And everything pointed to nothing other than an absolutely horrifying mediocrity (a conclusion that has since been oft repeated in misleading ways). From a genealogical investigation into the Hitler family tree unto the seventh generation (which showed nothing that offered even the hint of an explanation for the extraordinary quality of this one member) to a horoscope commissioned from experts (the stars too were helpless to explain the lack of proportion between human predisposition and superhuman achievement) to the ostensible supposed possible probable educational influences (though not mentioned in *Mein Kampf*) on the "young ringleader" and adult malingerer—we took into consideration everyone and everything that might have contributed to the rise of the person in question above the realm of the average (drawing as everyone knows a blank—scholars of the era are still feeling their way in the dark). Insufficient talent to offer the germinating love of power the refuge of art. Below average in every respect. Everything emanating the fustiness of low birth and niggardly education. Intellectual malformation via trashy novels rabble-rousing talks pamphlets picked up on the street cheap brochures eavesdropped barroom discussions. The biography of a street-corner loiterer: lousy food and flophouses his character-building milieu; life in the trenches street fights in the slums and beer-hall demagogy giving a final polish.

We tried to get ourselves off the hook with daring feats of intellectual sleight of hand. Boldly we declared that the meteoric flight by which this underling had become the Führer who led the German people straight to catastrophe was in fact not all so extraordinary. Quite the contrary—if you took the historical context into account. If you took the items one by one and peeled off their crust of legend the causal links among them appeared natural and logical. (Musil's historian.) What was surprising about the rise of this arrogant popinjay returned from the steel-storming front in 1918 armed with his dogs' whip and artistic forelock shading his fanatical gaze (this "stigmatized aging bellhop" as colleague Fritz Reck-Malleczeven once described him with unsurpassed accuracy)? What was surprising about his rise to become Führer and Chancellor of the Third Reich a so-called cultured nation? Nothing. From 1919 to the best months of the Weimar Republic the few confidence-inspiring figures who had preceded him had had far less of the charisma the Zeitgeist demanded. The Zeitgeist wanted (and got) mediocrity. As for the cultured nation: perhaps it was precisely the middle classes' humanistic education that paved the way for this upstart: after all both before and after the Great War classicism had remained a romantic ideal and every student had been spiritually armed with images of heroic national tribunals whose acts of violence were portrayed as the finest and most glorious in any country's history. Besides this rise from nothingness was in perfect keeping with the Americanist mythology that was all the rage at the time (according to which every paperboy enjoyed a fair chance of becoming a millionaire or president; in the down-and-out Europe of the inflation years this represented an auspicious bit of eschatology). Adolf Hitler then was "nothing more" than the self-made man who rose from the gutter to prosperity—tailored to fit the epoch. He was also a very lucky dog who was borne aloft by every ebb and flow of Zeitgeist sentiment—he didn't miss a one! (And it must be said he had extraordinary talent as a rider of those waves: no gentle rippling of collective emotion beneath the winds of the age was too slight for him not to turn it to advantage.)

But what sort of a person was it who could exploit these circumstances so effectively at the expense of millions of dead and crippled mutilated maimed survivors and their descendants? Adolf Hitler the man? Was he really "nothing" but an unscrupulous adventurer borne aloft by events of the time?

The last installment was over. Elef Sossidi and Herbert Blank quickly ran off to recover from the strain of working with so much distasteful and difficult material. Even the technicians left looking disgruntled. (How mixed their feelings were I cannot say.) I was alone in the studio surrounded by piles of the Nazi literature that our British controllers usually kept under lock and key but had given us for use in our series. Suspended in the vacuum between release and exhaustion I flipped through a photo album entitled *The Führer at the Front*. The usual: gunsmoke-blackened mud-plastered infantrymen ascetic faces beneath too-large steel helmets cheering their revered visitor from bomb-cratered flak-pocked shit-oozing holes in the ground. Mere lads awkward in oversized uniforms their starved cheeks flushed with pride as they receive the Iron Cross from *his* hand. Endless convoys snaking through the Kirgiz Steppe filing past *him* en route to their own destruction: eyes fixed on *him* in the worshipful slavishness of dogs. Nothing new. Though at the same time so strange one can't cease to be amazed: no doubt much the same thing went on from Alexander the Great to Napoleon. Why?

Aha: an utterly incomprehensible image. The complete General Staff is assembled around him. No naïve greenhorns these. Not born cannon fodder. Not obsequious lackeys faithful unto death. Not mindless subservients. This is the cream of Germany's military forces. Equal to any other elite group on earth in intelligence knowledge mental discipline self-confidence critical stance . . .

and they hang on his lips as though he were proclaiming a new gospel. By rights they ought to despise him. Ought to have bumped him off long ago: he is meddling destructively in their work. As a general he is a catastrophic failure. A bad joke. A fool. A dilettante devoid of conscience. And they gaze at him transfixed as though he were bringing them news of their own salvation.

I realized we hadn't understood a thing. With our questions our analyses our chatter we had missed the mark the real thing. What was the real thing? I was stumped. Once again I found myself falling back on that worn-out makeshift explanation: the demonic. Which could not be seen in any of the pictures no matter how long and hard one stared. The inhuman. The monster's "negative charisma": the undertow sucking people's egos from them like the magnetic mountain in the fairy tale sucking the nails from passing ships. And consolidating them in a single monstrous collective superego.

As they reclined at their leisure suddenly one of the water porters approached, kissed the hand of Ahmed al-Danaf and said to him: "Here you sit peacefully as the water flows at your feet, and do not know what has taken place."

—FROM THE FOUR HUNDRED AND FORTY-EIGHTH
OF THE *THOUSAND AND ONE NIGHTS*

By the end of my few days at the Cologne Carnival I had developed an honest affection (in my own way) for the three men of the Prince-Virgin-Peasant triumvirate. Their courage moved me. I admired the unflagging persistence with which they lived out their fantasies: though—alas!—for all too short a time. I regretted for the sake of our film that climatic inclemencies had nipped Shrove Monday in the bud this year (as other inconveniences doubtless would in years to come: a Gulf War?

other world-historical events?) but the thought of the trio made me regret it all the more. They would not see their life's blossom at the peak of its full-bloomed glory. Canceling Shrove Monday robbed them of the apotheosis of their sovereignty over the Carnival madness. Of their roles as saviors. No exorcism. The absurd was not ennobled as the grotesque nor the monstrous as the laughable; no unfettered exaggeration erasing denying ridiculing reality and thus offering liberation from it. None of the orgiastic laughter driving out the demon. Carnival is a product of folk wisdom devoid of sentimentality. It lets its fetishes vanish through trapdoors when their roles have been played. These three stars were extinguished with no fuss and bother.

Still these three brave souls gave me several valuable insights. Nothing earth-shattering (except perhaps that the gospel of laughter still hasn't had its Sermon on the Mount) but many amusing trifles. For example the meaning of pomp: showy splendor. What a serious business this playfulness is (a good seventy thou for a fool's getup). Anthropologists tell of clans in the tropical rain forests with a special way of waging war: all year long they hone their skills manufacturing useless objects of incomparable beauty; then assemble on a predetermined day to show off the fruits of their labors; then throw them onto a pile one after the other and burn them. Whoever can show *and destroy* the most beautiful objects is the winner. (A conception of art without the Great Fetish Art?) I began to understand the meaning of the royal robes the ermine the crowns tiaras scepters thrones and all the other showy splendors of the Old World: symbols of an order that left room for playfulness. For imagination. Irrationality. Lovely illusions in which power plays at being powerful. I realized what the ascetic uniforms worn by Comrades Lenin Stalin Mao and their minor imitators were really expressing. Anonymous power. The merciless rigor of abstract order. Ruthless will to manufacture an absolutely ideal world. An order with no room for playfulness. Without imag-

ination. Without irrationality (though not without artistic pro-
clivities). Without laughter.

The brave triumvirate in Cologne shifted the world back into
place for me on their hinges of reality and illusion. They turned
illusion into translucent reality—and revealed reality's illusory
character. When the Prince allowed himself to be borne aloft
on the roars emanating from thousands of black mouth orifices
in the gray dough of his worshippers he could sense the devilish
offer being made him. Sense that he could consolidate this wave
of love—this wave of soulfulness—within himself lead it and
mislead it at will. He could taste power's temptations. But as
a fantasy creature he was distanced from this power. His role
gave abstract form to this make-believe. Dispersed the satanic
seductiveness of the illusion created by its costume. The splendor of his regal fool's robes pointed to the symbolism of his
masquerade. Power burning itself out in illusion.

And this brave trio was prepared to relinquish its splendor
without regret. It was still painful (one can't say this often
enough) that Shrove Monday had been canceled. No reckless
waves of laughter would burst from the thousands of black
mouth holes and crash over the tumultuous throng of maskers
like the myriad-voiced song of the frogs of Băneasa. After a
few sporadic outpourings of merriment in beer halls factories
festival halls the people of Cologne would go back to the drab
gray of their everyday lives. The streets of this city of elves and
St. Ursula's eleven thousand virgins would once more fill with
the lava flow of vehicles and fission-fungus lives. Rabelais and
Brueghel would remain safely tucked away in libraries and museums. And the demons would once more be broken down into
individual selves single I's: captives of reality and bound by
reality's spell.

When the work of Prince Virgin Peasant went on so far past
midnight that the evenings all blurred together (and the days
along with them) I sat in the luxurious Mercedes and let the

214

monologue of the fleet owner break over me; and held a Sparkette in my arms with her head on my shoulder. The Sparkette
was not part of the triumvirate's entourage. She was one of the
dancers specially engaged by one of the numberless clubs that
devote themselves to Carnival merriment year after year and
do so with the same zeal with which their members (as my
informant put it) "pursue their professional lives." That is: with
the austere seriosity of the middle-class German elite. The Sparkette had been chosen from a large pool of applicants. The most
important qualification: she could do acrobatic dance. The next
prerequisite was a measure of social polish. The Sparkette was
to be friendly witty and at the same time reserved. Reserved
though not too reserved for the Carnival season's somewhat
relaxed mores. But there was a line she was never to cross. A
respectable kiss was just right for a miss. But beyond that:
nothing doing. The Sparkette came from a good family and
was studying music theory at the university. Her liking for
acrobatics was a sportive one. Besides which it was a good way
to supplement her allowance. And of course it was an honor
to be chosen to represent a Carnival club. A memory to last a
lifetime.

The dancers' costumes varied according to the color schemes
of each Carnival club. All of them had a touch of Frederick the
Great military spiff about them from the waist up; below things
took a more Russian turn with short stand-up skirts and red
ankle boots. The headgear topping off the identical braided wigs
varied from three-cornered hats to felt tumors representing Napoleonic bearskin caps. The task of the Sparkette—like that of
Their Madnesses—was to create atmosphere. A dancing duet
—the Sparkette had a partner—was one of the various offerings
(soapbox orators comedians choral groups soloists group
dances) designed to while away the time before the appearance
of the royal trio and to build up suspense. The Sparkette's solo
was the high point. An act of heraldry as it were: a final apothe-

osistic proclamation of the longed-for epiphany of Prince Virgin Peasant. A medley of acrobatic feats fit for a circus: jumps whirlwind pirouettes splits handstands and daredevil poses bore witness to the dancer's tremendous skill and drew thunderous applause.

The Sparkette in my arms with her weary head on my shoulder was twenty-three years old: just two years younger than my eldest granddaughter. She performed five nights a week for six weeks in a row for a total of seventy appearances. She had gotten through two-thirds of them but she had reached the limits of her endurance. The Sparkette was showing signs of fatigue. My friend the convoy director had taken her under his wing. After the last evening performance she was allowed to ride in the Prince's limousine and when His Madness had been delivered to his hotel my friend drove the Sparkette home. He and I both agreed that we had grandfatherly responsibilities toward this weary girl. While he chattered away in the front seat I offered the Sparkette warmth and a place to prop her head in the back. The girl's thick blond braids were real. Her young body was firm and elastic. Her strenuous dancing had left her sweaty with the sweat of youth. A "fresh clean scent" such as one reads of in newspaper ads.

The Sparkette trusted me immediately. She said I reminded her—no: not of her father or grandfather but of an actor. "In the most beautiful movie I ever saw. The man was a bus driver in Monte Carlo and had to give up his job because he'd had a heart attack. He stakes the compensation money at the casino and breaks the bank and with his winnings he buys himself a loose woman whom he wants to bear his child. But since he thinks he's too ugly he takes her to Italy to look at paintings so that the baby in her womb will be beautiful. And he is so sweet and kind to her that after a while she really falls in love with him. And he dies while he's waiting in the hospital for her child to be born." She's talking about a film made by my

friend Géza von Radvànyi: *L'Etrange Désir de Monsieur Bard.*
Made in 1953. The actor who played the poetical bus driver
was Michel Simon. The Sparkette hastened to assure me that I
was not quite as ugly as he was but at least as kind and sweet.
And with that her young head settled on my collarbone with
a sigh. My chin lay propped on the part in her blond hair. The
convoy leader went on monologuing at us:

". . . You say you write books. Well I haven't read any of
them you'll have to excuse me folks like me don't have time
for things like that. All the entertainment folks like me can
afford is a bit of TV in the evenings so as not to lose touch with
the world. It's the best way to keep informed. Especially about
all those terrible things. Cruel things. Ugly things. Makes more
of an impression in the mass media. But it's depressing. Well
you know sometimes it feels as though the whole world with
all its cruelty is being loaded on our backs like the man from
Atlas Travel with the globe I'm sure you've seen it. Didn't use
to be like that. Used to be everyone minded his own business
and had plenty on his hands as it was and now it's as if you're
supposed to worry about everything that's going on all over
this shitty planet. Every little thing that has nothing to do with
you: people starving in Biafra and the atomic bomb and that
the Prince of Wales broke his arm playing polo and all the Stasi
spying in the East. They say we're living in a democracy. And
at the same time when you think about it you can't even influence the garbage collection. People like Kohl and Bush and
Gorby and whatever they're called act like they could control
how things go. That's right: taxes! Ha ha! Taxes they know
how to dish out. That's one thing they can do for sure. Even
when they've promised not to. As for me personally . . ."

I personally have taken the Sparkette in my arms and am
conferring with my body. How curious it is that this much-
tormented snipped-apart variously patched and provisionally
stitched-up sack of skin and not much hair filled with spongy

bones and weary flesh should still be home to certain stirrings as though it were independently capable of memory: as though it had not yet been fully pacified; not yet quite filled with the tranquillity that comes with the peaceful evening of life. Without bitterness. Without regrets. With the deceptive distance of natural alienation. What was it that once upon a time had held me so peremptorily in its grip? It had become unreal. As though I'd spent three-quarters of a century of physicality pursuing something that hadn't been real and now my old bones are unwilling to accept this lie. After many thousands of days of life they still demand their due. Well versed in the bazaar of quotidian reality they keep piping up with demands. I don't want to pry too hard into the authenticity of my body's unexpected response upon feeling young flesh in close proximity: isn't it simply an echo of past stirrings? A ghostly voice from a bygone era? One thing I know for certain: whether real or feigned—it belongs to my body and not to me. *I* am no longer one with it; I've already stepped half out of it; long since bade it farewell: when I am aware of it at all I observe it with scientific interest (and with the merciless gaze of the irony my being is steeped in). Grimly I observe its disintegration: how its muscles disappear its skin puckers its bones grow brittle. I feel no enmity toward it for bringing me only torments these days and no pleasure and calling attention to itself only with this pain and that failure this inadequacy that threat. Nor do I bear it a grudge for having held me in its power all my life. Despotic in the days when juices were still flowing; their alchemy made me perform the strangest most illogical acts commit the most shameful deeds. (And today with its increasing disintegration it is free to extinguish my life flame at any moment.) Naturally I didn't always see its power over me as despotic. At times I was proud of how well turned out it was and thought it at my disposal ready to serve my wishes even in excess of its endurance. Youthful days in which my body was *me* signified *me* acted felt pleasure and suffered as *me*. Distant days in which the pride I took in it—in the *me* that was both of us—fanned out like a peacock's tail. Then again the occasional failure given my excessive demands signified a metaphysical defeat and nearly brought me to the desperate point of laying hands on it with lethal intent. (A pimple on one's nose is enough to do this, says colleague Stendhal.)

My old body. It has played its role gamely. The things I could lay on the scales if I had to give an account of the weight or insubstantiality of my earthly existence! It willingly performed its duties: procreation and destruction. And what account do I owe my body? Have I treated it as the hundreds of health-promoting rules of conduct disseminated via television radio daily weekly monthly periodicals prescribe? Have I spared it by leading a temperate life preserved its youth by doing calisthenics? Or ruined it with gluttony and debauchery? Overtaxing it insanely when sports were seen as an essential part of existence and then in recognition of its mediocrity neglecting it altogether? Perhaps a form of navel-gazing other than the literary sort I've chosen—one devoted entirely to the body and its spiritualization—would have made it an instrument of the intellect on a higher level; but I saw it through an epoch-embezzler's rationalistic eyes as mechanically operable matter and nothing more . . .

Idle considerations now. Now it is too late. Now I can no longer make it serve my will. I control it so little that I can no longer recognize its memories as my own. I am no longer what gives it meaning its lord and master. I am no more than a rent-paying tenant. Subletting from my own decaying physis. Yet still a plaything of its alchemy.

The Sparkette in my warm arms had her eyes closed and was breathing peacefully. She might have been asleep. And it happened that she raised her young face toward mine in a sleeper's gesture. It was a pretty little face of the usual sort: the face of a fresh blond girl of typically west-of-the-Rhine at-peace-with-the-world composure (she would have been to colleague Goethe's taste). And once again I had to tell myself it is the face of a woman in which the Tempter sets his traps. Certainly one body answers to the call of another (even mine; though at my age only with memories). But the mind does not engage until one looks into another person's eyes: only there does one find what my colleague Chamfort names—along with the contact of two skins—as the second original component of love: the exchange of two fantasies.

It happened that the Sparkette lifted her face to mine as if in sleep and now it lay in horizontal surrender beneath my gaze; and I understood that—perhaps in a dream—she was offering her lips to me. The unpainted lips of a young girl. (The moment her last performance had ended the Sparkette had cleared the garish makeup from her face.) The lips of a blonde: pale pink voluptuously swollen like the tails of two shrimp placed side by side (from the breakfast table at the family hotel). Aesthetically in accord with the blond lashes that—closed in sleep—appeared to point to them yet in a sort of depraved contrast to them: the licentious rosy tumescence of this pair of lips mocked the chasteness of the lowered lashes. My imagination took wing. I bent down over the shrimp tails and gently pressed a grandfatherly kiss upon them. The Sparkette replied with an affectionate murmur: a faint nasal meow that expressed more her half-slumbering luxuriation than pleasure at the touch of my lips; but at any rate seemed to find the conjunction of the two agreeable. I pressed a second gentle kiss on the pair of shrimp. "Don't be so lazy!" the Sparkette exclaimed energetically and seized the back of my head like a handball and pressed it against her parting lips. As if on command our tongues entwined (snakes' mating ritual).

The delicious shock and wave of heat that instantly swept

through me were strictly the business of my memory-steeped body. I—I mean *I*—reacted in a different way altogether. Alarm bells were going off. My qualms—I am ashamed to admit— had almost nothing to do with marital fidelity. The first shrill warning: if it were actually to come to a serious erotic scuffle would my body keep the promise it had made with its feeble response to this call from the past? The second: if the scuffle became intense and led to a showdown in the Sparkette's digs (or my own virginal room at the family hotel) wouldn't the poor child in the bloom of her smooth-skinned youth in the end find it unnatural to copulate with a Methuselah (an eco- logical desecration as it were despite my repertoire of routine services or perhaps all the more so because of them)? My imag- ination conjured up a few scenarios out of colleague Sade's *One Hundred Twenty Days of Sodom*: pushing sexuality (embarrassing enough in its own right) to the point of appearing ugly or even unbearably grotesque. Third (though not last): wouldn't such a conclusion destroy my chances of looking back fondly on the tender father-child relationship implied in these warmth-seeking half-hour cuddles on icy January Carnival nights? At my age one collects different trophies from those of the so-called prime of manhood.

Though I did take pleasure in the mollusk-soft vitality behind the shrimp lips. For a brief moment I and my body were in harmony and I felt profound gratitude for this reconciliation and devoted only one ear to making sure the fleet owner in the front seat continued his patter:

". . . now that Saddam Hussein has dumped this load of crap on us right when we had our hands full with our brothers and sisters in the East we have only ourselves to blame. Even the Yanks can't point the finger at anyone but themselves. Eight years of supporting the man any way they could so that he'll keep the Persians away from the Gulf and now he's a criminal because he wants to get there himself. Two-faced hypocrisy that's all it is. That's just the way the world's put together these days—"

but then the door of the car was wrenched open and Prince Carnival stuck in his exhausted head beneath its bell-dangling fool's cap. His gum-flashing put-them-in-the-mood smile was frozen on his face as though a mask. And I gave the Sparkette grandfatherly goodbye kisses on the tip of her nose and both eyes and toddled off to join the television crew in the mouse-gray Volkswagen bus at the end of the convoy. Prince Carnival my savior. It was three in the morning after my fourth night in icy Cologne and I was looking forward to my virginal bed at the family hotel and the generous breakfast the next morning—the morning of the day that was to bring me home to my Tuscan tower.

Hereupon Nuzhat al-Zaman said to her brother Sharrkan and the four kadis: "Here ends the second farewell of the first chapter."

—FROM THE FOUR HUNDRED AND THIRTIETH
OF THE *THOUSAND AND ONE NIGHTS*

The year is progressing. Summer is scorching our meadows yellow. Here the summer sun scorches rather than smoldering in greenhouse humidity as in India or as in the fruit-heavy summers of my enduring blue yellow red homeland (blue sky yellow grain red for love's heartblood). If things there really did resemble that fairy-tale land I sang into existence the air trembled with heat just as it does here; but nothing burned. The meadow grass stood hip-high. With each gust of wind the thicket of stalks bent their heads in histrionic undulation: making obeisances to the darkly gathering clouds in a sky that promised the blessing of rain. Afterward the blades would right themselves and nestle with a scatter of drops against the slender stalks topped with panicles trembling delicate as radiolarians at the once more resplendent sky. Cornflowers and poppies gleamed in the green carpet. How wonderfully soothing was the warm shadow the woods cast on it. (The woods of summer: the echo of the cuckoo's cries not sufficient to scope out its breadth.)

And here in my Tuscan tower I am beset by the question: What am I doing here? The shadows are as sharp as silhouettes cut from black paper. The summer its own skeleton. The sky is blue like a whetstone. The sun sharpens its knives on it. The cypresses are black torches flanking the sacrificial altar of the stony earth. The grape leaves are thickly coated with dust: the thirsty find no succor here. (Even the language is merciless in its inexorable clarity though it doesn't take much emotion on the part of the speaker to make it sound operatic.) They say the beauty of Tuscany lies in its noble poverty. (The butcher in our village of barely six thousand souls drives three high-powered cars; the hairdresser—daughter of a former *mezzadri* and married to a cottage industrialist—keeps a yacht docked at Viareggio.) I gaze out exercising my old eyes. When B. asks me if I love Italy I reply with feeling that I lost my homeland and found a fatherland. (The pathos comes over well in Italian.) And it is perfectly acceptable to see one's fatherland clearly yet love it all the same. I was like a plant in barren soil. How paradoxical that I should thrive so well here where the soil is anything but rich. But it is old soil. Rich with ancestral bones. The fine ritual of *humare* has made it fruitful. I adore Italians. They are my brothers and sisters. Their unspoiled humanity brings me back to the trust in the world I felt as a child. Let me attach a green white red banner to my coat of arms. From my tower window I can look out over the hills of the Arno Valley all the way to the Pratomagno and feel: This is my country. Yet wonder: What am I doing here?

What Am I Doing Here? is the title of Bruce's last book. Published posthumously. A collection of short pieces. Pastiches. Episodes from the life of a globe-trotter. A few marvelous interviews. Chatwin the journalist. *The world (Life; Reality) is like this because it presents itself to me as to all other people.* Preserved with deep-freeze precision. Exemplarily disciplined pen. Glass-clear. Masterfully brief. The work of an O.W.A. Curiously sexless. Knife-sharp intelligence and sublime tact that might make one think of a virago. Hermaphroditic. Seen together with his eternal youth (achieved by early death) these characteristics take on a godlike aspect. They remind me how mortal I am. A garbage dump of lived-out lifetimes.

B. is clever enough not to poke around in it too much. In particular she avoids my German intermezzo. (What did I do there?) When the subject of Germany comes up she bristles. She has no pleasant memories in this regard. Wartime experiences endured as a child (soldiers tramping through her parents' house welcomed by her Fascist stepmother her father off fighting in Africa). Growing up with the legend of heroic resistance. *(Bella ciao ciao ciao!)* A life in countries where the people are not sympathetic to Germans. And then tormented by the gnawing suspicion that I might be more German than I want to admit. Certainly I'm far from denying what's German about me: the language. I argue its splendors to B. One of mankind's grandest creations. Its words with unplumbed meaning. Its grammar a world order. Even melodious (except when barked brusquely by Germanicized Wends and Slovintzi). And this language separates me from B. She doesn't speak it never learned it. It is the dimension of me that has remained foreign to her even uncanny.

She can know what I write only indirectly through translations; until then it remains abstract.

Moreover Germany is the setting of that portion of my biography that determined my German image. My ignominious yesterday.

All it draws from me now is a weary smile when I think of how I myself once locked horns with it. My encounter with Otto von Hapsburg brought home to me what I was up against. It's my *image* that's at stake. My German image (not the only one I have). Faced with His Imperial Highness in the guise of a professional conference participant this image—resurrected from the garbage dump of my consciousness—kept me from posing a not-too-idiotic question that might have ended that crescendoing silence after His Imperial Etc.'s lecture and the imminent realization that we were about to send brightly iridescent soap bubbles sailing out the window of the steamship company and over the Danube region. All right: I'd missed my chance. Ludicrous to think it might have been an opportunity to say something (or cull something from His Imperial Highness's reply) with even trifling significance for me for my present my past my future life. For a vassal's pride in exchanging words with the sovereign it was three-quarters of a century too late. All the same I was haunted by the sense of a metaphysical falling short as though I had thoughtlessly forgotten a word that might have unlocked the universe; an "Open Sesame" to the meaning of my existence of all my deeds that would have disclosed itself to me had I only stood up to face that ordinary man radiating the aura of a long-gone Europe. Everyone there knew perfectly well who was standing before them: heir apparent to so-and-so-many kaisers' kings' princes' and dukes' crowns. A European myth with which I could feel certain ties. He would have been the emperor of my world (if . . . or rather: if not . . .). He would have linked me to my ancestors: living image of the

humare that had fertilized the soil of our culture over the centuries
. . . And so on.

But these are depth-psychological charades; anyone who gets
a kick out of cracking hollow nuts is welcome to try deciphering
them. ("Oedipus: motherfucker seeks father figure.") In more
trivial terms something occurred that presumably happens to
everyone at some point: you trip over a stumbling block and
get shaken back to consciousness: "Whoa there son! Where do
you think you're going? What are you doing here (or there) in
this marvelous world of historical events and Marlboro wide-
open spaces? Could it be you belong somewhere else altogether?
Could you be living your life in the wrong place with the wrong
goals letting life pass you by? Letting your ego pass you by?
Everything you might have been and are not . . ." And so on.

In short: I was confronted with myself. Through this encounter with my image.

*You have no doubt read in the great Book that this world is home not only
to men but also to the race that is known as spirits and djinns, who often
appear in human form.*

—FROM THE FIVE HUNDRED AND SEVENTIETH
OF THE *THOUSAND AND ONE NIGHTS*

The word "image" was not yet part of the German language
at the time when His Imperial Highness and I were born. Only
with the onset of Americanism did it (like so many others)
establish itself as a hybrid (like rabbits in Australia). In our

226

time—I dare to rub shoulders with H.I.H.—people were not masked by their images. They had reputations (the worse the better). And there were personalities: outstanding individuals of certain qualities and characters you would either love or hate in any case acknowledge. Nobody would try to build up for himself the reputation of being a personality. Nowadays everybody does. Every man woman and child has an image and ought to take pains to keep it in good working order: *for this is the reality of that person* regardless of what he or she thinks of it. Whether or not it's wrong; whether or not it corresponds to a given reality—it is part of the reality of CNN and Co. and the daily weekly monthly periodicals which is the only reality most human beings know: the only real reality. So be it! I who keep the harlequin suit of all my previous lives for around-the-house wear have no mere single image at my disposal but a whole handful. In the autocratic reality of the mass media I am a fictional version of myself—but it is *my* public reality. I have three of them (to name only the most important).

They come from three language zones. I live in all three simultaneously in a multiple present. Each is heralded by one of my books. Not in the chronological sequence in which they were written but according to the advent of these works in each linguistic realm. Since they have to be translated they appeared in temporal leaps that do not correspond to my biography. At various junctures and with quite different books I made my mark in the German Italian and Anglo-Saxon literary industries and each time showed the reading public a different face.

Whether it is my true face is another matter. For even an old man like myself is still in evolution. Particularly in his writing. The discrepancies between when the books were written and when they appeared—dates often separated by years—are enough to create anachronisms. My images fit the me currently inhabiting my tower more or less the way a too-short comforter covers an uneasy sleeper: while the distinctive head half-buried in pillows remains hidden from sight one can discern poking

227

out from beneath the bedclothes a shoulder here a leg there there an arm and perhaps a naked arse. In any case: since the most interesting thing about me—personally as well as literarily—are my exotic origins (less geographic than temporal: an alien in more than one epoch) I can categorize my three most important images according to my mythical blue yellow red banner. The first—as it were the blue stripe—is Anglo-Saxon.

In my mind I can hear the triumphant rejoicing of my (long since deceased) pseudo-English governesses. But my image in the Anglo-Saxon world was formed not by my linguistic abilities but rather by a novel written only partly in English. The title raised some eyebrows: *Memoirs of an Anti-Semite.* Though it isn't autobiographical and contains no more autobiographical elements than any other novel of a confessional character (I call them hypothetical autobiographies) people were and are quick to read it as genuine autobiography. The narrator is a man discreetly possessed of the courage of his convictions (with no intention of glossing over events and certainly without a trace of embarrassing remorse). Fit to appear in respectable society: a writer with good literary manners. (Colleagues Burckhardt and Hofmannsthal would have given an approving nod.) The subject—anti-Semitism: a word that calls to mind the most monstrous of the abominations of world history—is touchy. Doing it justice without calling in the artillery of the Apocalypse (giving entelechy a kid-glove treatment as it were: the tree in the seed) was a feat that found resonance among the largely unromantic Anglo-Saxons on both sides of the Atlantic. Ever since the eyes of the world were opened to the atrocities of Auschwitz Treblinka and so on people have been asking themselves the same question: How was such a thing possible? I undertook to show what child's play it was for such events to take place. Nothing more. With just a pinch of black humor. (What would the world be without it?)

So much for the man of letters as he appeared in that book. The picture of the man himself does not contradict this persona.

228

I'm always on my best behavior when I make an appearance in the Anglo-Saxon realm. Not as an artfully ideological down-at-heels bohemian. But not dressed in a Stresemann either. I don't appear to be wearing a costume when I appear in a double-breasted suit and a neatly knotted tie. My English is exotic but fluent and expressive. But for more than this I am grateful to my governesses of yesteryear who acquainted me at an early age with the totems and taboos of the Anglo-Saxon psyche and its paranoia. Only seldom do I offend against the tacit rules. In any case my identity as a "bloody foreigner" gives me certain liberties. (". . . they rely for communication on a warmer personal relationship than we English find necessary . . .") In short: my Anglo-Saxon image presents me as civilized upright cosmopolitan humorous and of artistic (socially valuable) substance. As such I might have faced up to Otto von Hapsburg without qualms. Unfortunately I had only my German image to offer him.

But before I get to this allow me to rearrange the color scheme of my mythical banner to give precedence to the red stripe of love. This love pertains to both my new and old homelands. In Italy my public image is based on my novel *An Ermine in Czernopol*. The book was fortunate in its date of birth here (books too stand under one star or another) which was just before the rediscovery of Eastern Europe. The Central Europe of the sunken Dual Monarchy in transfigured form. (Hapsburgland.) My book is about its legacy between the two (first) world wars. (All bad things come in threes.) Although it is anything but nostalgic it stirs up memories of great losses—an idea and an ideal. Czernopol is a legendary city of many cultures in which (to requote the immortal words of colleague Celan) "people and books lived." *Paradise Lost*. In this sense it is also a novel about the loss of childhood. In Italy it was received with great hospitality. Kindly reviewers brought in my colleagues Joseph Roth and Robert Musil by way of comparison. That's giving quite a generous estimate of my literary rank (though making me straddle the fence as it were). And then there's the impression I make in person: my appearance fits to a T the cliché of Dual Monarchy relic: rustic but with well-ironed creases. (Only my Imperial-and-Royal mustache has gone: the first of B.'s adjustments.) But the truly decisive thing is my social standing. Which I owe to B. Hereabouts (and not only here) B. is a luminary. I share in her light. Her countless admirers and friends have grown fond of me as well. I love Italy and Italians. The Italian origins of my name let me think of myself as their blood relative. My Italian too is exotic yet also fluent and rich in expressive potential. My stash of anecdotes such as one can expect to find (and generally does) in Central Europeans (this enchanted Bruce and irritates B.) assures me a prominent place in fireside chats. I am well liked; am considered charming and witty. A man with a cosmopolitan's polished joviality. Add to that my novelistic fame. With this persona as well I might have approached Otto von Hapsburg combining a proper degree of respect with self-confidence of my own. But as I've already noted . . .

Yellow is the color of envy. A German color. In the German-speaking world my epiphany occurred with *Maghrebinian Tales*. Roguish unabashed satire in the style of an Orientalizing Swift. Since their publication nearly half a century has elapsed. Meanwhile I have written a good dozen other books. They have about as much in common with *Maghrebinian Tales* as—here's another reach—colleague Hofmannsthal does with Roda Roda. Or Joyce with P. G. Wodehouse. But it's not such a rare thing for the name of an author to get stuck to one of his books in particular. In Germany my name is stuck to *Maghrebinian Tales*. People still read them. By interweaving a handful of old jokes anecdotes fairy tales fables to construct a make-believe Orient that mirrors our own Occident (*Maghreb* is Arabic for "sunset")

I managed to write a German classic. And thus created a personal memorial that corresponds in nearly every detail to the disreputable ignominious insolent sly-fox self-important swindlers who populate that satirical fairy-tale land. The Maghrebinian, *c'est moi*.

I won't try to deny I did my best to live up to this image. It was a dissolute era. The war had just ended and I was bursting with testosterone. Perhaps these aren't grounds enough to accuse me of all the picaresque amorality that can be filtered out of a collection of off-color jokes Hasidic and Sufi anecdotes and Balkan folklore. Oddly enough it was precisely this book that made me German. It created—by no means my intention—a complicity of winks and knowing nods between me and the readers of *Maghrebinian Tales* which gave them all the freedom to pound their paws on my shoulder and say "Hello there, old schlemiel!" This can be put down to a mix of unfortunate familiarity and a wish-fulfilling love for everything that's how one wants to be but doesn't dare. My later books permit no such identification. The German reading public was disappointed. My image became ambiguous like an out-of-register offset print. For this I have no one to blame but myself. As for the more serious failings I've had reason to blame myself for (and reproach myself for bitterly) the matter was settled in the intensive-care unit at Santa Maria Nuova. The absolution I granted myself may not be valid in the eyes of the Church. But it left me exhilarated with relief.

In such wild haste did they take flight that the shoes and sandals slipped from many a foot and many a head lost its loosely-wound turban.

—FROM THE SIX HUNDREDTH OF THE *THOUSAND AND ONE NIGHTS*

I was brought to the intensive-care unit many years ago after my first major operation. It was dramatic. No opportunity for a heightened sense of being alive preceded it; the need for surgery arose far too suddenly. No imagination–fueling curiosity; I had too much pain. The anesthesia was a welcome release—at least to begin with. They sliced me open took one horrified look and sewed me up again. A single glance at the malignant growth in my entrails (a side effect of earlier cobalt radiation treatment) sufficed to convince the surgeon that there was no point in tinkering further. He said as much to B. in a few blunt words. Cancer in a stage of voluptuous proliferation. (Even the seam up my abdominal wall later showed how unlikely my survival was judged to be: the intern assisting at a later procedure who daintily stitched up the scar in petit point—they'd had to slice it back open—called the work of his predecessor *"un lavoro di materassaio"*—the work of a mattress maker.) Nor was the anesthesiologist very scrupulous either. It isn't every day that a patient being wheeled out of the operating room bellows like a rutting stag. I can still hear my own voice reverberating from the corridor's walls and arched ceilings. Then B. took me in her arms and all was well again—for a while.

232

Even when it came to the follow-up treatments the staff of this luxurious (and very expensive) private Florentine clinic performed their duties perfunctorily. On the third day I was overcome with agitation. I tried to pull myself out of bed. I was gasping for breath. I broke out in a sweat heart pounding complained of heartburn. B. was at my side. She recognized the danger: a heart attack. The head doctor's unctuous display of sympathy did not placate her. Until you have seen B. in a crisis situation you cannot know the true meaning of energy determination competence. A scant half hour later I had been transferred from the luxury clinic to the intensive-care unit at venerable Santa Maria Nuova. (I have since become a frequent guest there for the treatment of the side effects of that first procedure.) So there I lay. Tubes sticking out of all my orifices (including a few newly created for the purpose). The many different apparatuses to which I was attached and the fluently technical demeanor of the doctors interns of both sexes attendants and nurses depersonalized the situation. These were not services being offered specifically to me but part of the institutional machine. Here I was not a private patient footing hefty bills who could lay claim to sanatorium-style amenities but merely a link in the process of a preprogrammed cure. The air of professional neutrality cultivated here was confidence-inspiring. Everything was carried out swiftly competently silently behind antiseptic masks and rubber gloves. I could surrender myself to the functioning of this meticulously regulated mechanism. The assembly line of medicinal progress was responsible for my survival.

Meanwhile however dramatic events were in progress in other spheres of my perception. My body was excruciatingly bisected. From the region of the diaphragm down it was paralyzed and heavy as the stone loins of the victims of magic spells in the *Thousand and One Nights*. The upper half was very much alive and racked with pain. And the two parts were like cities at war.

As in etchings of medieval sieges cannonballs flew back and forth along dotted lines and every one of them hit home. I suffered beneath the mutual enmity of these two cities. I suffered with open eyes for it was not a dream. It was reality experienced with wide-awake vigilance (though possibly in a dreamy magical light made by God knows what narcotics). The cannonballs of the enemy camps went right through me. The earth was churned up by them like the crater-pocked landscape of Flanders in the First World War (pictures of which I had consumed during my childhood in the agony of my great prescient curiosity). This Flanders was my body. Was me.

This geography differed from my mythological one. The Bukovina did not exist in it. I could not sing myself like a folksong. It was a moral battle and there was no mitigating circumstance for my being as I was. I had nothing to gild myself with. Not even a great misdeed. Only embarrassing trifles. Maghrebinian misdemeanors. Petty crimes for which I could not be convicted. Sadly they lacked both the charm and the humor of the Balkans. My blue yellow red mythology failed me. I had appropriated a myth not rightfully mine. I was without a homeland. The cannonballs of my two halves came from my wasted life. I'd let my ego pass me by and it had crashed into me with the full force of guilt.

What a holy fool! As if I didn't know how deviously the feeling of guilt was interwoven with every one of my fibers! Jesus Christ died on the Cross for me; but that He had to do so makes me one of the ones who nailed Him to it. Even when I was still a child the Ten Commandments trumpeted their accusations in my ears. I don't need to dig so deeply into the life of mortal man which has been shit to the brim with guilt. On all sides moral and ethical traps and snares. The ten-times-ten commandments of civilized social cohabitation begin with the obedient use of a child's chamber pot and end with contempt for

234

the *pappagallo*. One way or another you're guilty. My image: acquired amid the ruins of Germany. From the age of landsknechts. Me. I. My ego. Myself: an epoch-embezzling Simplicius Simplicissimus. Guiltily enslaved to dissolution in a dissolute world (which soon recast itself in respectably bourgeois terms: the triumph of the ladies' hats). I had been a roving mercenary in a war (variously waged by military or pseudo-peaceable means) that went on for more than thirty years. A baroque figure: fraudulently swaggering beribboned with falsehoods ornamented with forgeries decked out with stolen feathers. But this was over and done with—or so one would have thought. The sentence had been served. I did wicked things and failed to do good ones and realized that this was wrong. Some of these failings pursued me for years. Some still torment me today. You'd think by now I'd have done enough penance wouldn't you? Well that's easy to say. In the intensive-care unit I was confronted not with transgressions against the restored rules of the wearers of ladies' hats or the refreshed prohibitions of Christian ethics but plainly and simply with *Myself*.

Who I was I knew all too well. I knew each one of my past egos that I had shed like skins (as only a writer can who has spent his writing life in their service). Unrelenting navel-gazer. I had the whole motley assortment of my images within me; coming to terms with them was tricky. I wasn't taken in by my own logic when I told myself they were only what I was in the eyes of others and did not correspond to what I had really been ten twenty thirty or more years ago (and before and after and in between). I was in terrible simultaneity.

I existed in all my forms in ubiquitous time. A company of ragtag recruits who on command leap out of the ranks one by one to bellow their names. My name. It struck me with the full force of guilt. Alas! not with regret for one's actions or inactions that lets one look back with a sigh: "If only I'd known then what I know today!" My guilt did not exhaust itself in the memories of episodic failings. It drilled its way into the core of my being. I experienced a moral death by suffocation. All my images banded together to strangle me. There was nothing to balance the scales against my dissolution crudeness ignominy fraudulence false pretense and deceitful promise. Even—above all!—my speculation in literary prestige was nothing but blindness and self-deception. That I would one day exist only on paper—purified in printer's ink from the impurities of my earthly existence—did not acquit me of my own charges. I imagined Ugo Mulas photographing me from the Beyond: using a camera with the multidimensional technical capabilities they have there. All the good things all the unsavory things in me about me all at once. Without the "side effects" of biography. Including everything: all my virtuous strivings and all the deceits my successes and my failures. All my images superimposed without causality: yesterday's identity not to blame for today's; today's not effacing yesterday's: each existing in its own right. Each one a skin. Taken together they are a single rounded entity: the onion that is me.

If Ugo with his heavenly camera had photographed me in the intensive-care unit he would have produced quite a curious portrait. From the lunar landscape of Flanders within me a Golden Jerusalem emerged. The city of Florence was symbol of a new existence. It took its place between the two battling cities and brought their war to a standstill. (I never discovered to what therapeutic—or rather pharmaceutical—trick I owed this change in my condition.) This Golden Jerusalem was summoned into existence by a jubilant resolution in me: if I was what I was then henceforth I would be that all the more recklessly and relentlessly. Literarily as well as existentially. If I was a lout and a troublemaker then henceforth I would more than ever take pains to grate on people's nerves with my provocations. If I was a liar and cheat then henceforth I would even better lie and cheat. If I was guilt-laden I would wear this guilt

236

like a crown. I began to think about a book whose last pages I was to write one year later on the gurney while awaiting my next operation.

When B. was given permission to visit me she found me reading the newspaper. We couldn't help laughing: she was dressed from head to toe in antiseptic garb so as not to introduce germs into the intensive-care unit while I was holding a newspaper that had come from the street outside: my fingers gray with printer's ink. I was back in the world. Part of the world again.

"I must tell you," Sindbad said, "that after my return from my sixth voyage I put aside all thoughts of making any further journey; for my age was beginning to be against prolonged absences, and I had no further desire for new adventures after the dangers which I had already run."
—FROM THE SIX HUNDRED AND FIFTIETH OF THE *THOUSAND AND ONE NIGHTS*

*D*efinitely it's a good feeling to know you stand in this world absolved of guilt. Even if you can't get rid of the sneaking suspicion that in truth you're out of place. Of course there are all sorts of marvelous things you wouldn't want to miss. Not just Carnival time in Cologne. In India too for example. A faith-obsessed land where no cleft tree trunk no concave stone no hole in the earth lacks its altar to some pagan god with a few blossoms a sputtering tallow candle an offering scrimped from a handful of hungry mouths; a land (what am I saying: a continent) a gigantic chunk of the earth's ocean-washed crust swarming with hundreds of clans millions and trillions of human creatures born naked and at the mercy of cruel Nature's iniquities; scourged by fears thirsting for miracles bowing down fervent with hope before hundreds of gods idols fetishes (primordial metaphors for the inexplicable crux of all existence; good for producing flights of fancy and insignificant when it comes to the transcendent mysteries of being); a grotesque tableau of images each a vehicle for never-before-divulged enigmas; a bizarre otherworldly realm whose exoticism is a constant temptation to overstep the bounds of the accessible world . . .

To B. I said: I can't get over it. The horrifying fertility of life on this continent where the eruption of forms every hour minute second drives frightened people to the most murderous asceticism the most ecstatic self-denial self-castigation self-mutilation deities born of fear of an all-devouring Creation . . . Could she my beauty-thirsty companion on life's journey see this in the figures we encountered everywhere: the religious fanatics both wild and mild: naked shaggy-haired ash-bestrewn mud-encrusted needle-pierced or blossom-garlanded—striding toward us fragrant with incense beneath the silver hair of inconceivably pure saints. Could she my cathedral figure—whom I know better than I know myself—could she see what a monstrous hoax this panoply of gods was (like all others) on a continent where the people are gentle and lovely as flowers or dissolute and ugly as devils and each accepts the other the way he is *because he is* and is the way he is; and where in the name of faith unlimited tolerance is cynically reconciled with the most brutal tyranny the most ignominious greed the most merciless cruelty—in short with the *world as it is;* and the deities behind it offer only an ironic reflection of this earthly world in a monstrous shadow play that promises the mortals bowed down in worship before it no other release than nothingness at the end of an eons-long road of return and re-return to the mad chaotic

238

copiously spawning and ruthlessly annihilating realm of the Great Goddess Kali.

Why journey to distant lands? I say to B. Isn't there enough to see right here at home? For example the world travels of the Holy Father to preach obedience *urbis et orbis* and praise the *Creator*'s wisdom while exhaust fumes from motor vehicles wither the last green leaf on the avenue trees and crumble the angels (long since faceless) in their cathedral niches. The hydrogen bomb might speed up the process; cement is a slower way to lay waste to the planet. Be of good cheer! I say to B. Your artist husband is no cynic. On the contrary: it takes piety to keep your eyes open as I do and gaze at all there is to see. Requires belief in a Creator of genius. He invented the perpetual-motion machine: an eternal play of becoming and ceasing to be. One can't exist without the other. Each participates in the other determines it brings it about. Neither may be omitted. *His* law is inexorable causality. Even violations of this law produce causality. The universe is a toy of unfathomable perfection and our task within it is a proud one. It takes us beyond our earthly existence to a cosmic realm: destroyers of the planet. Man was created to bring the *Creator*'s game to outer space. Humbly we are to say in reverence: *"His will be done!"*

I say this to my wife to give her courage. Liberate her. Certainly not cynically. For of course I wouldn't leave her at the brink of the abyss without pointing out the rainbow on which she can cross to the other side. But I'm afraid she doesn't need me to point it out. It was drummed into her as a child that Promethean rebellion against the inexorable divine order is man's birthright. And that he has a number of escape routes to choose from. The hermit's life isn't the only one. (Where? In Tuscany? In the ashram of Pondicherry?) No: he is permitted amusing games. First there's thought. Then the more riveting Faustian game: the quest for knowledge. And the best plaything of all? Technology! (The stickiest of the Creator's lime twigs:

biricchino biricchino! His most refined method for achieving *His* goal: the more successful man is at perfecting the world the more irreversibly he destroys it.) And last but not least: the delightful game of Art! Not just producing but consuming it as well: worshipping the marvelous "side effects" of post-Promethean rebellion against the world's imperfections and the struggle to transcend it; man's superhuman strivings to build a more beautiful more perfect world. The world of beautiful representations: better crafted more moderate nobler than Nature's shoddy work. A world of order. And justice. Space achieves moderation through geometry. Time is structured by music dance the enchanting angels' tongues of my colleagues the poets . . . and so on down the gamut of muses.

Who am I to scorn the devotion with which mankind has set about erecting monuments to *Him* in *His* infinite manifestations: the lion- and griffin-guarded temples of Babylon and Egypt the light-flooded marble poems of the Hellenes the dancing-god-encircled idol-encrusted monster temples of India the thousand-columned giant crabs of mosques from Kairouan to Isfahan the Mayas' Cyclopean stairways to heaven the sacred gardens of China the sand symbols of the monk priests of Kyoto; and of course our own splendid cathedrals with their stony population of apostles saints kings queens and all manner of crumbling angels in their niches: all of them old venerable patinated. (Artistic value increases with age: God is most beneficial to the tourist industry when the tokens of *His* worship date back to times when belief could still have a clear conscience.)

And how could I fail to note that the sweetest of all fictions we enlist against the bestiality of God's world is love. I often speak of its antagonist: hate. (The subject of love has been rehashed too often.) I maintain that even hatred is Janus-faced: both ugly and handsome. I call evil hate the worst of the original sins devised by God: it's been an intrinsic part of human nature since caveman days and haters still rage with undiminished fury

240

against anyone different: the enemy by virtue of darker or lighter skin a longer shorter flatter pointier crooked saddle-shaped bulbous nose a different language different customs rituals totems and taboos. Good hatred (say I) should turn against its evil cousin and against what gives rise to it: obtuseness stupidity maliciousness bigotry intolerance arrogance lack of humor. A Promethean hate. I'll leave it to whoever feels moved to spin yarns about love's different sorts and species—above all the less common ones like pity mercy patience the virtues that come to mind when you want to build a rainbow bridge over the mocking abyss of Creation.

And everything is accepted in good faith. (I'm not the first to say these things.) So I needn't bother to say the most sublime safest most profitable love is that of *Him* the Creator Himself —the love of *God*.

In Bucharest in January 1990 I spent an evening at the Italian embassy at a reception for a delegation of aid workers from Sardinia who had been commissioned by the Knights of Malta to take a transport of food winter clothing and medicine. "One drop on a hot stone" their leader declared. "Besides which everyone's having distribution problems. A ship carrying eight hundred tons of emergency supplies has been lying at anchor in Constanța for weeks. None of it can be unloaded: there's no way to transport it. We don't know what to do with our stuff either." The aid workers appeared clad in traditional Sardinian costumes: charity with a folkloristic touch. Of the Romanians present (who in my day liked to announce their national pride with equally picturesque traditional peasant's garb: the costumes of the ancient Daci from the Column of Trajan in Rome) not one was thus attired. The delegate of the brand-new Farmers Party exhibited his close ties to the people with dress unusual for a member of his species: a red-and-black buffalo-plaid jacket. The other government representatives contented themselves with East Bloc ready-to-wear. Only the upper echelon wore standard Western conference mufti. "There's one of the men who *just happened to be present* during the four minutes in which the new government was formed right after the coup" a fresh-out-of-the-oven ministry official I'd met the day before whispered in my ear. That the new representative of the people's chained will had once when an opponent of Ceauşescu been blacklisted was common knowledge; whether he had been—or still was—a spy no one could say. I went over to the object of this most subtle denunciation and engaged him in conversation.

Nothing but elegant small talk. As suited the elegant milieu. The blackness of the police-patrolled street outside might have been of Muscovite iciness: inside everything was cozy and luminous. (Crystal chandeliers from the blessed age of the boyars.) The buffet on a table a fathom long was well laden. Liveried servants darted about refilling glasses and the Sardinians' colorful costumes helped create a festive mood reminiscent of a Zeffirelli opera production—rather dicey to reconcile with the actual purpose of the Sardinian mission. For the fresh-out-of-the-oven political bigwig these seemed to be natural environmental conditions. Seeing me as an agent of culture (I'd been introduced to him as a writer) he commented approvingly on how in the countries of the East—though admittedly for the moment only in Hungary and Czechoslovakia—now that the yoke of bondage had been shaken off intellectuals artists men of letters were at long last being accorded their rightful place in government: foremost among them Václav Havel and his beer-drinking companions in Prague. He read gloomy skepticism in my eyes and interpreted it correctly. With a gesture that traced out a sort of treble clef in the air thick with cigarette smoke before his silvery necktie he conceded: Well of course only time will tell how long this egghead interregnum might last (and unfortunately not the competence or incompetence of these stalwart sons of the muses). Goes without saying that pure foolishness—an ethically impeccable will to adhere to absolute ideals—wears out fast. (Thinking of my Hamburg days I conceded this truth with a regretful nod.) All the more reason, quoth this representative of the people, that this elite not be relieved too quickly by experienced craftsmen of the—alas! alas!—not very immaculate craft of politics. It would be tragic were the old hands to get their hands on the rudder again. Anyway for the moment (the two of us saw eye to eye on this) we were as it were just one step away from Plato's Republic. (I suppressed the urge to offer a structural correction.)

Beside us stood a journalist of unknown origin who was casually listening to our conversation; the parliamentarian and I exchanged a knowing glance.

"Unfortunately I am devoid of artistic talent" the politician said. "Otherwise I'd scarcely have gone into politics. I envy you artists for your ability to affect people so deeply. Take for example our poet Cornea." We both gave worldly-wise smiles. I said: "In my case warning is superfluous. I wouldn't dream of giving up my charmed existence as a literary man. It keeps me suspended between realities like Muhammad's grave. Quite aside from the fact that I would be utterly inept as a politician. I wouldn't have a chance." He made a gesture suggesting a bow. There wasn't a trace of irony in his smile. "I knew you were an intelligent man. One who isn't going to miss his real chance." Then he introduced me to his girlfriend.

The girlfriend was a striking woman who exuded the aromas of American beauty products that were cheap but until recently hard to come by. She was from Timişoara where she had experienced considerable drama while leading (in her words) a valiant student organization. She refused to comment on the Romanian students' relationship to Hungarians living in their country. "It was a people's uprising that did not differentiate between nationalities and religious affiliations" she proclaimed starry-eyed. (How many died? Twenty thousand? Two thou-

sand? Two hundred? Three? Political morality was a quantitative issue.) "And as for religious affiliation" she went on: in
the absence of profound religious belief all efforts to create a
harmonious future would be futile and meaningless. She showed
me a golden cross dangling in her décolletage harmoniously
complementing her bracelet and earrings.

And now at last I realized what sort of chance I thought I'd
missed in my encounter with Otto von Hapsburg.

*But the Sultan now spoke: "Since the lad is to be a hero, the blows of
fate will mean nothing to him, for the vicissitudes of fortune serve as lessons
to the sons of kings and teach them to act wisely."*

—FROM THE NINE HUNDRED AND NINETIETH
OF THE *THOUSAND AND ONE NIGHTS*

This unostentatious gentleman stood before us with incomparable poise in that hope-depleted gray afternoon at the Danube
Steamship Company headquarters. He was the only one unaf-
fected by the excruciating silence that followed his son's invitation to the audience to comment on the future of the Danube
region. He was not tormented by doubts; not worried about
the impression his speech had made; not plagued by thoughts
of his own success or failure; not tainted with the zeal of one
determined to sway others to his view. Unshaken in his convictions. Especially unshaken in his belief in his good cause.
Imperturbable in his trust in the hand that guided him (the hand
of God).

All these qualities distanced him from us. In his plain lack of ostentation he appeared as an earthly presence among us but he was distant. He stood not quite in a heavenly realm but in a sort of intermediate otherworldly sphere. I had a vision of him standing before a firing squad: before such self-possession the rifles would sink to the ground. A pyre could be no match for it. Although its source was his unshakable Christian beliefs the element of martyrdom was lacking. He was not rejoicing at the proximity of the Beyond. His admirable sobriety was of this world. And yet he himself was not. Nor was he dripping with Christian Love. He seemed to have transcended it entirely. Thus he was also cleansed of hate.

This distanced him from me all the more. I am not ashamed to hate. I don't try to hide it. I let it slumber its way through everyday life but it is a light sleeper. Like mother birds who are instantly awake and ready for combat at the slightest chirp from their brood. I show a brotherly tolerance for the hatred felt by others even when it is directed toward me. That snowy night in Berlin the feminist television moderator's hatred clung to me as though I'd broken a spiderweb and was trailing its threads through the black-and-white night on my clothes hair hands forehead. For this I bore her no grudge. My hate was better than hers. My clinging blemish was soon washed away in the purity of that night. The night was starless and as densely black as basalt and it seemed the snow was being expelled from its shadows as though the night was purging itself of the last remnant of light left from the day's drab gloom; the purged light had been purified to an immaculate brightness flawless gleaming; and the contrast between them was free of antagonism: bright and dark complemented one another and in the lovely unity of this snowy night I thought of Ugo Mulas and what had been so endearing about him: he too was enchanted by the play of opposites and loved the clear notes that are precipitated from obscurity.

Confronted with this gentleman in an inconspicuous elegant

conference-goer's suit; this nominal heir to all the crowns of a vanished arch-European empire whose genteel appearance made it clear that nothing was further from his thoughts than a will to political power and whose ingenuous notion of politics as the art of the best good intentions left him heartrendingly alone in a world where good intentions wear out quicker than you can say Jack Robinson; this man who was the incarnation of his own purity (flesh and blood like B.'s wonderful grief at what has been lost)—the purity of the splendid utopias that for millennia mankind has devised to oppose barbaric Nature—confronted with this truly noble man my hatred lost its bitter edge. Became pure. Was transmuted into gentle play. Directed no longer at him but at the world in which he was so pure and noble because he was not of this world. A singer-into-existence of his own world. I sensed Bruce's presence.

My O.W.A. writer-colleague Chatwin. I could see his adolescent's head before me sharp as a new-minted coin. A stable currency. Sun-bright. Bruce Chatwin the "Golden Boy." The alert always slightly crooked smile. The piercing gaze above it. The unquenchable curiosity in the sea-blue eyes (which once had gazed themselves blind on too much art). The calculating machine behind his peasant brow. And I imagined the look of perfect mutual understanding we would have exchanged (over the gap of decades that separated us) about the admirable figure of the imperial son who had brought us this message: that Christianity reawakened to life (never having died out entirely in the first place) would make the Danube peoples receptive to the ideas and ideals of the Pan-Europe movement. Bruce too would not have responded to the call for discussion—but for reasons other than my own. His irony had a different source. More rooted in the actual. More immediate. It hadn't grown as mine had out of so-and-so-many lived-out lives in the simultaneous present. It was very much in the style of his time: "cool" in the world. Mine came from a romantic rebellion

246

against the world. And that was precisely what might have shown me the way to clarity. Untroubled by my German image—on the contrary: wonderfully at one with it. After my triumphant resolve to accept myself as I was in the intensive-care unit at venerable Santa Maria Nuova in my Golden Florence I ought to have stood up broken the excruciating silence and said:

"Your Imperial Highness has called up images of a glorious future for a Danube region contritely returned to a godly world in which Church and State are the two axes whose structural power neatly organizes the amorphous gruel of humankind into hierarchies and allows it to crystallize into a civilized society. Everyone here today would agree that this conforms to a Europe-wide conception of order and that efforts to organize according to it are among the noblest tasks of the Pan-Europe movement and of all other noble epoch-embezzlers as well. The world as God willed it the world of order justice and love the world of Occidental values and traditions a world of humanity our debt to our forebears. A world of pious *humare* where even the Danube peoples bury their dead who all too often (except for members of the old and new nomenklatura) have been left lying about for stray dogs. The silence of this audience privileged to hear Your Imperial Highness's words clearly reveals its hesitation about this lovely vision. As if it were not a viable possibility but only a fond wish. I believe I can give a deeper reason for this silence—though I can hardly hope to be as successful in this as our charming translator was [a brief bow to Countess Waldstein] in her marvelous renderings of the heartening words of the speakers preceding Your Imperial Highness." A hint of a bow in the direction of the Hungarian Czech (Slovak? Yugoslavian?) minister.

Pause. A deep breath. Then bravely onward: "I must ask Your Imperial Highness as well as members of the audience to bear with me. This carnivalesque soapbox speech is intended

247

to fill the void of silence that was our response to your ideas on the projected future of the Danube region. We lack the humble acceptance of the absurdity in God's unholy game. What was being asked of us is that we trust in the God of order justice and love. Your Imperial Highness, you stand here before us as a pure embodiment of what we lack: delight in God's game. Awe-filled reverence for it. This behooves the heir of noble ancestors who by God's grace were installed as apostolic majesties over the former Holy Roman Empire—in particular the Danube region. The son grandson great-grandson and great-great-grandson of emperors believes firmly in the God of order justice and love even though the Lord God of Sabaoth moved by whim one not-so-fine day withdrew *His* grace from the House of Hapsburg and banished the insignia of apostolic rule (crowns imperial orbs and swords) to the museum's collection of cultural relics. A tourist attraction. Part of the inventory in the temples to culture. Though the resultant upheavals—above all in the Danube region—made the number of dead lying out in the open increase substantially. The very opposite of order justice and love. We mere mortals must be forgiven for questioning not only the wisdom of this sort of playful intervention in world structures but also this very conception of God. One might think we were speaking of a Hapsburg household deity whose motives (in principle good) may not be questioned since this would undermine those of the apostolic rulers. Alas these good intentions are not always as well realized as one might like. In *His* polyeidic form as God of order justice and love the *Lord* seems as it were to have gotten into trouble repeatedly over jurisdictional matters. To produce Justice *He* needed order and turned to the colleague in charge of this. The colleague from the Order department could carry out *His* assignment only by means of the tried-and-true method of power. Regrettably power has a woman's base character. It wants to be loved but above all wants itself to be capable of love. This doesn't always work. Love doesn't always follow the Almighty's trodden path. It is said that he—or she—who loves will be loved in return. That's what The Mother of Pondicherry wants us to believe. Your Imperial Highness's forebear Joseph II is often mentioned as an illuminating witness to this phenomenon. And did not the Germans initially love—forgive me—the Führer and Chancellor Adolf Hitler who loved them so much? But alas this reciprocity is frail. Mankind—the mass of bubbling kneaded human dough—is of feminine gender. And as we know *La donna è mobile.* When the love that subjects feel for their despot begins to flag (perhaps because the will to perfection of these benefactors of mankind cannot be realized or because—in the name of the God of order—justice and even the tyrant's brotherly love for his subjects has come up short or because the holder of power falls victim to hubris and declares himself God or because while the Führer or Duce or Caudillo or Conducător is busy building monuments that will testify to his magnitude power has been entrusted to the anonymous termite force of chief clerks—in short when the subjects get the feeling they are not loved so tenderly as their despots proclaim) then, if *monseigneur* permits, in no time all hell breaks loose. The love of the head bureaucrats turns to hate. And then power shows what it can do. Soon there are so many casualties no one gives a thought to humane burials. Bodies pile up until they're carted off to mass graves. The nearly epidemic proliferation of mass graves in today's world and their ever more quotidian status thanks to the journalistic thoroughness of television daily weekly monthly periodicals suggests that perhaps even the Hapsburg household deity of order justice and brotherly love —our Christian God Himself—has wound up under museum glass along with the imperial regalia as an ornament of the Great Fetish Culture—not as a pillar propping it up—and that the Big Creator means this abandonment as a terrible admonishment to us for having been all too faithful servants of the House of

Hapsburg and for having thought of *Him* in this homespun and frivolous Viennese way."

Wait for the shock to hit. Stalwartly onward: "If I take the liberty of calling this a soapbox speech it's because I can't seem to forget the carnivalesque character of God's world. I'm tempted to think that's what *He* was aiming for when *He* put it together with such extravagant humor and inventiveness. In particular when *He* decided to let some kind of ape develop into *Homo sapiens*. What a cornucopia of fantastic costumes and dare-devil adventures even a quick glance into the annals of *His* history reveals! What a robust role the House of Hapsburg plays in the more recent part of it! And yet this historical cavalcade is lame compared to the insanity of the present. Please don't ask me to list our crimes against God's nature. Let's keep to the subject of a world of order justice and love as willed by man. We frivolously jeopardize this triple task. We all know thanks to television daily weekly monthly periodicals what great deprivations this planet has endured and with what terrifying speed the increase in human population worsens our plight. The mass media disseminate a reality that is too harsh too real too *natural* for a God of order justice and love. Yet the leader of world Christendom has been doing his jet-propelled best *in urbe et orbe* to see to it that this all too proliferous human species not be hindered in this steady expansion. Even if there's no way to sustain it in a manner befitting human dignity. Not to speak of order justice and love. Even when the act of procreation was not consummated in love but imposed by marauding soldiers on unfortunate and non-consenting women. How can this happen in the name of order justice and love? We must assume that the charismatic personality installed on St. Peter's throne has a broader and deeper understanding of *the Lord God* than we the spiritual rank and file can hope to achieve. He probably sees *Him* not as a lofty fiction whom we enlist against cruel Nature because we cannot bear to see its horrifying truth. Not as the

One in whose bosom we shall be comforted after our journey through the horrors of *His* creation. Rather our sacred Polish father knows that the God whose unfailing representative he is on earth needs that teeming life in order to keep *His* creation going on. Fueling it with the flesh and bones of the living. A voracious devourer of life who invented the perpetual-motion machine of procreative destruction. *For without this He would have no reality.*"

A dramatic glance around the room. Onward: "It is obviously God's will that life on earth should proliferate and increase in no matter what quantities or misshapen forms thereby assuring the eternal cycle of becoming and vanishing and thus also the notion of the Creator Himself. It is pleasing to God that the planet be inundated with the largest possible number of new-borns—these are needed for the divine work of procreation and destruction; it might almost be the *Creator*'s intention to keep these far too many in misery and ignorance and to fill them with the rage and malice that turns them into marauders and murderers: ever more perfect instruments of destruction.

"The Lord God of Sabaoth *wants* vassals. He needs them for *His* monstrous game. A game of ingenious simplicity: to destroy life and to cause life to arise from this destruction. Unto all eternity. The formula may sound monotonous but the game itself is anything but boring. On the contrary: its variety is breathtaking. Carnival revelry such as even fever dreams cannot produce. All the world takes part in it. A universal carnival from the galaxies to the louse that Martin Luther attested bore witness to the Creator's ubiquity. All the world invokes the image of the Holy Father of love-order-and-justice-loving Christendom in order to camouflage *His* real face—in the meantime putting 'saber sword and spear' as the song says (also fighter and bomber jets) into the hands of *His* vassals so that *His* will be done."

Brief pause; slight stirring in the audience. Undaunted onward: "The silence here in the Danube Steamship Company if I am not mistaken did not have its origin in the fear that the Danube peoples with their sense for the surreal long ago embraced this expanded concept of God which includes the burlesque and now are happy to play their little games in the context of *His* bigger one and to let *Him* have *His will be done* as *He* pleases. If I were a cynic I might say that this could be cause for rejoicing. Indeed it might even bring about a new piety: a staunch acquiescence in every gruesome game under the rubric *God's will*. Let us rejoice. Anything goes. No problem. We may follow colleague Kundera's suggestion and take one another by the hand and dance our way through the diurnal reality of Biafra Cambodia Disneyland NASA the Berlin Wall erected and torn down the ozone hole: Your Imperial Highness Herr Dr. Hapsburg hand in hand with Their Madnesses Prince Virgin Peasant from Cologne; the Carpathian Genius Nicolae Ceauşescu with Pope John Paul II and the scientist Madame Elena with the most recent Nobel Prize winner in genetics; I with the triumvirate of quality postwar German literature Böll Grass Johnson; Liz Taylor with The Mother of Pondicherry; Madonna with Cardinal Ratzinger; Saddam Hussein with the TV anchormen on CNN and ABC and their scoop providers the CIA and FBI and so on. Lamentably this mix won't make us merry. The mirth would be poisoned. We'd be dancing in a frenzy—as colleague Kundera knew all too well—each dancer isolated in the discord of his ego. That would spoil the meaning of our dance. God's will cannot be accomplished by individuals. *He* needs masses. *His* game is based on quantities, not the isolated *I*. It's the bloody *I* that forbids us to enjoy the Almighty's work. We hate the Other. A discord that doesn't allow for happiness. The original source of all we suffer and endure. That each of us is both an individual and a creature of the herd instinct tears us apart. That we cannot give up our egos or survive without the others debilitates us. We hate the herd yet stay with it—until there comes a moment of questionable bliss and one charismatic oversized *I* tears our egos from us and hands them over to the demons: *God*'s accomplices—not the fictitious kind good *God* who sends hosts of angels to challenge evil but the *one great* Destroyer of Life who cannot be exorcised with the fiction of a fallen brother who can no longer be placated with animistic polarities of light and dark. Ormazd and Ahriman. *He* and Lucifer. And a humanity whose purest souls offer themselves up on the cross for the fiction of the good loving Father."

Pause for breath. Stubbornly onward: "I have no right to expect Your Imperial Highness to show understanding for this inner rift. *Monseigneur* is a profoundly devout Christian. Feelings of responsibility for your neighbor aside you are not haunted by consciousness of a guilt for which there is no forgiveness: hatred directed at God Himself. Hatred for *Him* Who put us in the world as hopeless schizophrenics. He who is blessed every Sunday and holy day not to mention other contemplative occasions—like weddings baptisms funerals memorial services that give him an opportunity to mingle his ego—cleansed of guilt in a divine act of forgiveness—in holy communion with the egos of his fellow-loners and with God does not know the sufferings of one who sees through the God of order justice and love to the *Creator of Chaos.* He lives in a bliss-suffused sphere between realities that lifts him above the world's ugly turmoil. In the sphere of bliss-inducing popular fiction. *Flame That NEVER Consumes Itself.* But for the one who sees through the fiction of the God of order justice and love—hate soon rattles his bones. And I'm afraid that all of us here fear this is especially true of the peoples of the Danube region who are scarcely in a position to leapfrog over harsh mass-media reality into the promise of a blissful Beyond and with its help return to the fold of their beloved Christian God of order justice and love. It will only make them go for one another's throats more furiously than ever. Thus fulfilling *His* will. Let's be cynical in *His* name.

Let's be of good cheer! Gaze boldly at the terrible countenance of the *Creator of Chaos*! Why not make it *His* female form (it being Carnival time)? An Indian: colleague Kali? Naturally we shan't approach her in Indian humility—it's hard for us to get by without a smidgen of Faustian rebellion. So it's face-to-face atop the pyramid of skulls. Let's get Shrove Monday off to a rollicking start with the godhead's complicity! Laughing with the hatred that comes from horror and drives us on to end the hoax perpetrated by our household gods. Finally call things by their own terrible names."

Significant throat-clearing. Preparation for the *Conclusio*: "Your Imperial Highness, please forgive me this heresy. After all it's Carnival when fools run wild. So I'm allowed to don the old hat of gnosis. Bare-chested so to say: It fits so well with my colleague Nietzsche's repudiation of the God of a Church that exports bad conscience and deals wholesale in forgiveness. The joyous dusk of life. An old man's ruminations.

"For my part I've put these conflicts behind me. Age sets me free. The unabashed use of a *pappagallo* symbolizes my liberation. Admittedly my moment of jubilant self-affirmation in the intensive-care unit of Santa Maria Nuova failed to give me the courage to confront you. Nor does anyone else here have this courage. And the reason is not because we are too polite to show that Your Imperial Highness's sweet utopia only makes us smirk. None of us is cruel enough to stand up and say we don't believe in the God of order justice and love—because we lack the leisure and need all our energy to cope with harsh reality. The everyday reality of disorder injustice lack of love. And because we are tired of the injunction to love our neighbor as well as we love ourselves and instead hate him (or her) and need that hatred to withstand the bestiality and stupidity of the human species. Our hatred is our only power. It alone gives us the force to say NO to the temptation of trying to escape the horrors of this world. To say NO to someone who promises

254

to lead us away from them. We would lose our egos in the bubbling dough of exalted crowds and fall prey to demons. To declare this openly would hurt Your Imperial Highness and this we do not want."

Brief final pause for effect. "The true reason for our silence, sir, is a very special form of reverence. Not the veneration for the presumptive heir of so-and-so-many imperial royal princely ducal crowns that enrich the shrines of our moth-eaten cultural heritage. What disarms us is your purity. Here you stand before us as the personification of all noble feelings—and we believe you. There is no sign of the usual 'benefactor of mankind.' No pretension. No sign of spiritual or physical power. No stigmatized dreamer either. No drippy love camouflaging the inborn hatred of the neighbor. Just someone who believes in the ultimate triumph of good over evil. No matter in whose name. Someone blessed with noble blindness. Refusing to see through the treachery of idols fictions myths images. Someone who still has the character to believe in himself and his creed. That's what makes us speechless, *monseigneur*. To be confronted with the embezzler of our forlorn qualities. We stand before you in the sadness of those who lost their fairylands and we are touched to think that you will pray for us too—though to no avail."

Deep bow. Off.

It had been the chance to speak these words I'd missed that gray afternoon at the Danube Steamship Company in Vienna.

Now in this time Shahrazad had borne King Shahryar three sons, and when she had completed the last story of the Thousand and One Nights she sent for them: the first walked, the second hurried behind on all fours, the third hung at the breast of its nurse. And Shahrazad kissed the earth at the king's feet and said: "O King of time, I am your servant and for one thousand and one nights have entertained you with the words of kings and peoples passed away, strange things and many that were worthy of reflection. For this, and for the sake of your children, spare my life."

*A*utumn is coming on. We're back in the big house again. The perfecting process is over. My tower has been abandoned. No more visual calisthenics. I've had my eyes examined and wear my new glasses on a cord around my neck. An old man. But there are consolations: young people are taking on the traits of my species. More and more reconciled with the chaotic present. A member of the film crew from the Cologne Carnival— colleague Helmut Frodl—sent a Danube beauty to lure one of his competitors to Budapest where he dispatched him with a coup de grace to the head carved him up with an electric saw and distributed the parts in municipal garbage Dumpsters. An O.W.A. if ever there was one.

The special awe this generation has for the Great Fetish Art is quite touching.

In June 1990 (just after India) I found myself in Romania again: in Constanţa. Another television assignment like Cologne. A survey conducted by the French *Antenne Deux* gave me a chance to show off my knowledge of my native land. We went around asking women how they had gotten by in the years of the dictatorship. A lady formerly prominent in provincial society nostalgically described to us the glory of bygone days in a harbor town full of interesting consular officers of various nationalities (preferably Italian) and marvelously dashing naval officers. This splendor came to a sudden end followed by years of adversity during which (before her husband—an engineer who owed his unemployment to his bourgeois origins—died) she had been forced to sell all her "real" carpets. She had survived only thanks to her marriage "far beneath my station" to an electrician. When he died he left her a two-room apartment and a small pension. No heartrending tragedy this; her tale was more or less typical of the flat-footed spiritual lives of the bourgeoisie.

The next was a prototypical harem beauty: roundly full-fashioned from top to bottom with magnificent black hair luminous eyes cherry mouth and a faint shadow of mustache beneath a finely curved nose. Gay as a goldfinch she told of three simultaneous lovers who made her life endurable: a Party functionary to protect her; a cook at a state-run restaurant to give her food; a customs official who spoiled her with luxury products (perfumes silk stockings and American cigarettes). After the coup she'd declared the Party official superfluous and given him the boot. The two others were still current. She expected of the newly established democracy that in future she could limit herself to a single lover.

The third woman we interviewed was a young prostitute: dirty-blond pretty as a picture slender limbs fine features. She'd been plying her trade since the age of fourteen. Now she was twenty-three. It was impossible to understand how such a creature survived the patronage of dock workers Russian Turkish and Bulgarian sailors East German vacationers from Mamaia.

For the defunct regime she had only a shrug—and the same for the current one. "Who's going to make trouble for a person in my profession? Customers come and go, including the worst ones. We are eternal." The circle is completed: Hamburg 1947. We were setting up a shoot in a hotel room in the heart of town. While technicians lit the scene I sat with her in the restaurant. The inevitable money changer swooped down. More obnoxious and repulsive than usual. She shooed him away with an indignant exclamation and a wave of her hand. As if this had been the signal everyone was waiting for a fellow in a circle of seedy-looking characters at the next table rose and came over to us. Before I could figure out what he was up to he seized my wineglass and splashed it into her face. "You dare to insult respectable people you filthy little whore . . . !" and so on with plenty of obscenities. I'm no longer in physical or mental shape to get involved in such brawls. Besides which I didn't know his relationship to her: he might have been a plainclothes man or her pimp . . . I pushed him aside took her by the hand and escorted her from the restaurant.

Upstairs in the hotel room and safe in the company of my strapping young film colleagues I wanted to comfort her. She was not at all mortified. She said it had been very wise of me not to have responded with physical aggression. "It could have turned out very badly." And as for herself . . . She began to recite a stanza of a poem in Romanian. "That sounds familiar. What is it?" I asked. "You must know it" she said. "Baudelaire." Astonished I asked: "And you know it by heart?" Perfectly ingenuous she replied: "We had to learn it by heart. There are hardly any books. Before it's passed on to the next person we learn it by heart." "We? Who is we?" She replied offhandedly: "Young people like me."

Nothing was more natural than that the classic *post coitum* conversation with the "fallen woman" should ensue. (Literature had established the same intimacy between us as the consumed

258

service would have done.) Didn't she have any other way to earn her living? "Nothing better than this," she said dispassionately. Didn't she have anyone to take care of her? A man who could protect her? No one she really liked? Loved?

Smiling patiently she waited for me to finish with my questions. When I got to the word "love" she said with a nonchalant shrug: "You know: I don't really believe in the true love that Mircea Eliade says shows up only once in a millennium. Would you give me a pack of American cigarettes?"

"Angels can fly because they take themselves lightly" colleague Chesterton says. That's probably what made me feel so close to Bruce (who took nothing more seriously than himself). It gave us great pleasure to exchange useless curiosities. He went into virtual raptures when I told him that about the only thing I remembered from my studies of mining geology were the names of the five sites where gold is found in the former Dual Monarchy: Schemnitz Chemnitz Nagybanya Ofenbanya Vöröspatàk (mineral resources of the Danube region). He tried to learn these names by heart which given the challenge they posed to his Anglo-Saxon speech apparatus was no simple matter. This only doubled his enjoyment. When he was on his deathbed and even phone conversations exhausted him he couldn't take my last call. His wife Elizabeth offered to pass on a message. I asked her to tell him from me: Schemnitz Chemnitz Nagybanya Ofenbanya Vöröspatàk.

As for me: the surgeon has assured me I have some time left. Maybe not long. In any case don't expect the genteel solemnity that is considered appropriate for a man with one foot in the grave. No anxious echoes of the hollow pounding of *memento mori* against my brain. From time to time in the questioning gaze of my sons and young friends I can see this provokes astonishment. "What is it like when you realize that tomorrow—or at the latest the day after . . . ?" The presumed course of this process is displayed in splendidly graphic terms in the frescoes of the monastery churches of my Romanian homeland: the body—bony and pale with a greenish tinge—remains supine while the transparent lilac-hued streamlined soul issues from the nostrils and rises weightlessly toward heaven. On the way either it is speared on the pitchforks of rust-red black devils with scorpion tails and badly tattered bat wings and thrown down to join the similarly damned in pits of flame and sinkholes of snakes; or else it is received by golden-haired angels with flamingo-pink pinions and escorted up a Jacob's ladder to God's throne. Since my stay in the intensive-care unit I haven't had to fret over which alternative will fall to my lot. It doesn't matter what might hand me over to the devils or deliver me to the angels: everything stops after the first picture. Perhaps what comes after will be as in the Indian view: a journey through many different existences leading to a final purification of the lavender-blue bubble containing the crux of my enigmatic *Ego*. Which possibly will be preserved in identical form in my next host body. Definable as the psyche of an individual who never fully achieved maturity and is sometimes passionately involved in reality but usually far removed from it—who sees his earthly existence as a sophomoric joke on the part of Creation and who as for the Beyond does not want to and cannot come up with any other picture than that of infinite blueness in which—like a helium balloon escaping from a child's grasp—a bit of im-material *ur*-matter temporarily assigned corporeality rises until it reaches its source. Perhaps there will still be some trace of it—for a while anyway—in the form of printer's ink on paper until it too is yellowed. Maybe not. Paying respects at a tomb-stone won't be possible in this case because there won't be one. This hospitable body once abandoned will be cremated. The ashes will fertilize the three linden trees that keep watch beneath my tower.

.   .   .

Since I don't want to depend on lingering traces of printer's ink on paper I've thought up a number of little games. B. who loves me disapproves. One especially irritates her although it is so to speak a game of reconciliation with the demonic. It is called *adat* a word I brought back with me from Indonesia once. It signifies a custom practiced with dogged persistence until its site is possessed of magical powers. A word said over and over again is enough. Well: the road from Rignano to Incisa that we often take climbs the flank of a steep hill in a gentle curve. Halfway up the curve stands a lone house. They say that once a bulldozer lost its brakes as it was descending the slope; the monster rattled downhill gaining speed spun out of the curve and slammed into the side wall of this house broke through it and smashed through a room before coming to a stop at the wall of the second. Fortunately there was no one inside—except for a baby in its cradle. The cradle was scooped up in the bulldozer's shovel and pushed against the wall. When they cleared away the rubble they found the child peacefully asleep in the shovel.

I have the habit of telling this story to everyone I pass the house with. B. has heard it so often that she'd like to forbid me to mention even a syllable of the incident. But meanwhile I've made a custom of it. Friends driving with us wait for me to tell the story of the miraculously rescued child. B.'s protests become all the more vehement—I've been working on this cult for years now—when I tell her it's a matter of raising the dead in advance. I am creating an abstract memorial to myself. No one who has driven with us to Incisa more than once will be able to drive past the house without thinking of the miracle of the bulldozer shovel and thus also of me (along with B.'s protests). The *adat* will survive me—and in it I will survive as well.

Superstitious B. doesn't like to hear me speak of my own posthumous existence in books and especially not this sort of ironic conjuring of my own transubstantiation into immateriality. *(Scaramanzia.)* She turns a deaf ear when I insist it wouldn't take much more than three or four generations performing the *adat* to make the place genuinely magical (even sacred). I have to admit the monotony of the game might eventually make it intolerable. So since our return from India I've spiced it up by claiming that the miracle of the scooped-up child ought by rights to be attributed to The Mother of Pondicherry. I make her a gift of my *adat*. It suits her better than me.

J'aimerais que ma vie ne laissait après elle d'autre murmure que celui d'une chanson de guetteur: une chanson pour tromper l'attention. Independamment de ce qui arrive, n'arrive pas, c'est l'attente qui est magnifique.

—ANDRÉ BRETON